Shaman

SAM POLAKOFF

SHAMAN

Published by Komodo Dragon, LLC
Forest Hill, Maryland

Book design by GKS Creative
Cover image used under license from Shutterstock

Author photo courtesy of Ed Polakoff
www.photosbyed.net

ISBN (print): 978-1-7338898-0-3
ISBN (EBook): 978-1-7338898-2-7

Library of Congress: 2019905649

First edition

Printed in the United States of America

www.sampolakoff.com

This book is dedicated to my wife, Denise.
You are my soulmate in this and in every lifetime.

Across the world, there are people who have learned, through the generations, how to access the spirit world. Via sacred rituals and beliefs, they are seers who become either healers devoted to good or purveyors of evil. These people are known as shamans.

PART I

CHAPTER 1

Mount Ausangate, Peru, present day

Alone atop the summit, Dan Alston gazed at the endless, embracing sky. The afternoon sun cast a pink hue along the edges of the scant gray clouds. Dan smiled as he filled his lungs with the crisp mountain air. There was nothing like a climb to exorcise the stress from the chaotic world of the US Senate. *Work hard; please no one*, he lamented. The life of a senator. *Fight, fight, fight and sometimes compromise.* The once-collegial institution had turned into a festering cauldron of partisan bickering. This just might be his last term. The prospect of campaigning once offered an adrenaline rush that rivaled a difficult climb. Not anymore.

Dan admired the snow-covered peaks of the Andes gently enveloping the color-laden mountains surrounding the nearby Sacred Valley. The vibrant hues of the so-called Rainbow Mountain shifted along the rock in striped shades of red, beige, and brown.

The sound of the wind caused his head to swivel, and he took note of the dark clouds threatening the valley below. Dan knew that weather in the Andes could change without notice, especially at twenty thousand feet. A light rain spattered across his face. He was cold and knew he had erred in ignoring Moises, their guide.

Moises and Dan's best friend, Eli Shepherd, had begun their descent ahead of the storm. They had to be close to safety by now. Inherently stubborn, Dan began to regret lingering too long on the summit. He couldn't help himself. Dan was certain a few more minutes wouldn't matter. He wanted to capture the breathtaking horizon in all its splendor for his digital library.

The growing intensity of the falling rain began to pelt his body. Each cold, assaulting raindrop stung like a flying dart from a native blowgun. The rock became slippery. He understood the descent would be tedious but manageable. High upon the face of Ausangate, even with the best equipment, the most experienced climbers occasionally succumbed to the treachery of the elements. He heard the faint sound of Eli calling from below. He wanted to respond to let his best friend know he was all right. The unyielding wind and rain made a reply fruitless. While his keen sense of focus remained intact, his body began to rebel, reminding him that this trip was commemorating his fiftieth birthday.

The Ausangate climb was his present to himself. His only child, Bri, was in the midst of law school at Georgetown; his wife of more than two decades, Maddie, had given up on their marriage after the last election, saying she no longer wanted to be part of the disingenuous Washington social scene. That left Eli, who had always been there—through school, grueling campaigns, divorce, and everything in between. He was as loyal as an old golden retriever.

Dan carefully lowered himself, axe in hand, pitons and crampons firmly engaged with the rock's nearly impenetrable surface. The rain was now falling in sheets. The water savagely raced down the face of the mountain. Dan's attempts to steady himself were difficult at best. He inched his right leg slowly downward, seeking a small outcrop of rocks upon which he could gain an advantage. His foot gently swayed along the surface, searching, until he discovered what he was looking for: a group of collected rocks plastered to the side of the mountain and held together by nothing more than a million years of erosion from rains, the likes of which he currently battled. He enabled both feet to hit the top of the rock and allowed himself a moment to rest and catch his breath. Two minutes, yes, just two minutes and he would continue.

Standing steady and hugging the mountain, his sense of regret had taken hold for not following Moises and Eli down the mountain sooner. Moises was particularly insistent, but Dan had been steadfast in his desire to enjoy the extra few minutes of tranquility. He looked up, taking solace in that he already had made significant progress toward basecamp. A bolt of lightning appeared, literally before him, followed by the crushing sound of thunder. When he was a boy, he used to think that thunder was God bowling. At twenty thousand feet, it sounded more like the world was about to end. Leaning against the cavernous rock, worry set in. The raging storm quickly reduced visibility on the mountain to nothing. He closed his eyes just for a second and attempted to gather his resolve to continue. With the rain and wind pounding down on him, he heard it. *That voice.* It haunted him. Was hypothermia causing him to hallucinate? A whispery, sexy, female intonation teased his senses. An alluring sound, it appeared at odd times: in bed, at the gym—heck, even once on the Senate floor.

Yāvenhawk, O Yāvenhawk
I am one with you.

The words, their meaning, and the voice meant nothing to him. The incidents were so entirely random, he trained himself to block them out of his mind. Today, he was unsuccessful.

Dan looked skyward to gauge the storm clouds and saw an angry predator on the summit. A terrifying gray wolf bared its teeth and snarled as foam formed at the corners of its mouth. Dan's head began to spin. It felt as if someone or something were consuming his state of consciousness. His vision blurred. *That voice.* It drove him insane.

Vertigo overtook him as the fragile grouping of rocks supporting his weight gave way to the harrowing storm and its accompanying rush of rain and wind. Dan clawed at the mountain, trying to hold on as his body slid down the wet rock. His belay, the anti-braking device designed to slow a climber's descent, failed. Dan's goggles were torn askew by the downward force and his right cheekbone was scraped raw against the cold mass of ubiquitous rock. His right hip and knee banged precipitously against the mountain's perilous ridge, ripping his pants with a sharp zipping noise. Dan felt his right shoulder dislocate and blood begin to emerge from the numerous cuts and scrapes. He couldn't gain control. He lost consciousness as the fast-paced slide continued, depositing his body onto a snow-covered ledge one hundred feet below.

A bloody, broken, and beaten soul, he conceded that the mountain won. He sat up slowly and assessed the damage. He knew his shoulder was dislocated and his lower back, right knee, and hip were sore, but he willed himself to rise, figure out where he was, and somehow make his way back to the safety of basecamp. He had a first aid kit and considered taking the time to tend to his open flesh wounds but determined that they weren't bad enough. As he got to his feet, he heard a growling sound. He brushed himself off and attributed the noise to the howling wind whipping through and around the rocks. He picked up his goggles, which had come loose during the fall, and spotted his axe resting in the snow a little further away. He knelt down to pick up the axe and as he rose, he found himself facing the wolf. Dan wondered how the wolf made it down from the summit. *Was it the same wolf?* As far he knew, wolves didn't populate Ausangate, especially at this altitude.

The wolf snarled and continued to inch closer. Dan felt his grip tighten around the handle of the axe. It was all he had with which to defend himself. He steadied himself and braced for the beast to attack. Dan raised the small axe above his head with his left hand and tried to cast his weight forward. His right foot slipped on a small patch of ice, and he went down face first in the snow and slush, back into a state of sleep-laden helplessness.

He knew this was the end and attempted, as if one would know how, to prepare to be mauled by the angry predator. He tried to lift his torso from the cold muck to face his attacker, but his head wouldn't move. His eyes wouldn't open. Everything went black. Just before the lights went out, Dan remembered hearing it again, the seductive voice . . . singing that haunting intonation: *Yāvenhawk, O Yāvenhawk. I am one with you.* Amidst the blackness, from the distant recesses of his mind, Dan Alston thought he heard the sound of an approaching helicopter.

CHAPTER 2

Northern Peru, 1472

Jade walked in solitude across the rock-laden path. The pink dicots in full bloom delighted her sense of smell. She paused upon hearing a rustling noise through the flowers lining the path. A small lizard danced in and out of the flowering plants. She smiled faintly because smiling was not in her makeup, yet she admired the tiny reptile's free spirit. Jade closed her eyes, inhaled deeply, and slowly let the air escape her lungs. As she paused to briefly rest, she reflected on the long sojourn on foot. The journey tested her resolve, but she knew she must not give in to weakness.

The Inca Empire measured distance in topo. One hundred and seventy-one topo, or 1,317 kilometers, from Cusco to Huancabamba Province was a trek most men in her village would have shunned, but she was young and strong. She possessed saiwa, the energy bridge connecting the upper, middle, and lower worlds. The accumulation of energy centered in one person was a rare gem bestowed upon her—a gift from above uniting the physical and spiritual worlds. She would not waste it. The time was at hand. Yanakilla would be waiting.

Jade wandered off the path through an opening in the foliage to a nearby stream. She leaned upon a Kapok tree, extended her arms skyward, and stretched muscles she forgot she had. Once she arrived at Yanakilla's village, she would rest in order to make the last leg of the journey over much less desirable terrain. Then, two hours later, she and her mentor would arrive at The Huaringas, the sacred lagoons, to partake of the waters of Laguna Negra—not for healing purposes, the objective of most who made the journey, but rather, the opposite. Jade wished to collect the sorrows, ills, and pain that others came to cast away.

Once she arrived, she observed that Yanakilla's village was poor. "Yana," as she was known to Jade, was the spiritual leader and healer of her people. Although the village had leaders and other elders, Yana, the sorcerer, controlled who lived and who died and the quality of the village life. Yana resided in an old stone structure that was small and damp and the envy of her people, most of whom had a fraction of the space in poorly constructed mud huts.

The rains of the Amazon had come and gone three times since Jade had last seen Yana. Jade assessed Yana's age to be early to mid-sixties, although truth be told, she could have been a decade older. Yana's face, ancient and weathered, looked like a decrepit animal hide. Her eyes, gray in color, were tired. Her hair, running the length of her back, was now more white than black, and her shoulders slumped forward, making her appear shorter than she was.

Yana had seen something in her, literally. Years ago, in a remote tributary of the Amazon, Yana had found her. Jade recalled how Yana had said she was drawn to her by the spirits, only to learn later that the tale of their alliance had been foretold decades earlier in a vision. At first, Jade knew not what to make of the strange older woman but over time, it was Yana who had unlocked so many of her mysteries. It was Yana who helped her see that she had been given the gift: saiwa, the energy bridge. Now it was Yana who would help her harness the power.

The older woman approached her slowly, her body no longer able to traverse the small dwelling with ease. Jade wondered how Yana would make the pilgrimage on a burro to Laguna Negra. That was tomorrow's concern. It was dusk, and the evening's plans included a meal of modest means and an early retirement. Jade was honored to share Yana's home. This was not the custom. Visitors to this village would camp out under the stars, except during rainy season. Then, and only then, would a guest seek refuge from a poor villager. Yana would not entertain the thought of her pupil sleeping amongst the wilds of Huancabamba. Jade graciously accepted. Her long journey from Cusco had seen many nights under the light of the moon. She would relish the comfort of Yana's modest home.

Yana woke her before sunrise to prepare for the journey. The burros and saddlebags were ready to go. Jade stepped quietly as she proceeded to mount her burro. The village was still sound asleep. Yana had explained that leaving before sunrise afforded them the better part of the morning to do their work. Jade knew that Yana believed morning time at Laguna Negra held stronger power, but really, she reasoned, the old woman no longer slept through the night and liked to get an early start.

As she mounted her burro, Yana smiled. To Jade, it seemed that Yana's rare smile accentuated the wrinkles on her worn and weathered face. They rode in silence with Yana leading the way. Jade understood the need for silence. Yana insisted upon it for preservation of solitude. The time was meant for reflection, enabling one to do her best work upon reaching the lagoon with the mystical power.

From past experience, Jade instantly recognized the raspy chirp of the oropendola, the black birds with their extended yellow beaks that made the long, stringy, hanging nests high in the trees to keep their young safe from snakes. The sound of the oropendola announced their arrival at the gateway to the mystical lagoon. Jade wiped her brow with her hand. Even though they were in high altitude, the humidity remained extreme. The combination of humidity and cooler temperatures native to the area left a constant fog hanging over the heads of visitors. Jade felt a fine mist gently grace her skin.

Yana motioned for her to follow down a barely visible opening in the foliage, one Jade would never have seen. At the Shimbe Lagoon, bright flowering plants and sunshine created an aura of divinity. Here at Laguna Negra, as its name implied, there was only darkness.

Yana did not speak upon dismounting her burro. Jade was familiar with the routine of traveling with Yana. Jade said nothing and following suit, secured her animal and ambled down the path toward the lagoon. Yana reached into her ancient sheepskin bag and withdrew a small vial containing *ayahuasca*. The mixture made from a vine of the same name was well known to the Incas of the Peruvian Amazon. Jade was young. In her village in Cusco, shamans consumed ayahuasca for healing and transformational journeys. She was familiar with the brew but had never partaken. She looked tentatively at Yana, took the vial, and paused with it in her hand.

Yana began to gently sing *icaros* accompanied by a wooden flute-like instrument. For some shamans, it took years to master icaros, but for Yana, the musical ceremony paying homage to plant life came easily. After inhaling the pungent aroma, Jade closed her eyes and threw back the dark brew as she listened to Yana shake her *chakapa*, the bundled leaves constituting a rattle. The ayahuasca was sticky and rolled slowly along the surface of Jade's tongue, leaving a bitter aftertaste as it made its way through her mouth.

Jade waited and wondered if the elixir would have any effect upon her. For thirty minutes, they sat aside the lagoon together in silence, staring across the murky water, watching the oropendola glide downward from the high rock formations surrounding the water and then gently down to its surface. Suddenly, Jade's stomach turned sour. She turned her head away from Yana and vomited violently. When she pulled her long, black locks away from her face and looked up, the oropendola had changed. The delightful black birds now appeared as pterodactyls. The prehistoric birds with long, webbed wings and sharp teeth swooped down close to her, causing her to jump back from a sitting position.

"The regurgitation is to cleanse your body for the remaining experience," she heard Yana mutter.

The rocks above the lagoon began to melt, rolling down the face of the ridge like lava leaving the open pit of a raging volcano. Laguna Negra turned black. The relatively calm water from a few moments earlier boiled as if it were in a village fire pot. The shriek of the pterodactyls pierced her eardrums as two of the dreaded creatures once again swooped down upon her. Jade's skin became hot to the touch. Like the rocks across the lagoon, she feared she would melt. She closed her eyes. Jade's heartbeat accelerated and sweat overcame her. Her stomach began to rumble and she thought she may be sick yet again.

Yana guided her to lie back flat on the ground and close her eyes. She tried to calm herself, but her heart was beating rapidly. After a few minutes, Jade settled down and when she opened her eyes and sat up, the dark, murky water of Laguna Negra had changed to a brilliant azure. Before her, a mountain of ice formed in the center of the water. It rose high and equaled the height of neighboring mountain peaks while puncturing the shroud of fog. The pterodactyls became blurry and faded, transforming in the sky to beautiful, majestic white seabirds with captivating wingspans. The birds flew with purpose, circling the tip of the ice mountain. But just as suddenly as it had formed, the mountain of ice receded back into the lagoon.

Once in the altered shamanic state, Yana instructed Jade to enter the water. Alone with Yana in the most remote portion of Laguna Negra, Jade removed her clothing and stepped slowly into the water. Icy needles pricked at her feet and ankles, and goosebumps enveloped her flesh. In a vain attempt to stay warm, Jade crossed her arms over her bare breasts. She wanted to retreat. Just below freezing, the lagoon's frigid water would not yield its powers contently.

"Keep going," the old lady chanted two and then three times in a row as she giggled out loud. To Jade, in her altered state and with ensuing hypothermia, it sounded more like a vibrating, evil cackle arriving from a distance. Now in up to her waist, Jade was instructed to submerge and hold her breath for as long as she could. Jade had never been this cold.

She had hoped the effects of the ayahuasca would numb the anticipated cold, but to her surprise, it did not.

Yana's voice was pervasive. "Child, if you are to become what you hope to be, you must gain control of the lagoon."

Jade persevered, calling on her power spirit in the form of the wolf. Together they rose above the icy lagoon while her physical presence remained in the water. With the wolf at her side, they floated fifty yards to a crater adjacent to the lagoon. With a rush, Jade felt the wolf pulling her underground through to Ukhupacha, the lower world, where she watched as burned-out trees and foliage appeared to her left and right, serpents whose length exceeded her own village whizzed by, and the souls of the damned called out to her for help. Jade had been here before but without the ayahuasca. Yana had shown her the way.

But today, aided by the wolf, her power spirit, she was mastering the trip to Ukhupacha. She inherently understood that her soul, like the many souls surrounding her, was fractured. Yana had led her to this point to continue a journey that had emanated lifetimes ago, a quest to perfect the wounds of her soul. Were she to live in the present without Ukhupacha's knowledge, her soul would remain in a damaged state, causing her to repeat mistakes of past lives her soul had lived.

Guided by the wolf, she drifted, almost listlessly, through cavernous, rock-like surroundings until suddenly she saw a glimmer of light in the distance. It seemed to flicker like the brightest stars she had seen in the nighttime sky. She floated through the corridors of the lower world until she came to the source, a smooth, rock-faced surface where the flickering white light expanded and contracted in bursts. Jade felt the warmth of the light's energy. The smell of the rock was pure, like the freshness of a waterfall in the early morning. The light transformed before her into the head of a serpent. Outlined in pulsating white light, the spirit-serpent, Amaru, had shown itself to teach Jade *yachay*, the power of the mind. Through yachay, she would reach a pinnacle of self-awareness.

With the wolf by her side, Jade stood before the light, not making a sound, as the serpent seemed to speak to her. No words were exchanged, but her body tingled as energy transferred from the light to her soul. She had found her destination. The shimmering light presented the Akashic Records, the historical preservation of each soul on earth since the beginning of time. These Records were open to allow Jade to learn from the mistakes of past lives lived by her soul.

Yana had explained that we are here on the earth at this time to heal the wounds, to create a better future for this lifetime and the next. If the wounds of the soul could be healed in this lifetime, then, Yana had taught her, the next lifetime inhabited by one's soul would be easier. Ultimately, the perfection of the soul would lead to peace in Hanaqpacha, the upper world. Jade knew that this learning experience would be invaluable. She also understood that this lifetime in Kaypacha, the present world, would not be her last. Her soul would inhabit other bodies and live other lives. In fact, in learning sorcery from Yana, Jade would be performing acts in this lifetime that were counterintuitive to the lessons of Ukhupacha. Her soul would have to be healed in a future lifetime. The upper world would have to wait. Revenge would be exacted.

Jade breathed deeply. She was in control and felt no fear about her surroundings. Upon this epiphany, she reengaged with her physical form and surged upward toward the surface of the lagoon, letting the air fully envelop her lungs.

Clutching a stone she had carved as a child as a vessel for her unharnessed power, Jade fed off the newfound energy streaming inward. The pain others had released in these spiritual waters was hers to possess. Like her mentor, she would become a great sorcerer. She would determine who lives and who dies. If she chose to, she would rule the world.

CHAPTER 3

Looking down at his hands and arms, Dan saw they were covered in soot. Wrinkled and torn, his khaki slacks were besmirched with black; his white shirt, normally pressed to a fault, was matted from the combination of sweat and the residue of burning buildings. With his sleeves rolled up to his elbows, he noticed his prized gold Rolex was gone. Maddie, his ex-wife, had given it to him on the night he had been elected to his first term in the US Senate. One loafer had a hole in the toe, the other, a missing heel. Walking was difficult but he dared not remove the shoes, for the path's surface might burn through his socks. His legs felt weak but he pressed forward down the street, only to notice fires, too numerous to immediately count, still burning.

As he walked, he dodged the bright orange embers flittering downward in the wind. The air was acrid with the scent of everything ablaze, including what he believed to be human flesh. Corpses lined the streets. He stepped over and around them to continue his investigation of the scene. *My God, some of these people are still alive!* Emaciated souls, barely alive, mouths agape, raised their hands slightly from the ground in gestures indicating pleas for help.

"Saaaave us," the voices groaned with an eerie tone. Dan offered words of comfort, but his voice was unheard by the dying. He listened for sirens, hoping the first responders might soon be here to help, but there were none to be found—just the audible wind fanning the ongoing flames and whipping in and around the remaining trees and shrubs lining this iconic street.

As he staggered further, he realized where he was. The White House was in plain sight. "Holy mother of God," he proclaimed out loud. "This is Pennsylvania Avenue!"

It had not been obvious as he made his way through the burned out street but, yes, this was clearly DC. Behind him was the Capitol and his own place of work at the Hart Senate Office Building and just ahead, 1600 Pennsylvania. Until the smoke had begun to abate, it was impossible to determine exactly where he was. As he looked up, he saw the familiar Romanesque clock tower resting atop the Old Post Office, now a Trump hotel. People fumbled their way out of the hotel's main entrance, all thin, many holding handkerchiefs over their mouths and noses in the vain attempt to avoid smoke inhalation. Dan inched down the street, stopping to take in the destruction and famine. Fountains in front of buildings along the street were all dry, the stone scorched by the angry will of the flames. Dan's mind struggled to comprehend why he was here and what was happening.

"Dan, Dan, over here."

He looked to his right and from across the street came a disheveled, skeletal version of his chief of staff, Talia Clayton. Dan was aghast at her appearance. Her strawberry blonde hair was enveloped in ash and part of her hair on the left side had been ripped away. Her hazel eyes were haggard and the freckles that dotted her angelic, pale complexion were covered by dried blood and streaks of gray slag. Nevertheless, he was glad to see her.

"Tally, oh thank heaven you are okay. What in the world is happening? I don't understand."

"It's all a message" she replied plainly.

He stood in the thick of the rubble, the smell of smoke incarcerating his lungs, and stole another look around him at the dead and dying. "A message?" he queried. "What kind of message and from who?"

Tally's image began to fade. Her body drifted away into the dense smoke. Her trailing voice chanted, "You know whoooo . . ."

Dan was beside himself. He needed to find help. Reaching into his pants pocket, he realized his phone was gone. He looked up and down the horrid scene unfolding before his eyes in the nation's capital. Moving toward the White House, he felt a tug on his ankle.

"Saaave us," cried the emaciated woman clutching his foot.

Dan began to perspire. His stomach turned sour. He regurgitated on the sidewalk as far away from the woman as he could. As he gently broke loose from her hold on his leg, his body lifted off the ground and began to hover over the scene. His ascension continued through the smoke, high above the skyline, until someone grabbed his hand. It was Tally.

"Dan, it is up to you," she whispered as another clump of her hair disappeared into the wind. Her right eye enlarged to twice its normal size. "Now, you must come with me," she decried in a deeper, throatier version of her normal voice.

Still holding his hand, Tally led him over DC, proceeding aerially, high above the Atlantic Ocean. The majestic water slowly turned brown, evolved into black, and finally evaporated before his eyes. Heading westward, the same occurred in the Great Lakes. Dan observed the scenes of fire, famine, and drought torturing every state across America. His body was being involuntarily lowered. Still holding Tally's hand, he glanced over to make sure she was okay. Dan stared into her troubled face and was sickened as her remaining hair flew away in the wind. Her face burst into flames until she was charred and unrecognizable. His mouth flew open, shrieking "Noooo," and her body exploded into a cloud of black dust.

Dan felt his body descend, slowly floating and then gently landing on a snow-laden cliff, on Ausangate with a majestic condor circling overhead, just watching him suffer.

The paramedics lifted his battered body onto the chopper and flew him to Cusco.

CHAPTER 4

"Someone has got be held accountable!" Maritza Coya said in an angry tone. She could feel the anger rising through her body, culminating in the onset of a powerful headache. She hated bureaucracy and moreover, incompetence really pissed her off. After dozens of unreturned calls and emails to Senator Alston's legislative assistant, Maritza grew tired of being ignored. Not known for being patient, she used her secret weapon to get through the gatekeepers. Tall and slender with long, flowing jet-black hair, Maritza, forty-two years old, was strikingly beautiful and exuded sex appeal. Her dark skin, full lips, and alluring brown eyes had made many a man melt in the palm of her hand. The only child of Peruvian immigrants, her mother had instructed her to use every attribute she had to get what she wanted.

Gaining access to the Hart Senate Office Building without an appointment had required nothing more than a good story, a low cut dress, and her perfect, prize-winning smile. Security guards posed few problems. She had a gift of hypnotizing people, men in particular, into giving her whatever she wanted. Once the receptionist in Senator Alston's office had told Joc Raymer, the senator's legislative assistant, that she was there, the game was essentially over. She saw him come around the corner intent on delivering the "I'm sorry, but you can't just barge in" speech but knew he would relent.

She had done her homework. She already knew that young Raymer had been tossed out by his wife for cheating with a coworker. Maritza was a vulture swooping in on wounded prey in the middle of a dusty and barren country road. Before he could speak, she approached him and took his hand, hauling it and Raymer gently into an uncomfortably close proximity for two people meeting for the first time. She made sure her perfume enveloped his senses as her long dark hair brushed his cheek and her generous bosom pushed up against his arm. This would be child's play.

"I am Maritza Coya from American Clean Food. I am hoping you can help me gain an audience with Senator Alston. People across this planet are starving. You don't want that, now do you?" she asked seductively as she locked eyes with his. Awaiting his reply, Maritza marveled at how easy it was to manipulate men whose brains were driven by nothing more than testosterone.

Joc Raymer returned her gaze and smiled the nervous smile of a high school boy with a crush. Maritza, shallow to the core, thought his shaved head and baby-faced features, with the well-manicured goatee, made him look like an idiot. He probably thought he appeared tough. Where she came from, guys like Raymer were there to be used, abused, and spit back out onto the hard pavement. To his credit, she admired, just a little bit, how hard he tried to stick to the party line. At the same time, his response was eliciting her brewing temper and frustration at what she and her employer considered a do-nothing Congress.

"People around the world are starving while the very countries that need our food impose excessive value-added taxes, duties, inspections, and all sorts of other roadblocks."

"I'd be more than happy to schedule time with you to listen to your ideas," Raymer stammered.

She collected herself and once again moved into his personal space. "I would like to discuss those ideas now, with Senator Alston."

"Perhaps you are new to lobbying. Generally speaking, you start with me. If I think you have something to offer, I will advance the idea to our chief of staff. Once she's convinced, then, and only then, will you get a meeting with Senator Alston."

Unfazed, she leaned in, getting close enough to whisper in his ear. "Trust me, I have something to offer."

She enjoyed the sad puppy dog look on Raymer's face. Once he offered to meet her for drinks at the Filibuster Pub after work, she knew he was now in play, a mere stepping stone to gaining an audience with the infamous Dan Alston, the chairman of the Senate Committee on Agriculture, Nutrition, and Forestry, the man they called "the last honest senator." Maritza had every intention of getting the good senator to see things her way, even if she had to endure meaningless sex with Raymer to get there.

For Maritza, chasing the dragon, a potent mix of heroin and crack, would transform the night into passionate lovemaking with a handsome emperor from another era in the serenity of his luxurious temple chamber.

CHAPTER 5

Brianna Alston, or "Bri" as her friends knew her, desired adventure. Her studies at Georgetown Law in Washington, DC, had caused her to reluctantly decline her father's invitation to climb Mount Ausangate in honor of his fiftieth birthday. That's literally where she would be now were it not for the need to listen to Professor Bowman drone on and on in a class entitled International Perspectives on Environmental Law. Bowman's nasal voice, mixed with a touch of whininess, grated on her nerves. A former EPA deputy in the Obama administration, he broached each new slide, all with much too much data and verbiage, with an attempt to generate enthusiasm for the mundane subject matter.

His presentation was supposed to cover environmental protection theory in third world countries, a topic for which she held immense passion. Instead, they were being treated to a lecture on decaying bridges in the Amazon. The subject matter had no relevance to the students at Georgetown Law, yet the speaker droned on and on. As Bri gazed around the lecture hall, she observed fellow classmates downing the last swigs of their coffee as thumbs danced across cell phone screens. Others struggled to keep their eyes open. Stenciled on the wall above Bowman's head was the Georgetown Law motto: "Law is but the means. Justice is the end." Bri sighed and wished Bowman would wrap it up.

In her state of abject boredom, to keep from falling asleep, she jotted down his every feature in her laptop's word processor. The eyes were deeply embedded beneath protruding orbital bones housing bushy eyebrows and giving the appearance of ever-present dark circles. His nose was long and rounded at the end. The Hollywood jawline now sagged in deference to age. His hair looked like it had been recently cut, exposing the enormity of his ears. The thin lips, at rest, crested downward. The suit was a dark charcoal. The tie, a light gray floral against a white Oxford collar. The suit was an athletic cut to accommodate his lean frame.

While Bowman bored them to tears, her mind wandered to the climb. She had begun climbing with her father as a twelve-year-old, starting on Mount Hood and then working her way up Pikes Peak a year later. She missed him terribly. Despite his divorce from her mother four years earlier, she had remained close to her father. They were both in DC. Her mother was jet setting around the world with her new boyfriend. *A bank vice president or something like that*, she thought. Her mom wanted a lifestyle with less drama than that of being the spouse of a US senator. An only child, Bri Alston was smart enough to understand that her parents needed her to help them through their ordeal. They parted on good terms, and Bri knew her parents still loved one another. They simply weren't in love anymore.

Bri didn't worry too much about Dad on Ausangate. Although it could be treacherous, as an experienced climber herself, she took solace in the fact that "Uncle Eli," as she called Dad's best friend, would always have his back. She insisted that Dad hire a Sherpa to get him and Uncle Eli safely up and down the formidable mountain. Dad had reluctantly agreed to the guide. She knew how stubborn he could be. She also understood that he wasn't as young as he once was. His mind might be telling his body a lie regarding its present capability.

Bowman finally realized he had run out of time. *Thank God!* She knew he would never tire from the sound of his own voice. As she stood up from the crowded hall and gathered her laptop and other belongings into her purple backpack, a chill worked its way up her spine. It was the inevitable feeling she got when things weren't as they ought to be. She was seated in the front of the hall. The room contained exits at the upper and lower ends of the staircases lining the east and west sides of the hall. She chose the lower east side exit. She made her way down the light blue carpeted stairwell and instinctively glanced over her right shoulder, noticing a man in a dark suit, white shirt, and black tie in the upper tier. She couldn't be sure, but it felt like his eyes were boring right into her. It was impossible to know every student at Georgetown Law, and it was early in the semester, but clearly the man in the dark suit stood out like a sore thumb.

She decided to hightail it out of the building, down the three levels of cement steps and safely into the crowd along New Jersey Avenue. Nerves rattled, she walked briskly while drawing her long dark-brown hair into a ponytail. She didn't want her hair to be windblown upon arriving at her pro bono job at the Foundation for Preservation, Peace, and Light, otherwise known as FPPL. She had counted on Bowman ending on time so she could stop for a chai latte. Bri was a marathon runner. She decided her long, athletic legs would whisk her eight blocks through Starbucks and to FPPL's offices on time—or close enough for comfort. Earl Sanderson, FPPL's director, would understand. Earl had history working with students assigned by Georgetown Law's Office of Public Interest and Community Service, and she knew he was fond of her in a parental sort of way.

As she made her way through the crowded sidewalk, she couldn't shake the feeling that something was amiss. Her father had always taught her to anticipate danger. "You can't climb a mountain in a vacuum," he always told her. She was reminded of his ever-present warnings to be aware of her surroundings and to act decisively to protect herself. *A predator could appear all at once.* That sense of danger was serving her well as she took note of the man in the dark suit, now donning sunglasses, pursuing her from behind. He was taller than she. His head was bobbing and weaving so as not to lose sight of her. There were always crazies out there looking to kidnap a senator's daughter. It didn't go to her head, but Bri Alston knew her lithe figure, long brown hair, and crystal blue eyes weren't working to her advantage when it came to avoiding the wackos.

Options, she commanded of herself. *Stay in the crowd. Skip the latte and get to the safety of the FPPL office. Make a cell phone call to 911.*

Bri concluded that all three measures would be prudent. She hurried down 1st Street NW. Her pursuer was closing in. Despite her father's teaching and her intellectual prowess, she was still twenty-three and scared. Amidst the cold DC wind, she broke out into a sweat, her brain went into a fog, and her legs felt twice their normal weight. She urged herself to find the strength to keep moving. *Breathe*, she told herself. Maybe she would duck down into the Metro station. Even more people there. There's safety among the crowd, she reminded herself. As she considered her next move, a heavy hand suddenly gripped her shoulder from behind.

CHAPTER 6

The room was a blur. Dan's mind was overcome by a sense of dread. Where was he? As he gathered his senses, he noticed his skin felt cold and clammy. His toes were numb. Two gray and blue woven blankets lay atop him. He lifted his head slowly and took a breath. The room had a sterile aroma reeking of isopropyl alcohol. He picked up a small square mirror from the wheeled tray table stretched across the bed and noticed he looked pale. His right cheekbone was sore. Dan took note of the stitches lining his jaw. An IV drip was flowing into his arm, restricting his movements. As the fog began to clear, Dan observed a sleeping Eli Shepherd, lightly snoring in the hospital recliner adjacent to his bed. Eli was bald but the remaining hair he had on the top and sides was graying and askew. Eli's slight, middle-aged paunch gently protruded from his trousers, placing pressure on the buttons of his green plaid flannel shirt.

Without moving his right arm that was tethered to the IV pole, Dan stretched the best he could. His back was sore, as was his neck. His right hip and knee howled as he tried to move. A thousand times worse than the most severe pain he had previously experienced, he thought, as he winced and settled back into a moderately comfortable position. To the extent he could see his own battered body, he observed cuts, scrapes, and bruises everywhere. Sliding back down into the bed, the pain seared through his right shoulder, urging him to be deliberate in how he moved.

A painful grunt escaped involuntarily. He brought his left hand up to his eyes and rubbed. His vision was distorted. His ability to think coherently was dulled. He looked over at his friend and noticed he began to stir. Eli stretched and opened his eyes. Dan appreciated his friend's dedication. Eli looked haggard.

"Normally, after a fight, I would suggest you tell people that the other guy looked worse than you," quipped Eli, "but in this case, it would be a lie. I'm pretty sure the mountain got the best of you."

Dan looked into his best friend's emerald eyes and tried to smile. The gash along his right jawline reminded him not to. "Where am I?"

"At the regional hospital in Cusco. You were airlifted here two days ago."

"Guessing next time the guide tells me to descend ahead of an approaching storm, I should listen."

"You know, for a US senator, you ain't too smart sometimes," Eli joked. He had always been known for his sarcastic sense of humor.

Through the receding fog, Dan's memory flashed a spark of recall. Moises and Eli imploring him to come with them back down the mountain . . . the warnings . . . the approaching storm. He thought he could outpace the storm after lingering at the summit. He was an experienced climber who knew better. Dan had discovered climbing in college. A high school star in baseball and basketball, he always enjoyed athletics and competition. Knowing he wasn't good enough to play collegiately, a friend suggested a school-sponsored climbing trip for beginners to Càrn Mòr Dearg in Scotland. From that first summit, he was hooked. In the ensuing years, he had broken away as often as possible to climb some of the world's most impressive peaks, among them Mount Fuji, Mount Olympus, and Kilimanjaro.

The Ausangate expedition was not his toughest challenge, but it did represent his first climb in Peru. Dan had been reluctant to invite Eli on this climb. Eli had said he could handle the physical challenge, but Dan worried that the middle-aged CPA who had little time to exercise was telling himself a lie. Ironically, it was he, not his best friend, who lay broken and battered in a foreign hospital bed.

Dan and Eli had spent the prior week in the region to adjust to the climate in advance of the climb. It was good spending some time in the region, seeing how the locals lived. Ausangate was situated in the Cusco district within the Cordillera Vilcanota mountain range. Part of the "sacred mountains," as they are known by those native to the area, Ausangate was painted with rich colors, layered one over another, that display all the brilliance nature could muster.

The "Rainbow Mountain" was also seen by natives as the sacred and wild masculine energy. In the foothills, it was common to see grazing llama and alpaca flocks foraging for nourishment. Dan knew these animals were used by locals to farm, and their wool became needed clothing required to brave a sometimes harsh climate. Hides became sandals. Droppings were used for fertilizer. Once their useful lives had concluded, these animals would be killed for food. A tinny-sounding intercom announcement refocused his attention.

"Dr. Chavez, su paciente en la habitación 4A despertó."

"Dr. Chavez, your patient is awake in room 4A."

Five minutes later, Dr. Chavez came through the door of his private suite. "Señor Alston, I am glad you are finally awake. It is not every day we get to treat a US senator who fell off our mountain." Chavez grinned. His dark complexion and graying mustache gave him an affable appeal. "I am Dr. Chavez. You have been in my care since your arrival two days ago."

"It doesn't seem like I've been unconscious for two days. Did someone call Bri? What about Tally?"

Eli jumped in. "Relax, Mr. Bigshot. A few hours after you arrived, a representative from the US consulate came by. The State Department was tracking down Bri at Georgetown and I spoke to Tally myself. She wanted to jump on a plane, but I told her to sit tight until we knew what the story was."

Feeling relieved, Dan tried to relax. The pain continued to intrude on the notion, but he looked at the doctor and pressed on. "When can I go home?"

Chavez smiled warmly and replied, "We'll see. A couple of days at least, I think. Now that you are awake, we will see how you do once you are up and moving about."

"Thank you, doctor. Slipping off the face was harrowing in its own right. I'd hate to think what might have happened had the snarling wolf gotten to me before the rescue team in the chopper."

"Wolf?" inquired Chavez. "Señor Alston, I have lived here my entire life. In fact, I have climbed Ausangate numerous times. I can assure you that there are no wolves on Ausangate."

"But . . . it was so real. At the time I blacked out, I was preparing to be mauled."

"My best guess is that you were experiencing a hallucination, probably emanating from the hypothermia or the concussion you suffered. Rest up. I will have some food sent in and return to check on you later."

As Chavez turned to leave, Eli got out of the recliner, looked up at his friend of thirty-plus years, and snickered. "Wolves, huh? What else did you 'see' up there? Flying monkeys, perhaps?"

"Now that you mention it, there was a condor, flying low above my head and circling . . . and that damn chant."

"Chant? Okay, I'll bite. What chant?"

Hesitantly, Dan described the wispy female intonation he had randomly experienced for decades.

"You must have hit your head really hard. Snarling wolves, condors, and seductive women whispering sweet nothings in your ear. The wildlife you can keep. The last part doesn't sound too bad," he smirked.

Dan decided to change the subject. "How long have you been camped out in this room?"

"Since you arrived," he replied. "I did extend our stay at the hotel, but I haven't been back there since you came in."

Dan tried to smile. Eli had always been there for him. When they became friends in high school, Dan's father was serving as governor of Maryland and his mother was the executive director for a statewide, nonprofit animal shelter. An only child, he saw precious little of them. He concentrated on his studies, the baseball and basketball teams he starred on, and, along with Eli, the vain attempt to score with every pretty girl on the private school campus. Without Eli, those years might have been unbearable.

When he began his business after graduating at the top of his class at Wharton, his father told him he was insane. No one starts a business right out of school, he yelled. But Eli, the number cruncher, helped him bring his vision to life. His startup, an online recycling business that meshed perfectly with Dan's passion for the environment, sold twelve years later for $1.2 billion. Eli earned his CPA and opened an accounting and business advisory firm. Dan became an angel investor and ultimately followed his father's footsteps into politics, starting in the Maryland state senate. Eli had been his emotional crutch through it all, even during his lowest point when Maddie left. It was why now, at age fifty, he forgave Eli's propensity for sarcasm and cynicism. They were like brothers. The thought of Eli spending two nights in a hospital recliner shouldn't have surprised him, but at some level, it did. Being honest with himself, he loved the man.

Eli's cell phone came to life. It was Tally. "Yes, ma'am, the good senator is awake and ready to assume control of his life," Eli joked and then handed the phone to Dan.

He pressed Eli's phone against his left ear and thought how good it was to hear her voice. He had always guarded against getting involved with staff. His father had regaled him with stories of sexual exploits that brought down more politicians than the fickle nature of the average voter. Dan had always been careful. When he was married to Maddie, temptations were easy to avoid. His love for her would never truly die. Even now, as an eligible bachelor, he walked the straight and narrow path of responsibility, accountability, and integrity. After getting Tally up to speed on his current physical state, he dove right into work. "Lining up votes for the Clean Water Act?"

"Dan," she said, "we can go over that when you are feeling better. First things first: Bri has been arrested."

"Arrested? For what?" His daughter had never been in trouble of any kind. *What could have transpired?* he wondered.

"Assault and battery," she replied. "I don't have all the details. DC police just called the office looking for you when you didn't answer your cell. Joc got the call and forwarded it to me. I'm heading down there now."

Dan Alston's overpowering love for his daughter caused a rush of adrenaline and a momentary pause from his body's assorted maladies. He sat up, ripped the IV from his arm, and looked over to Eli. "Come on, we're going home."

CHAPTER 7

Cusco Village, 1472

Jade stood in the small waterfall underneath a hidden embankment. Here, she washed away the grime from the long journey home. The dusty trail left a film on her long, black hair, and she yearned to free herself from the burdens of the trail. Standing in the downpour rustling over the rocks above while the river swirled around her knees, Jade felt something she had never before experienced. Somehow, the journey to Laguna Negra had changed her. She felt powerful, invincible, and perhaps even immortal. She tilted her head backward and let the rushing water cleanse her face and hair. *Yaku . . . the water, a gift to be treasured.*

Jade had plans for the day, none of which included her role as Acila, which was the designation given to young women her age with the expectation they would live in isolation learning how to cook and weave with the intent of being married off to a noble or perhaps being sacrificed to Inti, the sun god. No, this was not for her. Her parents were long gone, killed in a vicious flood when she was eight. Raised by the village shaman, she was taught to be independent. She would honor her independence even if it meant rebelling against Sapa, the supreme leader.

Her independence came at a cost. Being without a husband meant no government allotment of land accorded to married couples. Life amidst the farming village as a single person normally predestined one to hard labor. Jade was not intimidated by this prospect. She had always known she was preordained for a greater purpose. Growing up the way she did, under the watchful eye of Maicu, the village shaman of Cusco, she was denied an education. This was a privilege reserved for the children of nobility. She, a commoner, and her childhood playmates were made to observe their parents at work, learn a trade, and prepare for a life of labor once they came of age. She had watched and learned from Maicu. Even as a young girl, she had felt the sphere of energy that surrounded her. Maicu saw it too and enriched her with wisdom. Yana provided a higher level of education, one that would eventually enable mastery.

Once dried from the river bath, Jade pulled the brown, leathery tunic over her head and straightened out the garment. A sash tied around her waist completed the outfit, which bore no design—a way to mark her on sight as a commoner. She pulled the sandals onto her feet and tied the thin straps around her ankles.

Today's chore would be to inspect the village crops on the common land overseen by her people, the lowest class of citizens whose job it was to grow the crops that fed the nobles and high-ranking officials. Jade was assigned the task of inspecting the crops and ensuring the stores of chuños, the freeze-dried potatoes, were intact. Once processed by the combination of the day's warmth and evening's chill, the chuños were jarred and preserved at higher elevations for later dates when they would be made into bread and stew. To properly satisfy the nobility residing in the palatial city structures, her inspection of the common lands would take the better part of two or three days. The crops of potatoes, maize, and quinoa were integral to the Incas' survival.

○○○○○

Jade sat atop a hill overlooking the fields, enjoying the light wind making its way through her long dark hair and gently rustling the tall, bushy, multicolored quinoa crop. From her vantage point, she admired the white, red, and yellow plants occupying the land as far as her eyes could see. The wind carried the distinct odor of the quinoa plants, which smelled somewhat musty to Jade. Having lived in this region her entire life, she knew the aroma came from the bitter outer sheath of the quinoa seed, the saponin, which would be stripped after harvest.

The Incas had mastered the art of irrigation. Quinoa needed less water than maize and the delivery system created by prior generations had the quantity perfected for each respective crop. Harvest time would occur in one moon. It seemed like yesterday that Sapa had sowed the first seeds as part of the opening season ceremony. Since Maicu passed away, Jade had undertaken this responsibility to earn meager amounts of food in return.

"You! Turn around . . . immediately," commanded Cunac in a stern, raspy voice.

Jade bristled at the sight of the neighboring shaman. Cunac had abused Maicu, belittling him at every turn, drawing Jade's ire. Maicu's fatal heart attack occurred in the aftermath of Cunac's harassment. Jade vividly recalled that night. The sacred fire in honor of Great Mother Earth and Inti, the Sun God, the singing of icaros and Cunac's ingestion of the ayahuasca. Maicu's back was turned toward her. She couldn't prove it, but she had always believed that Cunac had regurgitated *tsentsak*, the magical darts possessed by all shamans. Tsentsak caused illness and even death. A healing shaman prevented them from leaving the body for illicit purposes and even removed tsentsak from victims to save lives. An evil shaman, or a sorcerer, used tsentsak with the intent to kill. Jade had always planned to follow in Maicu's footsteps as a healer. Maicu's murder and Yana's mentorship had changed everything. Jade understood that her soul would not be perfected in this lifetime. Her soul would one day be reborn into another body, in another time, to live in quest of righting the wrongs of this and prior lives.

Rising slowly, she looked at Cunac. He repulsed her. He was a tall, stocky beast of a man with wavy salt and pepper hair parted in the middle and kept in place by a brown headband with three long feathers, each dyed a different color. His graying beard and shocking coal black eyes with flecks of gray, along with his hooknose, made him look all the more imposing. Jade was not afraid. Cunac was her motivation. His evil nature inspired her to study under Yana, to gain the advantage. She blamed Cunac for Maicu's death and the poverty of her village.

"You have stolen food from the poor people of Cusco for the last time. I shall see that you are punished."

Jade strode toward the imposing older man and spat at his feet. "I have stolen nothing," she protested.

Cunac grinned and kicked his foot toward her, raising a cloud of dust, and said, "There is no one else here but you and me. It is my word against yours. You will be punished. I will administer your public flogging myself, in full view of your fellow commoners."

Her initial reaction was pure, unfiltered rage. She wanted to eviscerate this man, take her knife to his throat and rip the flesh from his bones. It was Cunac who stole food from her village. Since he had killed Maicu, the most benevolent man who ever lived, Cunac had become shaman for Cusco and the neighboring region. He was a powerful man who no one would challenge.

In response to the unfounded accusation, Jade said nothing. She closed her eyes, summoned the wolf, her power spirit-animal, and tried to contain the rising fury others had once possessed but abandoned at Laguna Negra.

CHAPTER 8

Maritza sat before her boss, Tyler Morrison, in the Washington, DC, offices of American Clean Food, which also referred to itself as ACF. The organization was only five years old, but it had made significant inroads as a lobbying firm representing the interests of clean food growers in the US. While she waited for Morrison to complete a phone conversation, she considered her situation and how much had changed. She was new to the DC political scene. Having grown up in Miami as the only child of Peruvian immigrants, Maritza was raised by well-meaning parents who each worked numerous jobs to try to make ends meet. Her father was a doorman at the Miami Ritz-Carlton. In his off-hours, he worked as a carpenter and did other handyman work. Her mother labored at the Ritz as a maid and also as a seamstress in a local dress shop. Consequently, they were never home and Maritza, at a young age, was left to fend for herself.

When her parents were killed in a freak accident, her sense of being alone was never more pronounced. A teenager had been texting behind the steering wheel and, in the process, mowed her parents down in the street. Maritza would have considered it an unfortunate act of bad luck were it not for the stories her mother told her. For generations dating back to their origins in Peru, family members had mysteriously perished in seemingly innocent "accidents." Her grandmother, an accomplished swimmer, had drowned in the Shimbe Lagoon, and her great-grandfather was washed down the side of a cliff during a particularly bad rainy season. The stories dated back to her family's times as part of the Inca civilization more than five hundred years ago.

To date, her career had mostly consisted of helping to launder drug money through high-traffic, cash-based businesses like dry cleaners and florists. To get her current job with ACF, she had engaged the services of an expert forger and hacker in Miami named Manuel Sanchez. It was he who created a "work history" indicating ten years as a lobbyist for Florida Fresh Fruits. Sanchez "erased" her real work history, cleaned up her credit report, and expunged her prior felony arrests. After all, if someone could steal an identity, she reasoned, couldn't the same principles be used to alter one? It took only sixty minutes to create a phony website with a stock photo of a businessman posing as the executive director of Florida Fresh Fruits. The same businessman wrote a glowing letter of recommendation raving about the miracles Maritza performed for Florida Fresh Fruits in Tallahassee. Just like that, she was hired on in DC. No one checks references these days. All she had needed to do was create the appearance of an appropriate background.

Morrison hung up the phone, apologized for making her wait, and got right down to business. "What if you don't get to see Alston in time?" ACF's executive director inquired. "Senate subcommittees have to submit budget recommendations in sixty days."

Maritza crossed her legs, sat up straight, and threw her head back ever so gently before replying, "I'm not panicked. I have broken through the first protective layer in Senator Alston's office. It won't be long before I get a face-to-face."

"Alston's committee and its influence are the keys to achieving literally all of our clients' objectives," proclaimed Morrison. Maritza smiled to acknowledge her acquiescence to the obvious. In DC, everyone spoke in acronyms. Maritza, in her head, had taken to calling Morrison "MOTO"—master of the obvious. He bored her. The job, however, and his existence in her world were necessary for the time being to complete her real objective.

"Our top people are working to finalize a brief for you to give Alston. I've seen the rough draft. It details the idiosyncrasies of every country in the world and what barriers they are holding up to prevent our clients from exporting food to people in need."

"Anything surprising?" she asked, knowing Morrison was a retired ACLU attorney who championed social causes and had no prior experience in clean food exports.

"It's quite an array of tricky issues. The list runs the gamut from excessive duties, value added taxes, quarantines from outbreaks that occurred decades ago, objections to genetically modified crops, pesticides, weeds, fungus, insects, and even crooked customs officials. Sometimes the governments of foreign nations simply hold up our food exports for completely unrelated reasons, leaving their own people to starve."

"Unrelated reasons? Like what?"

"It's unbelievable, but a foreign country might want to export something to the US—like steel, for instance. They hold up our exports of food to their country for a trade agreement to buy more of their steel. Shortsighted, if you ask me." Morrison had a full head of gray hair brushed back with a minimal amount of gel. The back hung over the collar of his plaid sport coat, not quite long enough for a ponytail. He pushed his hand up his crinkled forehead and sighed. "That's why your work is so important. Alston leads the Senate Subcommittee on Agriculture, Nutrition, & Forestry. He can cut through some of the red tape."

Maritza delivered her trademark smile, the one she knew melted the hearts of men. Morrison was old, but he was no exception. He and his organization were nothing more than a bridge to a world where wrongs from long ago would finally be made right. She had to keep herself from laughing at Morrison, the old fool in his yellow polka-dot bowtie. She would get in front of the good senator not for ACF's purpose but for her own. Alston would learn soon enough that it was she, Maritza Coya, who would control the fate of mankind and what they ate, not some high and mighty senate subcommittee.

She bid Morrison adieu and made her way out of the Romanesque office building in the northwest part of DC. She hailed a cab and while she rode in the back on her way home to the apartment on DuPont Circle, she contemplated her mission: break the curse. As unbelievable as it had sounded when she first met with the psychic in Miami, she came to believe in its story.

The proof was in her own family's history. She recalled the numerous stories of tragic deaths, all of which she could now attribute to the curse. At one point in her life, it would have been unimaginable to Maritza that she once lived as the daughter of a shaman in fifteenth-century Peru and was now being asked to right the wrongs of that period. Her visit to the psychic was originally regarded as a joke, something to do one day when she was bored. She didn't even take the first meeting seriously. But something compelled her to return. Maritza's mind wandered back to the last session.

The story was told of two shamans living in the Inca Empire, one good and one evil, and a young woman named Jade whose father was the good shaman. He had been murdered by the evil counterpart. Maritza was intrigued. The psychic had told her that she and Jade, the good shaman's daughter, inhabited the same soul through reincarnation. The soul would remain in a state of unrest until the wrongs of the past were corrected. At first, it was difficult to comprehend. Maritza put all the disparate pieces together and it began to make sense. She considered her family's history of tragedy, the untold grief dating back generations, and now she held the key to ending it all.

CHAPTER 9

"I can't believe you beat up a guy from the State Department," Dan said while laughing with his daughter as they finished dinner in her Georgetown apartment. He and his "little kitten," as he had always called her, arrived at a place where they could joke about her first arrest. The State Department envoy wasn't as amused but did admit he could have taken a less clandestine approach to his mission. After returning from Cusco and learning the backstory of why Bri had been arrested, he reflected on what a strong and independent woman his daughter had become. Bri was an undergrad student when he and Maddie divorced. Parents breaking up is tough for kids at any age, but for a young college student, an only child, in her formative years, the situation was particularly concerning. This was especially true for the daughter of a US senator where home life was never what one would call normal.

He and Eli had landed at Andrews Air Force Base the previous day. Dr. Chavez had protested mightily against his abrupt departure from the Cusco hospital, but Dan insisted he would rest on the plane and in the ensuing week after returning home. Truth be told, despite feeling sore all over, he was doing remarkably well for a guy who just turned half a century old and survived an encounter with an angry mountain and its accompanying storm. Bri had offered to bring dinner to his place, but he insisted on visiting her. Their respective DC homes were only ten minutes apart. Even though he maintained a house in nearby Olney, Maryland, the condo afforded him the advantage of being on time every day without having to deal with the brutal DC rush hour.

Besides, Bri's apartment felt more like home than his own place of refuge in DC. He kept the bare essentials in the place: bedroom furniture, a couch, a flat screen, and a modestly stocked kitchen. Bri had the knack of making any place she lived in, even for short bursts, feel like a home lovingly made over many years. Like most college students, she had her share of parental hand-me-downs, but she proudly decorated the walls with views of breathtaking mountain ranges she had climbed with him—pictures she took herself. Dan loved that Bri shared his penchant for photography. Growing up wealthy had left Bri with the ability to spend a little more liberally on décor than her fellow law school students. Dan admired his daughter for not letting money go to her head. He and Maddie had done a great job of teaching her the importance of being humble, selfless, and independent. He watched her clear the dinner dishes and silently thanked God for his daughter, a blessing in his life. Lying face down in the frigid snow on a ledge of Ausangate, he had wondered if he would ever see her again. The thought was abhorrent. Now, together again here in DC, his heart was filled with love and admiration for his little kitten, as always.

"Dad, do you want an after-dinner drink?" she called from the nearby kitchenette. "I keep a bottle of Johnny Walker here just for you."

Dan's father, once governor of Maryland, had told him that every winning negotiation and special occasion should be capped off with a scotch. He was only fifteen when the governor offered up a Cutty Sark. At the time, he recalled thinking that the stuff tasted like what battery acid might. Over the years, he had acquired a taste for it. "Sure, you talked me into it," he replied.

They sat together in her living room, he on a white microfiber armchair and she on a blue, peach, and green floral sofa. He removed his brown penny loafers and placed his feet on the accompanying ottoman. Scotch in hand, his body began to feel the effects of yesterday's travel. Mentally, Dan Alston was always on top of his game. Physically, he was experiencing exhaustion on top of the aches and pains from his injuries. *Fifty*, he thought. It was a number he had always associated with old people. Now it was a sobering fact of reality.

"Classes going well?" he inquired.

She nodded, took a sip of her chardonnay, and said, "Some are more intriguing than others."

He smiled at his daughter. "You know how when you are in school, bored out of your mind in some class they force you to take, and you ask a classmate, 'Why are we here? We're never going to use this stuff?' Well, the truth is you're never going to use that stuff." Bri giggled in response to his frank admission. This type of communication was one of the things he loved about Bri. They could speak honestly about anything.

"How's work going at FPPL?" he asked.

"Okay. Earl has me researching legal precedent to establish arguments for busting trade agreements so he can get large quantities of needed grain to foreign countries."

"What exactly is he trying to achieve?"

"Beyond the obvious? I'm not sure. I know he had a meeting with a lobbyist for something called American Clean Food here in DC. Ever heard of them?"

Dan scratched his head, furrowed his brow, and searched the recesses of his mind. It sounded familiar, but there were so many organizations based in DC focused on social causes, he couldn't keep track of them all. "It doesn't ring a bell. If I think about it, I'll ask Tally. She interacts with the lobbyists far more than I do."

"Well, I can tell you this: I was there when the lobbyist came into the office. She was a looker—early forties and might be date-worthy for the most eligible man in town," Bri chided.

Dan formed a somewhat embarrassed smile at the suggestion of dating. He hadn't wanted the divorce. It was Maddie's idea. He had always given her everything she wanted, even when it came down to their marriage. Since their demise, he had thrown himself into his work. In four years, he could recall exactly three dates, all of which were fix-ups from concerned friends. Two resulted in one-night stands and the third was a dud that flamed out before the main course at dinner arrived. Bri had his best interests in mind. He knew that, but he still loved Maddie. Eventually, he would need to accept that she had moved on, a feat he also needed to accomplish.

"Not saying I don't want to meet the beautiful lobbyist, but a senator dating a lobbyist could place me in a compromising position. Your grandfather taught me that when it comes to the political spotlight, always walk the straight and narrow path." He rubbed his temples to ease the tension of an oncoming headache.

"Are you okay?" she asked.

"Yeah, yeah, just a little thunder boomer forming. They have been coming on fairly regularly since the fall."

"Docs say anything about that?"

"Head CTs came back fine. All normal aftermath in light of a trauma like the one I experienced. My other issues seem to be more pronounced, however."

"Other issues?"

Dan sipped his Johnny Walker and let the scotch soothe his anxiety as he began to recall the visions, the female voice, and the apparent out-of-body experience he had endured forecasting the world's end. He concluded the recitation with the story of the snarling wolf on Ausangate. As he spoke, he watched his daughter's face express the incredulity of what she was hearing. "You think I'm nuts, don't you?"

"No, not at all. You've never shared any of this with me. I'm fascinated. Does Mom know?"

"No, I never told her. She would have told me I was working too hard, drinking too much, or both. I figured silence was the path of least resistance. I never told anyone before now. Actually, I tried to tell Eli in the hospital, but I think he chalked it off to post-trauma delirium."

After Dan told her the entire history of events—seeing visions in his sleep and hearing the female voice in his sleep, at the gym, and even on the Senate floor—she shook her head as if amazed.

"Well, since we are playing true confessions, I have been seeing a psychic."

"A psychic? You mean like a gypsy fortune-teller?"

She laughed. "No, Dad, not a gypsy fortune-teller—a lady with a gift. She can tell you more about yourself than you might think possible. She's been a big help to me. Maybe you should talk to her."

"Picture the headlines: Senator from Maryland visits psychic to battle visions and voices. If that got out, I wouldn't have to worry about whether or not to run for reelection. The media would decide for me."

"Maybe I could talk to Madame Cece for you, you know, without mentioning your name."

"Well, I appreciate it, Kitten. Let's just see how things go over the next few weeks."

"So you are electing to do nothing and hope for a different result."

He fashioned a lopsided smile, his eyes twinkled, and he said lovingly with admiration for his daughter having called him out, "Yup, something like that."

○○○○○

It felt like forever since Dan had been in his own office. Between recent government travel, outside meetings, the vacation in Peru, and the added days in the Cusco hospital, time had just whizzed by. He needed to catch up with Tally. She was as indispensable as one could get. Ninety percent of the business of his office could effectively be run without his daily input, but he knew the major decisions were piled high. As was their custom, he and Tally sat at the round mahogany conference table in Dan's office. They each pulled up to the table in one of the plush black leather chairs reinforced by antique brass studs along the arms and seat and matching perfectly with the burnished look of the dark wood table.

Dan looked across the walls of his office as he sipped the hot coffee an aide had just set on the table. The framed wall map of his home, Maryland, bore the title, "The Old Line State." On the adjacent wall were pictures of himself with various dignitaries—President Trump, President Obama, several key senators who had become close personal friends—but his two favorite photos were displayed front and center: his dad and him in the governor's mansion in Annapolis, and with Bri in her cap and gown during undergrad ceremonies at the University of Maryland. He took a moment to reflect on his life and, gazing down at the azure carpet, decided that all in all, he was a pretty lucky guy.

Tally sat across the table amidst the stack of file folders; each, he was sure, contained the vestiges of a problem he would need to address. Her strawberry-blond hair fell over her shoulders in waves. The dark blue dress she wore had a moderate neckline accompanied by a petite white-lace trim. A string of small pearls completed her ensemble.

"We have three major issues to go over, Dan."

She continued to brief him but suddenly, without a hint of warning, his head became heavy and his mind filled with fog. Tally's voice sounded tinny, as if it were coming from an ancient PA system. His vision blurred and dizziness befell him. Nausea consumed him. He closed his eyes in hopes that the moment might pass quickly. He hoped Tally didn't notice something was wrong. In his mind's eye, all he could see were the visions of Tally in that fateful night. In a flash, the image of her hair falling out in clumps and her head exploding in a cloud of black dust took over his brain. The explosion, as he quickly relived it, caused his body to jump.

"Dan, Dan, oh my God. Are you okay? Susie, call 911."

Dan began to regain his balance and a sense of normalcy. He heard Tally order the receptionist out front to call for help. "No, don't. I'm okay. Just a dizzy spell. I'm fine now."

She viewed him tentatively and with concern said, "Leave the coffee. Let me get you some water to sip. Do you want to lay down on the couch?"

He declined, preferring as always to hulk through anything that stood in the way of progress. Tally left and returned with a bottle of spring water. She stood behind his chair as he sipped the water. After a few minutes, he was ready to resume the briefing. *What the hell? Was that a migraine?* Unlike the prior episodes over the past several years, this one took a physical toll unlike any other. Maybe it was the injuries; maybe it was his weakened state. He'd think about it later. Right now, he had to get his head back into the briefing.

Tally started again, tentatively. "There are three major issues but honestly, they can wait a little longer if you want to go home and take it easy. Can I call a doctor for you?"

"No, no, let's get down to it," he managed to reply with as much conviction as he could muster.

Tally went through the three issues. The first was the approval for the committee budget on Agriculture, Nutrition, and Forestry. As committee chair, he had to weigh in on the final submission before it went to leadership for compilation. Many senators in his shoes received an executive summary choosing to avoid the time-consuming chore of reading a voluminous report detailing the rationale for each expenditure. Not Dan—he would review the entire brief in all of its monotonous grandeur. After all, that's what his constituents were paying him to do. Evasion of duties simply because he could get away with it was not in his makeup. He knew no one would squawk if he chose to bypass the lengthy report, but he just wasn't wired that way. His original intent was to read the report on the long flight home from Peru. His premature exit from the hospital and the need to rest on the plane derailed that notion. Now he was behind and would need to work late into the evening.

Tally continued to discuss upcoming votes on two bills, one for $1 trillion in infrastructure rebuilding and the other to stabilize healthcare. Philosophically, these were easy issues to process. He knew where he stood on each matter. The devil, however, was in the details. If all bills were simply about one thing, life would be easy. To get votes, colleagues threw all sorts of unrelated subjects into a bill, hoping to sneak them through the process. Consequently, these draft bills would also need to be read in detail. There went any downtime planned during the coming weekend.

Dan thanked Tally and placed the thick files on each matter into his briefcase. He closed the door behind her and sat down on his black leather couch. He inhaled deeply, loosened his red and white striped necktie, and thought about his last campaign. He had stirred the masses. He was still young and good looking, and he spoke with confidence. A successful entrepreneur who was passionate about social causes, he pledged to help clean up Washington and had three ideas with which to accomplish the objective. One, make all spending bills about only one thing—no more "tack-ons" to get votes. Two, strongly regulate lobbyists who were paid to sometimes influence senators from doing what might be counter to the needs of their constituencies. Third—and he felt most strongly about this one—impose term limits on all US senators and congressmen. If the president was subject to two terms, why should senators and congressmen serve forever, some into their eighties and nineties, unable to attack complex issues with the same mental acuity they once possessed? The odds of accomplishing any of these game-changing objectives were extremely long, particularly the term limits. But he had to try. He was there to make a difference. He had to stay true to himself or he would no longer be able to look in the mirror and like what he saw.

He took a deep breath and exhaled forcefully. Another sip of the spring water and then over to the phone to return calls from many colleagues and key constituents worried about him in the aftermath of his accident. He had to keep in mind that, for a few days at least, he was a leading global headline. When he ran for Senate, he wanted to make news, not be the news. He got off the couch and made his way toward his desk, a restored antique that had once been used by Harry Truman. As he traversed the blue carpet, the dizziness once again consumed him. His head felt heavy and his breathing became constricted. He stumbled toward the desk, reaching out his right arm to brace from falling, and steadied himself as best he could. His mind went dark while images of emaciated people crying out for help amidst the ruins of cities across America flooded his brain. The sound from the scene was a static, crackling noise suggesting fire. The scent of ash and burning flesh filled his nostrils. Dizziness gave way to full-scale vertigo. The office began to rotate, and he parked his rear end on the front edge of the vaunted desk. He placed his hand to his eyes in a hollow attempt to shield himself from any more of the destructive images. And then his head began to clear, his sense of balance returned, and just when he thought everything would be okay, he heard it. That voice. The haunting intonation for which he had no logical explanation.

Yāvenhawk, O Yāvenhawk
I am one with you.

CHAPTER 10

Frustrated, Tally sat at her desk, laptop open, seeking answers. Something about Joc's morning pitch felt off. Until now, the craziness of the day hadn't allowed her time to think about it. But now, at 7:30 p.m., the last of her staff had departed. Finally, a few minutes to herself. *American Clean Food?* She had never heard of it. Nor this new lobbyist, Maritza Coya. Tally checked the federal registry required of lobbyists and found just the basics: name, rank, and serial number. Aside from some vague information on Coya working for something called Florida Fresh Fruits, there was scant information available.

As she frequently did when she worked late, she kicked off her high heels, went to a mini-fridge, pulled out a yogurt, and mixed it with some granola she kept stashed in a filing cabinet. Forty-seven, divorced with no children and no life other than serving the good senator, Tally instinctively knew she needed something more. Like many single women in DC, she silently pined for Dan Alston. After all, he was as true as water from a mountain spring. Unlike her contemporaries, she worked with him every day, side by side. She knew him inside and out. She knew his strengths, weaknesses, and vulnerabilities, what he liked to eat and drink, and really, his entire personal history.

Her mind drifted back to their first campaign together. She was hired on from a PR firm to help with campaign strategy and optics. Tally reported to Dan's campaign manager, Sully, as they called him. The old curmudgeon was a brilliant strategist but not much fun to hang out with. They were all on the eastern shore of Maryland, just outside Ocean City in Wicomico County. A rally was held in concert with a crab feast. After the final song was played by the last of the four country bands and the event officially ended, she and Dan lingered with event organizers for two hours, drinking Bud Light poured from plastic buckets and nibbling on shrimp steamed in beer and Old Bay seasoning. Her friends from college had called her a beer wimp. Her petite frame never could hold much. Two or three and she was gone. She never drank on the job, but that night she let herself go. The campaign was drawing to a close and they were all exhausted.

Sitting next to Dan, she had let her true feelings show. In the haze of inebriation, she made a pass at him, suggesting subtly that her hotel room door would be unlocked that evening. She placed her arm behind his back and laid her head on his shoulder. She could still vividly recall how rigid his shoulder instantly became, as if the mere presence of her body next to his was repulsive. No, she knew better. While she always resisted the urge to beat on herself, she knew why Dan had rejected her. He was that one-of-a-kind all-around great guy. He loved his wife and doted over young Bri. Silently she thought, there would be another opportunity someday. Maddie was out of the picture. Dan may decide not to run for reelection. She just had to be patient.

Years later, she still held out hope. She stared at the laptop. A blank Google search box stared back. In her quest for answers on Washington's newest high-powered lobbyist, she had come up empty. Who did she know who might be able to help? Of course, Dan had a million connections, but asking would just introduce him to the concept of Coya. This was a notion she preferred to avoid, at least for the time being. She wanted time to properly vet the lobbyist and her organization's interest before involving the senator. The next logical step was to simply address the situation the way she did every other one: take it head on. Even though for some inexplicable reason she didn't want to, she would have her assistant reach out to Coya for a meeting. Nothing elaborate . . . ten to fifteen minutes max. Just enough time to get a feel for the person, the organization she represented, and her motives. Tally's people radar, as she liked to call it, was right more often than not. In this particular case, the radar screamed trouble.

CHAPTER 11

"What exactly is a clean food box?" inquired Eli Shepherd to his prospective client.

"Think of it as our modest effort to save the world, one person at a time," replied Earl Sanderson. "It's why I came to work for the Foundation for Preservation, Peace, and Light. I've dedicated my career to being the patron saint of lost causes. I guess the board figured I would be perfect for the job," he mused.

Eli smiled spuriously at Sanderson's banal attempt at humor. "If I am going to help FPPL as a trusted business advisor, it is critical that I learn everything material about the organization."

"Of course," replied Sanderson. Eli watched as Sanderson swept his hand through his wispy gray remnants. The guy must be naturally anxious. He was sweating profusely. Granted, it was unseasonably warm for Maryland on this fall day. Eli's office overlooked Lake Kittamaqundi in Columbia. When the sun reflected off the lake, it seemed that the entire building felt warmer. Eli momentarily gazed out the window and saw a group of mallards swimming happily on the outer edges of the lake. He had always loved the outdoors. His appreciation of nature was the primary reason he selected the office building in downtown Columbia for his accounting firm. Columbia was the second largest city in Maryland and was more or less equidistant to both Baltimore and DC.

Eli refocused on his would-be client and resumed the quest to climb the learning curve. "Tell me what you guys are doing now."

Sanderson shifted in the chair, crossed his right leg over the left, pulled up a drooping argyle sock, and began droning on about the operation in its earlier days, as well as aspirational goals. "Our organization is a nonprofit founded on the belief that no barriers should stand in the way of feeding the poorest people, even in the most desolate places on earth. It would astound you how difficult it can be to achieve the simple goal of sending food to hungry people."

"Barriers? Like what?"

"Mostly export regulations, trade restrictions, you know, things of that nature. My board recommended I hire a lobbyist to cut out some of the red tape. Frankly, I had never thought of hiring a lobbyist. I thought as executive director I would be the main person fighting the good fight every day in DC. After all, I did spend thirty-five years with the Peace Corps."

"So, what did you do?"

"I relented. Our board chair insisted that my background was best suited to design strategy and work operations. My history is traveling the globe and doing everything from disease prevention to feeding the hungry and negotiating with local village leaders to allow our help. Effective lobbying is, I am told, an art unto itself. I placed a series of inquiries around DC and ultimately found a lobbyist experienced in the food sector."

Sitting straight up in his leather side chair, notepad perched firmly in his lap, he pretended to be taking copious notes. Little did Sanderson know that Eli had the ear of the FPPL board chair and had personally recommended American Clean Food.

Sanderson went on. "We received a half dozen interesting responses but in the end, we hired ACF. Our board chair had heard that they had a lady who pulled off miracles in Tallahassee. The decision was really out of my hands."

Eli lamented to himself how weak Sanderson appeared. As a leader of an organization, one must show some degree of backbone. *Oh well, Sanderson's timid manner would likely serve him well in the long run.*

"Let's go over sources of funds for your operation."

"Mostly, we are fighting in a competitive space with other world hunger and peacekeeping efforts for corporate donors and federal grants. This is where I am spending most of my time."

"How do you convince donors to give to your cause versus dozens of similar causes?"

"We emphasize the 'clean food' aspect of our work and the intended long-term effects. Many competitive organizations are merely money collectors redistributing funds to other charities. Donors can never be sure what their generous monetary gifts are buying."

"And how is your operation going to overcome the same problem?" Eli flipped pages on his notepad, pretending to capture every detail. Given his penchant for remembering everything, the note-taking was just a ruse.

"Simple. We will develop and manage our own supply chain by establishing close relationships with logistics companies specializing in the warehousing and transportation of temperature-controlled food products, or what they call 'cold chain.'"

Eli needed to shift the conversation back to his purpose without it seeming obvious. "So, enter the clean food box."

"Precisely," replied Sanderson. His eyes lit up when Eli reconnected to the early part of their conversation. "A clean food box could conceivably contain fresh fruit, vegetables, protein, and a bottle of spring water. We envision creating millions of these boxes and shipping them to places where they are most needed."

"What happens when demand exceeds supply?" asked Eli.

"Oh, we know that will happen. Our objective is to have the clean food box program serve as sort of a precursor to the long-term goal of teaching people around the world to plant and farm with modern techniques and equipment. You know the old proverb: Give a man a fish, he eats for a day. Teach a man to fish, he eats for a lifetime. That's more or less our battle cry."

Eli nodded and smiled to convey his alleged admiration for the humanitarian effort being laid out before him by Earl Sanderson.

"How many employees do you have?"

"Right now, we have myself, an administrative assistant, and an operations manager."

Eli felt his sense of excitement building. He delighted in this part. Maybe it was just his nature, the irascible part of his personality. The thrill was unmistakable. Just knowing that he needed to use someone and that the other person was completely oblivious to his scheme. Man, he loved that feeling!

"Feeding the world is a huge endeavor, Earl. I can see this costing millions to operate each year."

"No doubt, but you'd be surprised at how much product and service we can get donated. We have already established a relationship with a cold chain logistics company that is charging us an extremely discounted rate. Food donations are already pouring in. The cold chain company is creating kits we designed that will comprise a single clean food box. But in the end, you are right, even with everything considered, it will cost tens of millions to conduct a proper operation."

"What about the legal aspects of the operation? With all of the operations details you described, and with such a small staff, you must have an international law firm helping you."

"Good assumption but no. We cannot afford one. Since we are so close to Georgetown Law, we have arranged to get free legal work done through the Office of Public Interest and Community Service. In fact, the student assigned to us is Bri Alston, the senator's daughter."

"What a coincidence! The senator and I are old friends." Eli found it hard to keep a straight face. This was too easy. He fondly recalled how he came to learn of FPPL. It was Bri who had told him all about her work for the young nonprofit in the aftermath of Ausangate. "Earl, I think you already know that Shepherd & Associates is the largest CPA and business advisory firm in the Baltimore–Washington corridor. As you might imagine, Senator Alston aside, we have countless numbers of influential business owners, politicians, and wealthy individuals as clients who could be prevailed upon to help you raise the millions you will need to get your clean food boxes in the hands of the world's hungriest people. You won't find a more qualified firm than mine to do your accounting work. To make the decision as easy as possible, because you are a nonprofit working for a cause I am keenly interested in, we will take on your account pro bono."

Sanderson smiled and extended his hand. "You are a good man, Eli. Thank you so much."

Eli was satisfied. The beginning of the end was now in hand. He escorted Sanderson out and mustered his most endearing smile as they shook hands. Eli embraced Sanderson's right wrist with his left hand to accentuate a show of collegiality. He returned to his office, sat in his leather chair, and swiveled to face the large picture window behind him, which overlooked the lake. It was the lunch hour and many people milled about the plaza in search of either food or fresh air, maybe even a moment of sanity from the occasional office-life doldrums.

His mind wandered back to the mysterious package he received a year earlier from Florida. The small bubble mailer had arrived at his office with no return address. Inside was a flash drive and a handwritten note. It simply said, "Play me." At first, Eli disregarded the whole thing as a clever marketing ruse. Some company that wanted to do business attempting a covert play to get him to watch an infomercial on his computer. He would have none of it. He tossed it in the trash. Two weeks later, a similar package arrived with the same note. Again, he threw it away, this time worried about malware.

Things changed when he received a voicemail from a woman who didn't identify herself but made reference to the mailers. She told him that the video on the drive would change his life profoundly and indelibly. She assured him it was personal and that one more flash drive was on the way . . . just in case he happened to have "misplaced" the first two. A day later, the same bubble mailer arrived once again. This time, he took the drive and inserted it into an out-of-service laptop he found in the IT storage area. One could not be too careful.

The memory of the short video would forever be ingrained upon his mind. A strikingly beautiful woman appeared on the screen with a message so disarming, he had trouble believing her. Something forced him to keep listening. Maybe it was her stunning good looks. Yes, he admitted to himself, he probably was that shallow. But still, she reached someplace deep inside him and when she finished, he longed to learn more.

Realizing that she might come across as a con artist, she had arranged for Eli to meet and discuss the video contents with a third party whose credibility would not be an issue. The end of her video message instructed him to contact a man named Quesaré.

CHAPTER 12

Cusco Village, 1472

With little time to react, Jade removed her knife from its protective sheath as Cunac made his way toward her. She told herself she was unafraid. As Cunac approached, Jade shifted in the dirt, feeling the hot earth beneath her thin sandals. She bent her knees and assumed the stance of a warrior. Cunac was a head taller and outweighed her by two times, but none of that mattered. She would not be taken alive. In the seconds before the physical encounter, Jade tried to recall all of what Yana had taught her. How to summon the power to command her foe and control the situation. She began to sweat. Cunac's feet stomped toward her and it was as if she felt the earth move.

The stench from his body, likely from a combination of sweat and the chewing of coca leaves, made her sick. Jade knew that people often used coca leaves in higher elevations for energy and to mitigate hunger. The coca leaves were a staple of living in a mountainous region. A side effect, however, was a distinctive body odor. The light breeze that was so relaxing just a few moments ago was pushing his putrid scent toward her face. Cunac, the region's most powerful shaman, was far more experienced than she. Her will to resist and manage the situation using her own shamanic powers was fleeting. Her knees began to buckle and she dropped her knife just at the moment that Cunac's beefy fist slammed into her jaw. Jade felt the back of her head crashing into the hard-pounded dirt path overlooking the quinoa fields.

Through the haze as she lay in the dirt trying to contemplate her next move, Jade heard Cunac with his small drum. He tapped upon it in rhythmic fashion, chanting the same pattern of words over and over again. After several minutes he stopped, and somehow the air felt heavier. The musty smell of the quinoa turned acrid. She lifted her aching head off the ground and through the fog, she thought she saw the water from the irrigation system evaporate and the plants begin to wither.

ooooo

Jade's jaw was swollen. It ached from the encounter with Cunac's fist. Her hair was disheveled and her tunic was filthy. Cunac had literally dragged her from the quinoa fields to the village. Semiconscious, Jade recalled a rope extending from her bound hands causing stress on her arms and shoulder sockets. She was next to him, perched on her knees with her hands now tied from behind. The rope binding Jade's wrists was tight and dug into her skin while the platform's hard wooden boards sent searing pain through her knees. She looked around. Every person in the village stood at attention as Cunac dominated the makeshift wooden platform to address the crowd.

"This woman," he bellowed. "This woman has stolen from you. She has taken the food from your own mouths. Entrusted to watch over the crops, she sold parts of the upcoming harvest to a neighboring village for which I am also the shaman. Before I could prevent it, this woman used sorcery to dry up your water supply. This means the upcoming harvest will yield little." The angry mob howled. Their anger was clear.

Jade bristled at the lies he told. She was a loner in her own village. *Who would come to her defense? If only Maicu were still alive.* She fought the urge to cry, an emotion she deemed unacceptable, and lifted her head to face the crowd and absorb more of the injustice.

"Once I discovered her deceitful actions, I brought her here to face you. I have consulted with Sapa, who has mercifully decided that she shall not be put to death for her actions nor even publicly flogged. Sapa has decried that the woman you know as Jade be subjected to a life of hard labor." Cunac then smirked and said, "Of course, in my village when people are caught engaging in illicit activities, the villagers administer justice in their own way. I, for one, would not stand in the way should one or more of you decide this is a just and fair path forward."

CHAPTER 13

She was dressed to kill and she knew it. Maritza finished the last of her makeup and stood in front of the full-length mirror inside her room at the famed Watergate Hotel. At forty-two, her looks had not deserted her. Tall and slender, Maritza's long black hair snaked down her shoulders, coming to rest inches above the small of her back. The gown was her favorite, the one she inevitably chose when she needed to make a strong impression on a member of the opposite sex. Red, with a subtle hint of black, it had a plunging neckline partially covered by her long locks. The colors of the dress were naturally complemented by her dark complexion and the matching shade of lipstick. As a final touch, she donned a stainless steel cuff bracelet and a thin black scarf. Satisfied, she reached over to the dressing table and applied just the right scent, Poison by Dior.

Although she lived in DC, a room at the Watergate was an absolute must for her evening plans. Through help from Tyler Morrison, she had scored a ticket to an exclusive fundraiser starting at the nearby Kennedy Center and finishing at the hotel. The Congressional Kids Cancer Caucus held its annual fundraiser each October. Tickets were available by invitation only. The room would be filled with Washington's elite—politicians, business owners, lawyers, anyone who was a somebody would be there. The caucus was cofounded by Maryland Congresswoman Stella Gresham, who, according to Maritza's research, had lost her five-year-old son to childhood cancer nearly fifteen years ago. Gresham's district was near the home of her close friend, Senator Dan Alston. The good senator was a regular at the annual TOY Night sponsored by the caucus. Maritza, who was childless, admitted to herself she really didn't give a damn about the cause. In fact, she thought their "TOY" slogan was a bit campy, "**T**ogether **O**ver **Y**ears, we will eradicate childhood cancers." Nevertheless, like all attendees, she was expected to bring a toy to be distributed to pediatric cancer wards in the greater DC area. To avoid carrying it to the Kennedy Center, she left it with the Watergate maître d' who had started a collection box to be transported to the Moretti Grand Ballroom for the second half of the evening event. She stepped outside the hotel and entered the first available vehicle in a long line of black town cars waiting to transport guests from the hotel to the nearby theater. With the mild October weather, she could have easily walked the short distance, but in heels she elected to ride.

The commencement of the evening was a private concert for caucus guests featuring the National Symphony Orchestra performing a musical tribute to pop icon Neil Diamond. Maritza didn't care for the music selection but being visible during the performance was a necessary evil. If anyone had consulted her, they would be entertained by Gloria Estefan. Upon walking into the theater, Maritza was directed to a roped-off area where cocktails were being served. She accepted a white wine spritzer from a liveried server and moved to a high-top table. Looking around, she recognized many faces but didn't see the one she was looking for. She hoped he would be alone, making her mission for the evening easier. As she sipped her wine, she heard a voice come from behind.

"Maybe we can share a table with this young lady."

Maritza turned and observed an elderly gentleman in a classic black tuxedo, accompanied by his wife. "Allow me to introduce myself. I am Morris Erskine and this is my wife, Mimi."

Maritza, of course, knew Morris Erskine. Everyone in the room knew the retired chief justice of the Supreme Court. *My God, he looks ancient in person. Much older than his eighty-five years. How can one man's face be that wrinkled?* Mimi was reasonably attractive for a senior citizen but Maritza chuckled to herself at the shade of red hair dye. She thought Mimi looked like an old madame from a Miami brothel. With a few minutes to kill, she decided to have some fun. She put her arm around the old man, let him absorb the scent of her perfume, and lamented in her most sultry tone. "Well, I hope you won't judge me." The retired chief justice, known for his sense of humor and proclivity to flirt, blushed and replied, "Why, no, ma'am. You are someone that no judge could keep on the bench."

Inches from his leathery face, Maritza smiled at him just as his angry wife pounded him on the arm and said, "C'mon Morris, I think I see the Johnsons over there."

Maritza stood by herself for a few minutes, nursing her drink and spying the crowd for Alston. The lobby lights flickered. Along with the crowd, she moved toward the seating entrance and presented her ticket to the usher guarding the doorway. She moved down the left aisle toward the center orchestra and discovered her place at the halfway point between the two main aisles striping the theater floor. As she sat down, a familiar voice beckoned from her right.

"So we meet again," exclaimed a delighted Morris Erskine. Maritza smiled. Mimi was pissed. Maritza didn't care; the old man was harmless. She glanced around, looking for Alston again and hoping he was by himself. She was craning her head, making it a little too obvious.

"Are you waiting for someone?" inquired Erskine.

Embarrassed, she settled back in her seat and forced herself to relax. "No, Your Honor, I guess I am a little starstruck. You know, just seeing who is here. I don't get to events like this very often. It's not every day you get to meet a former chief justice of the Supreme Court." She smiled in the seductive way that she had long ago mastered. Erskine need not be suspicious of her.

"What was it you said you did for a living?"

Maritza gave the thirty-second elevator speech on American Clean Food, reciting, more or less, the same nonsense anyone might read on the mission section of their website. This seemed to appease him. Maritza was pleased when Mimi, agitated again, pulled his attention back to her. A second later, she saw him. Decked out in a tuxedo and walking down the aisle with that little twerp Talia Clayton. *Damn, what was she doing with Alston? Were they a thing?* None of her contacts had said anything about that. Just looking at the petite figure of Talia made her blood boil. Her dress was a simple design, white with a soft pink accent, which complimented her bouncy strawberry blonde hair. A single strand of Akoya pearls hung from her neck. Even with heels, she didn't look right next to the much taller senator. Maritza resolved to deal with that little priss later. She had prepared for the possibility he might show up with a date. She watched as the unlikely pair waltzed down the left aisle all the way to the front row. They were seated in the middle. Guests of honor, she supposed. The theater lights began to dim. A woman Maritza figured to be around forty-five years of age took the stage and assumed her position in front of a standing microphone. Stella Gresham introduced herself.

"Good evening and welcome to the tenth annual TOY Event sponsored by the Congressional Kids' Cancer Caucus. The toys you have brought tonight will delight sick children across the Capitol region while the money you generously pledge will assist us in research toward cures for a host of deadly childhood cancers."

As Gresham continued, Maritza tuned out. While she supposed she should have more compassion for why everyone was gathered in the elegant concert venue, she just didn't care. She fidgeted in her seat as Morris Erskine intentionally moved his left elbow over the shared arm between their two chairs. His arm was now invading her personal space, probably hoping for an errant feel. Mimi shot him a look. Mercifully, Gresham stopped talking and the houselights dimmed. She shifted uncomfortably in the upholstered chair as the orchestra opened the show with Neil Diamond's "America." As the music began, an enormous US flag unfurled from the top of the stage. This part of the evening was foundational. She couldn't wait for part two. That's where things would get interesting. First, however, she had to get Talia Clayton out of the way.

The special performance concert was scheduled for only an hour but the National Symphony Orchestra played for close to ninety minutes. Maritza had no idea there was so much Neil Diamond music to pay tribute to, but as the evening's program had told her, Diamond wrote and sang hit songs across parts of seven decades. The performance came to a crescendo with a song called "I'm Alive," which Maritza thought was somewhat amusing given the reason for the benefit. When the music ended and the houselights came on, Gresham once again took the stage and let everyone know that the string of black town cars was waiting out front to transport them to the Watergate for the dinner, auction, and cocktail hour. Like in a wedding, the front of the auditorium was permitted to exit first. She sat impatiently and did her best to keep her body perched to the left to avoid unwanted contact with Erskine, the old perv. Maritza couldn't help but stare as Alston walked up the aisle with his annoying little companion.

Thirty minutes later, the throng of people had invaded the elegant Moretti Grand Ballroom at the Watergate Hotel. Maritza took note of the dozens of round tables draped in white linen and accompanied by hushed tones of modernistic black and white diamond-shaped art on the walls. The black leather chairs looked slightly more comfortable than the stiff parlor chairs one was typically subjected to at these kind of events. Seats were assigned, yet Maritza had taken care of that. Hours before the concert, she had come down to the ballroom as it was being prepared by the hotel staff and conveniently relocated someone assigned to Senator Alston's table to her assigned table in the back of the room. The young man in charge offered some mild resistance but folded like a house of cards when Maritza explained she was the person in charge of the organizing committee. All that had been required was a wink and a light touch on his shoulder. It was imperative that she be seated near the senator.

The moment at hand, Maritza strolled casually toward the front of the seven-thousand-square-foot ballroom. Alston and his chief of staff were already seated. Her assigned seat had been moved. *Damn!* Someone was in her place. She couldn't make a fuss. The one open chair at the table was next to Talia Clayton, who would now be seated between herself and the senator. She quickly reassessed the situation and decided it could be most advantageous. She took her seat and introduced herself. Senator Alston smiled at her like a schoolboy and reached his arm across his chief of staff's face to shake hands. She held his hand for an extra few seconds, just long enough to make him feel her presence and to annoy Talia. When their hands parted, she looked at Talia and disingenuously apologized for her reach, smiling a spiteful smile. She immediately sensed this woman's dislike for her.

A pitcher of iced tea was in front of her. The opportunity was evident. She turned to Talia and said, "I see your glass is empty. Please, allow me to pour you a refill." She smiled in an attempt to disarm her obstacle but knew she had not been effective. Adeptly, Maritza took the small black cap off a tiny, quarter-inch vial she had concealed under her stainless steel cuff bracelet and emptied its contents into Talia's glass. The cryptosporidium parasite would cause the little bitch to quickly excuse herself for the rest of the evening. Maritza smiled as she envisioned this pipsqueak darting to the ladies' room for the beginning of what would be a long night of uncontrollable, explosive diarrhea.

○○○○○

It was approaching midnight. The mild October temperatures had made for a perfect evening concluding on the hotel terrace, which offered a stunning view of the Potomac River. Maritza leaned over the rail, letting the mild breeze gently move her hair over her shoulders and across the black scarf. Most of the guests, primarily an aging old-money crowd, had long since gone home. She had been drinking throughout the evening but only sporadically, with full glasses of water in between. She wanted to be social, but lucidity was required. Growing up in Miami, Maritza knew how to hold her liquor. She inhaled the pleasant evening air and felt the presence of a man approaching from behind.

"It was really nice getting to know you at dinner tonight. Your mission at American Clean Food is a worthy one. Advocating for a solution to world hunger is a noble cause."

She turned toward him slowly. She wanted the breeze to carry the scent of the Poison to her prey. She paused and took a long, hard look at Dan Alston. Sandy blond hair, with graying temples and a cleft chin, he really was a handsome man. As a mountain climber, he had to be in good physical shape. To Maritza, from casual observation, there was no doubt.

Alston continued. "We should get together in my office and see if there isn't some way I could help."

"I appreciate that, Senator. Your involvement will be pivotal to resolving a problem that has been going on for many lifetimes."

"Please, call me Dan."

"Thank you, Dan." She let her eyes melt into his. "Would it be okay if we left the business talk for another time?" Maritza turned her back against the rail and pulled Alston close to her. A nearby speaker on the terrace played Sinatra. *Strangers in the night.* Placing her arms around his neck, she guided him into a slow dance. The warmth of his body touched her soul. She felt something peculiar inside, a weakness of some sort. They swayed to the music as she moved her mouth to his and kissed him, gently at first and then with her tongue, penetrating his lips, intermingling and causing her own passion to rise beyond what she thought possible. She'd had many men and this was a job, not a romantic endeavor. Still, she was moved by his kiss. It threw her off her game but only for a moment. They parted lips and she looked deeply into his eyes, a haunting shade of light blue with a hint of gray. They appeared to hold the wisdom of centuries past with a story all their own to tell.

"I hope you don't mind," she said softly, not even needing to fake the emotion. "I'd been wanting to do that all night." Slightly taller, he returned the long gaze and kissed her in reply.

"Do you like scotch?" he asked. "They have a great whiskey bar here."

"I couldn't imagine anything more perfect."

The Next Whiskey Bar, as it was called, contained small oval tables with oversized, stuffed red chairs that looked like something from a sci-fi movie depicting a future world. The curved walls held spirits from floor to ceiling and gave the illusion of going on forever. Scotch wasn't her favorite, but tonight it was what she would be drinking. She was confident in her ability to keep up, drink for drink. Dan brought two Johnny Walkers from the bar and they retreated to a table in the back, seeking some modicum of privacy. She would get him talking. Men loved to inadvertently brag to women they had just met, especially over drinks. He would ask her questions about her life but she already knew she would have to reply only in the most cursory fashion.

"Can I tell you something most people don't know?" he inquired. After the third scotch, she could see he was tipsy. "Being a US senator is not all I imagined it would be."

"How so?"

"Well, for starters, it's impossible to get anything done. Opposing political parties don't agree on much and always want something in return for support of a good idea."

"I don't think that's a huge revelation. The average voter sees the dysfunction in Washington. Will it ever change?"

His words began to slur. "I have some thoughts on the matter. Like term limits for senators and congressmen. Why should we serve endlessly when the president can only serve two terms? Eliminating the continuous need to get reelected removes an inherent conflict of interest."

"You don't mind leaving the Senate? Introducing such an idea is bold for a sitting senator."

The waiter, a tall and very thin young man clad in a red vest, offered round four. Alston looked at her asking only with the expression on his face whether she wanted more. She replied by moving her hand under the tablecloth and caressing his inner thigh with her long, wispy fingers. As the waiter retreated, she stood up, bent over his right shoulder, her long hair brushing against his face, and said, "One more scotch might be nice, on my balcony. Room 1472." And with that, she could feel his stare bore into the back of her perfect figure, well-displayed by her favorite gown as she made her way to the elevator.

ooooo

Maritza left the door open. She already secured the bottle of Johnny Walker Black and had it waiting patiently in the room for the last drink of the evening. She slipped out of her gown and into a black-lace negligee falling just above her knees. After pulling the covers down from the king-sized bed, she took the bottle and two glasses and moved to the balcony overlooking the river. She sat, legs crossed, and began to feel a slight chill as the early morning hours rolled in. The scotch would warm her. She knew she would not be outside for too long. She heard a gentle knock on her door and resolved to ignore it. Maritza enjoyed building intrigue, especially with men when she needed to accomplish a purpose. She heard him call, almost sing out loud, "Hello." She decided to let him find her, admiring the view and patiently waiting.

When he discovered her on the balcony, her back to the slider, he ambled up from behind, leaned over, moved her hair and softly kissed her neck. Maritza felt a tingle go down her spine. She, the one who was always in control of every situation, attributed the sensation to the cool night air and the warmth of the scotch. Without saying a word, he took off his jacket, removed his bowtie, and unbuttoned the top button of his shirt. Before sitting, he kicked off the black dress shoes and took the seat opposite her at the tiny balcony table. Picking up his scotch, he held it high to clink glasses and took a sip.

"I haven't had this much to drink in a long time," he said with a sheepish grin on his face. "It was nice to let go for once."

Her sense of control returned, squarely in position and ready to exert its dominance. "I'm glad I just happened to be at your table tonight." She took the last sip of her drink, placed the glass down, and rose from the chair, taking his hand and leading him to the bed.

The lights had already been dimmed. She stood with him and helped remove his clothing. She took her time. Every action was deliberate. The worst thing in the world would be for Alston to view this as a one-night stand. She had no intention of developing feelings for this man. He was there to be used. Toward this end, Dan Alston would need to fall in love with her. For Maritza, this was a job, a voyage that extended across the boundaries of souls. She would win at all costs.

With their mouths locked together, she let his hands explore her body. He slipped the negligee over her head. Locked in an embrace, they were one as they fell slowly into the confines of the soft mattress. She rolled on top of him, fully intending to dominate, but to her surprise, he maneuvered gracefully to reverse positions. On her back, she felt him enter her and submitted to a pleasure she hadn't experienced in a long time. All of her training, her experience, her indomitable will to win receded in a climax of worry and concern. *Why,* she wondered, *had this man neutralized the powers that had always come to her so naturally?*

CHAPTER 14

What had he done? The guilt was overwhelming. He was single, he had slept with other women since the divorce but, for some inexplicable reason, he was rattled to the core. Instinctively, Dan knew he had done something wrong. It was barely sunrise on a Saturday morning. He should have taken a cab back to his DC condo, but he needed the escape offered by the early morning chill. Walking along the National Mall, Dan looked up at the Lincoln Memorial and reflected on the prior evening's events.

My God, she was beautiful. If he were being honest, probably the best lover he had ever known. The passion exhibited in her every move intrigued him; the perfume, and the sound of her sultry voice whispering in his ear. It was strange yet in some undefined way, familiar. He couldn't explain it, but being with Maritza somehow felt preordained. *No, no,* he commanded of himself. *You cannot have feelings for this woman.* His personal code of ethics simply wouldn't allow it. His father, the governor, had warned him of the dangers of politically oriented romances. And this woman is a lobbyist, for Christ's sake. *I must be out of my mind.*

Dan walked up the cement steps and approached the enormous statue of the man to whom he was most often compared, Honest Abe. He looked up at the stoic face of the sixteenth president and quickly concluded that Abe looked disappointed. It was undeniable. Lincoln's gaze told the whole story. *How could you?* Lincoln's face declared. *You, the most decent of men, the shining house on a hill providing the beacon of light to all who are lost. You are not worthy!* Lincoln's expression did not change, but Dan stood there, alone at the memorial, and heard Lincoln's deep, scratchy voice chastising him nonetheless.

Dan was thankful that it was too early for anyone else to be around. Truth be told, this wasn't the first time he had visited Honest Abe in the wee hours of the morning. Somehow, he believed Abe would understand. He was the ultimate sounding board. A light breeze blew some fallen, brown maple leaves into the open edifice. The chilled air brought on a mild dizzy spell. Guessing he was just hung over, he tried to ignore the sensation. His legs felt wobbly and he dropped the tuxedo jacket that had been slung over his arm. The world began to spin. Dan staggered toward the mall and sat down on the top of the cement steps near one of the Greek columns in case he needed something to lean on. A sharp pain materialized behind his right eye and his head took on a dull ache. *Shit, a migraine.* He began to feel nauseous and decided to just sit back. He moved his arms behind him to serve as a prop for his upper body, stretched his long legs down the steps, and closed his eyes.

As he willed himself to relax, the breeze whipping softly against his face, he thought he smelled something burning. He opened his eyes. The early morning sunlight blinded him. The migraine, he knew, was causing sensitivity to light. He shut his eyes again. *Deep breaths*, he told himself. *Breathe in, hold, exhale, and repeat.* His body started to relax. Still, he could smell it. Something was certainly burning. He opened his eyes, squinting to guard against the bright morning sun. He placed his hands above his eyes, as if somehow this might reduce the glare. He lost his balance and started to lurch forward. Catching himself before he slid down the steps face first, he decided it best to sit back down and wait for the migraine to pass. He closed his eyes again and listened. If something were on fire, sirens would be evident. Nothing. Maybe he had imagined it. As he tried to reconcile the smell, a wicked vertigo overtook him and caused the world to start spinning violently. Dan became frightened as he perceived the five-hundred-foot Washington Monument about to fall toward him into the reflecting pool belonging to the Lincoln Memorial. In fear, he placed his right arm over his eyes. He laid all the way back and tried to keep his mind still.

Dan was losing control and he knew it. *Where to this time?* Over the past few years, it had been the female voice, hallucinations of the world coming to an end, being in remote mountain caves, beneath the earth's surface and even in the heavens. It always started with a migraine and generally followed the consumption of too much alcohol or not enough sleep. Stress had always been the assumed culprit. His entire body broke out into a cold sweat. Pins and needles caused his arms, legs, and buttocks to tingle. The burning smell became more intense. His eyes were slammed shut but he saw it, clear as day, a field of swaying grain, pitching forward in the wind as far as his eyes could see. In the back left corner of the cavernous field, the crop was ablaze. The flowering heads of the colorful crop burned easily while igniting the dry stalks. The scorching of the quinoa field left a distinctive aroma, something akin to burning musk. Dan watched the flames consume the entire rolling crop, eliminating the food supply for the nearby village. *Village? What village?*

Where had he gone?

Drenched in sweat, the vertigo began to subside and he admitted to himself he had no earthly idea.

CHAPTER 15

In her entire life, Tally had never been this sick. She barely won the race from the Moretti Grand Ballroom to the sanctuary of the hotel commode. On the cab ride home, she texted her apologies to Dan and prayed the cab would wind its way through the congested DC streets in record time. She made it into her condo, left the gown on the floor, and slipped into an old pair of sweats, preparing to ride out the storm. After the maximum dose of Imodium, she was still going, long after there could have been anything else in her stomach.

Twelve hours later, she still felt horrible. She contemplated a trip to a nearby urgent care but concluded that they would tell her what she already knew. She had a stomach bug and needed to rest and stay hydrated. Reaching into her fridge for a bottle of water, she resolved to stay in all weekend. Tally never afforded herself the luxury of taking a sick day and although she could easily work from home, serving as Dan Alston's chief of staff meant being in the thick of the myriad activities taking place on any given day. Scheduled meetings, strategy sessions, phone calls, and fires needing to be extinguished were tough to handle from outside the office.

Standing in her kitchen, she closed the stainless steel door to the refrigerator and felt her stomach begin to churn. Leaning against the black granite countertop, she placed her right hand on her abdomen and gently rubbed, loosely expecting that this would somehow ease the unavoidable, umpteenth rush to the bathroom.

Ten minutes later, Tally settled onto her plush gray leather sofa with her water in hand. Barefoot with her hair piled into a messy bun, she was comforted by her favorite black University of Maryland sweatpants and bright red terrapin fleece top. She was ready to just close her eyes for an hour or so. Joining her was her ever-faithful companion, Ziggy, the gray tabby whose brilliant green eyes and Egyptian Mau markings made him a unique member of the feline species. He rolled over on his back like a dog seeking a belly rub and revealed the white underbelly that ran all the way up to his chin, accentuating the burnt orange hue of his small nose. "You seem to be the only man in my life right now," she remarked to the cat. Ziggy responded with an affectionate head-butt and began to purr. He placed his white-mitten-clad front paws on her leg and yawned.

For the past few years, it had essentially been her and Ziggy. Her ten-year marriage to an insurance broker had ended badly. John was eight years her senior and wanted a wife to be there at the end of the day to cook for him and share his nine-to-five lifestyle. She had placed her career above the marriage and admitted her mother's warnings about the man had been spot on. Since then, she really never made room for a relationship. Who had the time? Besides, she loved her work and if she were being honest with herself, she loved Dan. *Don't screw up a good work thing by getting involved with the boss*, she reminded herself. Dan was contemplating making this his last term. That would be her opening. Until then, Ziggy would have to do!

Tally laid her head back on the navy blue throw pillow and replayed the prior evening in her mind. When the concert concluded and they moved from the Kennedy Center to the Watergate, she had felt perfectly fine, delighting in the comfort and warmth of being on Dan's arm. Then, out of nowhere, that witch appeared: Maritza Coya, the lobbyist who materialized in Washington out of thin air. How in the world had she scored a ticket to the exclusive TOY event? And furthermore, how did she wind up at their table? Every ounce of her screamed that this woman was up to no good. Tally considered the possibility that Maritza had somehow poisoned her. *But how? Why?* Clearly, Coya wanted to get close to Dan. Tally herself was viewed as an obstacle. When that bitch shook hands with Dan and held his hand, she wanted to wretch. All in front of her face. And that perfume! Talk about overdoing it. Then she had poured the iced tea refill. Could she have slipped something into the tea? Tally admitted to herself she hadn't been paying much attention to what seemed like an innocent gesture of kindness. Then again, she had been fooling with that ugly cuff bracelet. She had said she had an itch and appeared to be rubbing her wrist with two fingers under the bracelet. Her long red fingernails were obnoxious. Obviously, they were fake, just like the woman herself. Could something have been hidden underneath the overbearing cuff bracelet? It was all so farfetched. There would be no way for her to verify any of this. Security tape? Interviews with the other guests at the table or the wait staff, maybe? As quickly as these thoughts entered her head, they were dismissed. Even to her, the ideas were nothing short of paranoid. Still, there was something about this woman she simply didn't trust. She vowed to ask around about Coya and schedule a short sit-down with her to learn more.

She and Dan had similar people instincts. She was sure Dan would see it the same way. She would snag a few minutes with him on Monday morning to validate her belief.

CHAPTER 16

"Madame Cece is just a silly nickname my kids gave me when they were young. My name is Cecelia, but my friends call me Cece without the 'Madame.'" She laughed and extended her hand.

Dan returned her warm smile and replied, "Well, thanks for seeing me and for the discretion."

It was late Sunday morning. Dan had been up before sunrise. As he aged, he just didn't seem capable of sleeping more than five or six hours. The early morning was his favorite time to catch up on office work or to hop on his elliptical.

Cece LaBello was the proprietor of The Oracle, one of Vienna, Virginia's most respected fine dining establishments. As instructed, Dan drove his car, a silver BMW 750i, to the rear entrance behind the avenue-style shopping center and parked by the loading dock. Cece was waiting for him by the adjacent door. They sat down in her well-kept and elegantly appointed office decorated with a nautical theme.

"I keep this office mostly to meet with food service vendors, but occasionally I do a psychic reading here. I must say, your daughter is a delightful young woman. I've enjoyed working with her."

"Thank you. Bri cuts her own path. She has never been bashful about exploring anything in which she has an interest. As I mentioned on the phone, Bri sort of goaded me into coming. If I am being honest with you,

I don't really buy into what you do."

She became a bit more serious, sat up straight, and replied, "Many people feel the same way. Mostly because they don't know what they don't know. With that said, I can only provide what comes to me, if anything. Interpretations will be completely up to you."

Dan was feeling uncomfortable as they sat at the round white ceramic table, the base of which was in the shape of an octopus holding the top with its tentacles. He was sure she could sense his anxiety because she asked him to wait while she brought out two espressos. She sat down across the table, moved the bouquet of fresh flowers, and said, "Admit it. You were expecting an old lady in a fortune-teller costume with a crystal ball."

"I'm afraid so," he confessed sheepishly. Cece was anything but the carnival fortune-teller. A blonde with a pixie haircut, she was a slender woman of maybe five and a half feet who wore a pair of faded jeans and a royal blue blouse. She appeared much younger than her probable age, which he guessed at early to midfifties. This speculation was from the picture on the distressed white bookshelf of her husband and her with grown children and a baby, which he assumed was a grandchild. The baby was wearing a burgundy and gold onesie bearing the logo of the Washington Redskins. Near the photo on her bookshelf was a plaque commemorating the Redskins' three Super Bowl championships. At least he and Cece shared an NFL rooting interest.

"I am a clairvoyant. I can see the future and sometimes the past. I don't communicate with the dead, which is done by a medium. I also do not use tarot cards. We will simply engage by holding hands and through a brief meditative state, I should be able to help you."

"Understood. Where do we start?"

"First things first. Some clients like to record their reading so they can review the session at a later time. Your iPhone's record feature can be used if you wish."

"I think I will, if you don't mind. If for no other reason than to share with Bri."

Dan fumbled with his iPhone, setting the app to record, and Cece took over.

"Just to state for the record, I am Cecilia LaBello, a psychic reader, and you are Senator Dan Alston. We have never met before today, and in the one prior phone conversation we had to set this meeting, you told me nothing about yourself, and your daughter, who is a client of mine, has told me nothing about you. Fair enough?"

"Fair enough," Dan stated for the record.

She took his hands in her own and closed her eyes. They sat silently for what seemed an eternity, and then Cece's eyelids appeared to flinch. Dan could see her jaw clench. Her brow wrinkled and the grip on his hands tightened. "I am sensing some ongoing anxiety related to . . ." She hesitated and continued, "Mmm, some unresolved issues perhaps."

"What types of issues?"

She kept her eyes closed and continued. "It's hard to say exactly. I see two people in conflict, you and a woman. There is an argument . . ." She kept her eyes closed and seemed to be in some sort of alternative reality. Dan was already dismissive of what he was hearing. A mere Google search would reveal his divorce from Maddie. Of course they argued. What married couple didn't? With all due respect to his daughter, this psychic stuff was a waste of time. He would not find the answers he sought.

Cece pierced his veil of doubt. "I see a wolf. He is angry. On a mountain, perhaps? It's raining and windy. A storm . . ." She paused again, as if waiting for the next piece of information to materialize. "And a large, majestic bird circling a mountaintop. An eagle? No, wait, the longer wingspan. It's a condor."

Dan was mesmerized. While the news coverage surrounding his fall from Ausangate was well chronicled, the experience with the wolf and condor was not. He had told only Eli in brief and Bri in detail. Dr.

Chavez at the hospital in Cusco was aware of the wolf, but Cece would not know any of this. He was sure Bri would not have divulged the details of their private conversation. She grew up understanding the need for certain things to stay within the family.

They were still holding hands when Cece abruptly disengaged. Her face took on a troubled look and she said, "I'm sorry. This doesn't happen often. I felt a tremor go through my body. It is attributable to some sort of violent episode in your past. You and a woman. It was . . . frankly, unlike anything I've ever experienced, and I've been doing readings for thirty years."

"But there is no violence in my past," he gently protested.

"Senator, I can only tell you what I see. You must provide the interpretation. I saw a violent exchange between you and a woman with long dark hair. I heard a voice. The woman's, perhaps. She was singing or chanting something that sounded like 'I am one with you.'"

Dan sat there, stunned. Not knowing what to make of it all, he knew that Cece was right about one thing: he didn't know what he didn't know. Through his entire life, there was no woman with long dark hair with whom he had experienced a violent encounter. *What could that be about?* Maybe a psychic trying to throw something generic out there, hoping it meant something to the client? *But she knew!* She knew about the voice and its haunting chant. How could that be explained? Apparently, the interpretation was up to him.

Not sure where to turn next, he left The Oracle praying he wasn't losing his mind.

CHAPTER 17

Cusco Village, 1472

Jade was sure her life was over. Her existence was relegated to slavery. A commoner, forced into a life of servitude, not for nobility but for the other commoners. Cunac had ensured that they would treat her poorly. She would have preferred a death sentence. She traversed the main village road, a bushel of grain heavy on her right shoulder. People jeered. A young boy hurled a rock that barely missed her left ear. Her heart was full of sorrow. There seemed to be no escape. She could move about the village, but Cunac had made it clear that no one would permit her to leave—ever. She contemplated sneaking away in the middle of the night. She would be welcome in Yana's village. But if Cunac found her, he would once again drag her back to Cusco to face a grisly death. Her shamanic training was incomplete, but she knew enough to inflict some damage against her enemy. Jade understood that the only difference between using the shaman's power for good or evil was intent. When she had first met Yana, her adoptive father, Maicu the good-hearted village shaman, was still alive. It was her intent to take his teachings and learn from him and Yana to emulate his healing ways. But everything changed when that beast, Cunac, came and filled Maicu with tsentsak, causing his demise by heart failure. Had she completed her training, Jade might have been able to suck the tsentsak from Maicu's body in order to save his life. *Ah, hindsight. It was always crystal clear.*

Jade made her way through the village. She was forever thinking, and a plan was beginning to take shape. She would not be able to reclaim her reputation, but she could fight back somehow. Tsentsak? She had never regurgitated the magical darts but believed she knew how. Cunac would likely be ready for such a maneuver. He was clever. No, Jade needed the element of surprise. And she determined she would need to kill him. Wounding Cunac would only inspire him to be more vicious. He had to die, even if it meant the end of her own life. Jade considered the use of ayahuasca as a means, along with the assistance of her power spirits, the wolf and the condor. In this altered state, she could leave her inhibitions behind, pull her knife, and slash the bulging vein in the thick of his neck. The coming night would be the perfect time. It was when Cunac would be most relaxed. The people of his village would be gathered around the fire, singing and letting the cares of the day drift. She would somehow evade the people of her own village, hike the short distance, and emerge from the shadows to strike from behind. The ayahuasca would give her the courage. She would have her revenge.

Jade proceeded to deliver her grain to the women who would prepare it for future meals. Content with the formation of her plan, she allowed her memory to harken back to a better time, peaceful and carefree days growing up under Maicu. Prior to her vision quest, where she discovered her own power spirits, Maicu had always applauded her tenacity. She thought of herself as stubborn, but Maicu told her that the ability to focus on learning something new and committing to things she believed in made her his little hawk. Thus, her childhood nickname from her adopted father became Yāvenhawk, to honor her ability to soar in the midst of her own beliefs. Meant as a term of endearment, he would sing her to sleep every night. One of her fondest memories, Jade never let go of the beautiful bedtime song. She sang it to herself whenever she needed a modicum of peace.

Yāvenhawk, O Yāvenhawk
I am one with you.

CHAPTER 18

After finally seeing Maritza's introductory video, Eli had immediately sought out the man named Quesaré. He found him at Towson University in Baltimore County. As he drove his 2018 black Acura TL east on I-70, Eli recalled having made his first contact with the head of Towson's anthropology department. Geronimo Quesaré identified himself as a distant relation of Maritza Coya. As a child, he had grown up in a Peruvian village nearby Maritza's family. Their parents were cousins.

Eli parked the Acura in the University Union garage, procured a parking pass with his credit card from the vending machine, and placed the temporary permit on his dashboard. The short walk to Caskey Hall along the black asphalt path lined with maple trees was a pleasant one. *College students look younger all the time*, he thought, but really, he was just advancing further into middle age, gilding his view of the world.

He climbed the dozen cement steps, pulled open the heavy yellow door, and entered the aging vestibule. A bulletin board featured a multitude of papers attached with thumbtacks offering everything from tutoring to school-sponsored trips to South America, Europe, and Asia. He passed through another set of yellow-painted doors and proceeded to room 116, the office that belonged to Geronimo Quesaré. Eli pushed past the vacant assistant's workstation and knocked on the doorframe to announce his presence. Quesaré welcomed him and motioned for Eli to sit at the small, round oak table at the front of the room. Eli sat down and took note of the office décor, if one could call it that. Quesaré had traveled the world, and his small office reflected his ventures with artifacts from just about everywhere. Paper and books were stacked on every flat surface and the room had a musty smell to it. The old campus building had poor ventilation. Eli removed his sport coat and warded off the emerging sweat from his brow with his left shirtsleeve.

Eli guessed that Quesaré was roughly sixty-five years old. He had long silver hair worn in a ponytail and possessed a long, aquiline nose. His face was deeply lined, especially around the eyes and mouth. Eli mused that Quesaré must have survived on a diet of fruits and nuts, because he was so thin that he appeared almost emaciated. Quesaré had left Peru at age eighteen to see the world and eventually landed in Baltimore where he founded Towson's Department of Anthropology. Eli was fascinated by the man who once lived amongst the Q'ero in Peru and studied under modern-day shamans. Today represented their second face-to-face meeting since becoming acquainted one year earlier.

"Eli, it is good to see you again. What brings you to Towson today?"

"Thank you for seeing me, Geronimo. I know that you brought Maritza and me together in the interests of your belief in reincarnation and the pursuit of a soul's perfection and that you have made it abundantly clear you do not wish to know anything about what she and I are working on, but . . ."

"But nothing!" Quesaré abruptly bellowed. "You shall honor my condition for helping you understand why you are now in each other's lives. I make no exceptions."

Eli paused, gathered his resolve, and took a deep breath before continuing. "I would never ask you to violate your morals. I just need to better understand that which you have already conveyed."

Quesaré appeared to relax just a bit. He arched one eyebrow and looked suspiciously at Eli before replying, "What exactly do you wish to learn?"

Eli decided to shift the conversation to something more mundane. He reasoned that if he could coax Quesaré into a tranquil state, his intended conversation might be more productive.

"I appreciate the contact information you gave me for guides in Peru. Moises was phenomenal at Ausangate, especially when the storm rolled in."

"Yes, I have worked with Moises personally on many occasions. Like his father before him, he is an excellent guide. But to the point, Eli, this is not what you came here to discuss, is it?"

Eli bowed his head somewhat sheepishly. Quesaré was too smart. He saw through the ploy to divert his suspicion. He looked up slowly and locked eyes with Quesaré.

"You helped Maritza see she once lived in fifteenth-century Peru as a commoner abused by an evil village shaman. You convinced me that I, in a prior life, had lived as her mentor, an elderly woman from the northern part of Peru, and you helped us understand that my lifelong friend, Dan Alston, lived as the evil village shaman who abused Maritza's past-life body. You explained things that touched us in ways we still do not completely comprehend. Why then, tell me, do we feel so moved to rectify actions of people we supposedly lived as hundreds of years ago?"

Quesaré looked at him quizzically. "There is no 'supposedly.' You did live as these people all those years ago. The Akashic Records do not lie. Every moment of your soul's existence in each lifetime is recorded and preserved in the Records. Reincarnation is very real indeed. The bodies we inhabit in each lifetime are merely flesh and bone. The soul, the true life force of human existence, continues on, lifetime after lifetime, in search of perfection. Self-awareness in this regard is a powerful thing. One can be moved to correct the sins of a past life or those mistakes can be repeated time and time again."

"It is incredible that a group of people who lived more than five hundred years ago in a different part of the world would now find each other in present day."

"But it is not unusual at all. In fact, it is quite common to reincarnate in groups. Your father in this life might be your daughter in the next or merely a good friend or perhaps a business associate. It is all part of the energy cycle taught by shamans in places like my native Peru."

Eli squirmed in the chair. He thought about everything he had learned since watching the video. In a past life, he was living as an evil woman sorcerer training a young commoner. Now, the reincarnation of that village commoner was engaging him to seek revenge on his best friend, the man who once lived as an evil shaman, one who tortured the village commoner after killing her adopted father. While he had been fully engaged in helping Maritza, he had to admit to himself that, at times, his present-day life and experiences caused an unresolvable conflict. It kept him up at night and was taking a physical toll on his body. Odd skin rashes, digestive issues, and tension headaches had become part of his norm. Still, the other side of the coin found his soul awakened by Quesaré's revelations. Throughout their lives, Eli found himself playing second fiddle to Dan Alston. In sports, in accomplishments and even love.

Maddie, Dan's ex-wife, had been Eli's first real love. He still felt the pain of that loss. After she met Dan and they began hanging out together, it became clear that she preferred him, the silver-spooned governor's son. Eli had been dumped. Dan and Maddie became an item and, as always, he had been forced to play the good soldier, pretending that it didn't matter. But all those years, his insides churned away from the pain of a shattered heart. The first conversation with Quesaré had awakened a beast within. The concept of revenge from both his past and present lives now consumed him, fueling his every move.

Eli lamented how easy it would have been to simply use Ausangate as a vehicle for Dan's demise. There were so many options: injecting his hospital IV with some undetectable lethal substance or even smothering him with a pillow while he lay unconscious. No, it was better, he reasoned, to continue to hold his trust, to lay the framework with Maritza for the ultimate strike. As he contemplated their plan to end Dan Alston and wreak havoc on the values he held dear, the bell from Stephens Hall, the university's oldest building, rang five times indicating the new hour was upon them. His thoughts were snapped back into the small campus office. He looked up at the weathered face of Quesaré, who was shaming him with his eyes.

"I sense from your demeanor that you and Maritza are engaged in some sort of sinister plan of which I want no part."

Eli sat up in the chair, placed his arms on top of the old, oak table and looked Quesaré squarely in the eye. He then proceeded to lie. "Geronimo, my quest is merely to help Maritza achieve some inner peace. I now understand the phrase 'troubled soul.' I was hoping we could dive back into the Akashic Records for more detail from that lifetime in 1472."

"Eli, I must strongly caution you about inappropriately using knowledge from the past to act in the present. As an Akashic reader, I intend only to offer you and Maritza a view from the past so that you may pursue the soul's perfection in this lifetime. I urge you not to take action resulting in the opposite effect."

Eli nodded in a feeble and unsuccessful attempt to pacify Quesaré. "I understand. Will you help me learn more?"

Quesaré stood up, extended his hand in a gentleman's obligatory but unwelcoming manner, and said, "No, I fear I may have already opened Pandora's box. The Akashic Records are not to be abused. They are to be honored, and I do not believe your intentions are pure. Do not call me again."

CHAPTER 19

It was early on Monday morning. Tally's stomach felt like it had been through a war, but at least she felt functional and maintained her determination to learn more about Washington's newest lobbyist. It was seven o'clock and no one else typically arrived this early, except the good senator. That was her intention, to grab some time with Dan before the day got away from them. Dressed in a new lavender blouse and an innocent small-stone sapphire necklace, she approached Dan, who was already immersed in his overwhelmed email inbox. She was surprised that he wasn't wearing a suit. Very unusual for a Monday morning. He had donned a baby blue polo shirt and a pair of tan slacks. His golf round later that morning at Congressional completely slipped her mind.

"Good morning," she said with as much cheer as she could muster. "I can't tell you how sorry I am for leaving so suddenly Friday night. Without going into the gory details, I think something I ate or drank made me sick. There was no option but to leave in a hurry, if you get my drift."

He looked up, removed his tortoise shell readers, and smiled warmly. "Hey, if you were sick, you were sick. I completely understand. You think it was something served at the dinner?"

She badly wanted to blurt out her suspicion that Maritza had slipped something into her iced tea, but she had no proof. The timing just wasn't right to reveal that notion. "Who knows? Maybe. Could have been something that didn't agree with my system. I assume no one else at our table had to leave abruptly."

He laughed softly to convey his sympathy and replied, "No, I think it was just you."

"Well, I felt terrible abandoning you. After all," she said sheepishly, "I was your date for the evening." Tally cursed her inability to contain her emotions as she felt her cheeks begin to blush.

"Don't feel bad. I wound up having drinks afterward with Maritza Coya. In fact, we were among the last to leave. She is quite an interesting person."

Tally's settling stomach suddenly reverted to a raging storm, not from the past weekend's illness but rather from anger. She needed to collect herself. The last thing she wanted was to appear to be the jealous sidekick in a high school drama. She had to proceed with every measure of caution.

"Oh . . ." she replied, trying her best to sound nonchalant. "What did you find so interesting?"

He showed the warm smile she came to love. His eyes seemed to glow and he simply offered, "She has this aura about her I can't explain. I felt something just being around her, some sort of inexplicable radiating energy."

Tally was mortified. *Could Dan be developing feelings for this witch?* Given this wrinkle, she had to reconsider her weekend plan to bring Coya into the office for a grilling. Maybe after she had time to learn more but not quite yet. Unsure how to reply, Tally decided to punt. "How are you doing with the migraine episodes?"

He filled her in on his weekend sojourn around the Lincoln Memorial, the episode there, and his Sunday morning visit with Cece LaBello. After ingesting Dan's unusual weekend, she decided at that point she would do what she could to help Dan through his experience with the migraines and related visions. If she were ever to be taken seriously in his eyes as a future spouse, she needed to be the one to help him through this troubling time.

"Ms. LaBello called me early yesterday evening to tell me she did some research on my behalf. She thinks I am what is called a clairsentient."

"Clairsentient? What is that? Like a clairvoyant? Can you see the future?"

"No, as I understand it, a clairsentient can experience the future, even the past and present, in a way that transcends normal psychic abilities."

Befuddled, she furrowed her brow and responded, "So she thinks you have some sort of psychic powers?"

"The way she explained it to me, it was like having the ability to 'see' in the manner of a psychic but also to experience more, like a sense of smell from, say, a burning building in a vision."

"Oh my God, do you believe it?"

"The pragmatic me says it's all a bunch of BS, but I can't deny that I have had these types of experience. In recent weeks, they seem to be more frequent and stronger in intensity. Ms. LaBello also said I would be able to sense energy from another person or even a building or an outdoor place. It might explain why I felt an energy emanating from Maritza Friday night."

Tally's insides again recoiled at the suggestion that Dan's migraine episodes and Coya might be related. She had temporarily put that woman out of her mind. Now it seemed that Dan was intrigued by her. Tally knew she needed time to contemplate what came next. Her initial reaction to research and discredit Maritza Coya was still, instinctively, the right move. She would now need to proceed with caution to avoid incurring Dan's blind defense of a woman with whom he had become enchanted. She resolved to be clandestine in her efforts to help Dan. She also decided to start a search for someone who might be able to help Dan better understand clairsentience or whatever he was dealing with.

Tally retreated to her office and began an internet search in her endeavor to help Dan. Just as she began reading the first set of results, Joc Raymer burst through the door. "Turn on the TV. You are not going to believe this."

Tally took the remote from the credenza behind her desk and powered the TV on. Every news channel was running the same story: Senator Dan Alston, it was being reported, was seen early Saturday morning in a drug-induced stupor stretched out on the steps of the Lincoln Memorial. Tally recoiled at the video, clearly made from a bystander with an iPhone. The optics were terrible. He looked like a junkie in need of a fix. In politics, things could turn on a dime. She made a beeline for Dan's office but when she peeked her head in, she realized he had already departed for his golf date in Bethesda. Standing in his doorway, Tally knew she had to mitigate the damage before Dan's sterling reputation was tarnished forever.

CHAPTER 20

Bob Alston, a widower, did his best to keep a low profile after retiring from public life more than ten years ago. His two terms as the governor of Maryland and the subsequent years of public appearances had taken their toll. After his wife of forty-five years died following a difficult bout with breast cancer, he simply wanted to retreat. He became a recluse of sorts, communicating regularly only with his son, Dan, and his granddaughter, Bri. His days were occupied mostly by reading and fishing. His expansive home in Crisfield, on Maryland's eastern shore, was the perfect place to avoid attention. At seventy-eight, he just wanted to be left alone.

Dressed in a pair of lightweight gray slacks (he abhorred shorts, even on the hottest days) and his favorite M.R. Ducks t-shirt, he reached for his baby blue floppy hat perched on a wooden peg on the back of the side door. With his fishing gear in tow, he made his way to the folding lawn chair on the edge of his private dock. It was here where he would kill a few hours and maybe even succumb to a nap. Although he occasionally fell asleep in the folding lawn chair, it exacerbated the problem in his lower back. Coffee would help in this regard.

Bob lowered himself on the chair, reached down for his rod, and cast the line into the water. He prided himself on catching a fish and preparing his own dinner. He settled in the chair and took in the view. The calm waters of Somers Cove were peaceful. A pair of laughing gulls swooped down around the water's surface, flittering through the high green seagrass and competing with Bob for fish. Although many beachgoers found them annoying, Bob admired the black-headed seagulls. Their dark eyes encased in a rim of white against the black face with the orange-red beak made them appear almost human in expression.

Bob was a child of privilege but always outworked everyone to show he wasn't just another silver-spooned kid. The laughing gulls understood. They fought for everything they got and in the end remained supremely confident in their ability to survive. Bob smiled at the gulls and pulled his floppy hat down in an effort to shield his nose from the sun's harmful rays.

The first nibble of the morning began to pull on his line. As he worked the reel, he felt a sudden, intense pain on the right side of his neck. He reached up to slap the unwanted mosquito, but instead he felt the small, sharp end of a metal dart. Disgusted, he pulled it from his neck, looking at it in a state of bewilderment, and then chucked it toward the water. Bob began rubbing the site of the intrusion. His head maneuvered in every direction in a vain attempt to figure out what had just happened. The futile effort fell prey to blurred vision and a searing heat that coursed through his brain. As he fell over onto the dock, the world went dark.

CHAPTER 21

Cusco Village, 1472

Jade was nervous but confident. Her hands ached from the obsessive sharpening of her knife. There was no margin for error. Cunac must die. She sat on the ground, damp from an earlier rain, and imagined the scene in her head. She could feel the pressure being applied from her hand to his carotid artery. In her mind's eye, she saw the blood spurt from his neck like a geyser as he fell to the ground amidst the stunned villagers gathered around the fire. Soon, she thought, this would all be a reality. She had to calm herself; there were just a few more hours until nightfall.

She breathed deeply and placed her back against an aging tree trunk for support. Jade closed her eyes and began to reflect on the opportunities that life had denied her. As a girl, she had so badly wanted to succeed Maicu as the village shaman. The thrill of healing once intoxicated her mind. After Maicu's murder at the hands of the evil Cunac, bitterness enveloped her every thought. Yana taught that shamanic training could yield either the power to heal or the means to seek revenge. *Healing versus sorcery?* The line, once clear in her mind, became blurred at times. In this moment, however, she was sure. Cunac had stripped her of everything she treasured: Maicu, her role in the village, and her dreams. Living her life on Cunac's terms was no life at all. He would have to pay. Death would be too kind a fate for this hateful soul.

The caw of a bird overhead stirred her senses. She looked up and noticed the sun had begun to set. A light sweat covered her body. A combination of humidity and nerves, she supposed. She stood up, stretched, and made her way to her hut. She had not meant to linger so long, and time was now running short. She would need to grab the vile of ayahuasca, ingest it, and walk briskly to the neighboring village fire pit. This is where her final act would be staged. Jade inherently knew she would not survive the night. Once she killed Cunac, the villagers would show no mercy in ending her life. She was at peace with this fate. This was simply the way it had to be.

Jade entered her small and modest dwelling. She moved a small grouping of bowls fashioned from clay and picked up the tiny vial of ayahuasca. She concealed the knife in a loop under her tunic and then opened the vial, throwing back the sticky solution into her mouth and down her throat with the intent it would give her the courage, strength, and agility to perform the task at hand. The liquid was warm and thick. The taste and consistency were similar to mucous and made her stomach curdle. She looked out the window. Daylight was almost gone. She would take a shortcut through the fields—a more difficult path, especially at sundown, but it was the only way to make it through on time to approach from the back of the campfire site, to the position normally occupied by the village elders and its shaman.

Jade took a last, lingering look at her hut. It was a spartan existence, but it was home nonetheless. She would miss it. With the ayahuasca beginning to take effect, Jade sensed the presence of her power spirits, the wolf and the condor. The wolf's eyes glowed brightly. *What a relief,* Jade thought. *His eyes will help light the way through the dark path of the fields.* The condor circled high above, its wings taking on an incandescent glow to guide her final journey in this lifetime. Jade admired the majesty of the condor's illuminated wingspan as a loud, shrieking caw came from above. The wolf nudged her left hip with its nose. It was time to go.

To gain access to Cunac's village, Jade would need to traverse recently harvested fields of maize and quinoa. As she entered the field of maize stalks, her legs were immediately scratched and cut by the sharp edges of the harvested plants. She felt the blood run slowly down her legs, but she paid no mind. The wolf plowed ahead, clearing a path for her to follow. It gazed above, constantly eyeing the condor and its illuminated wings to guide him. To Jade, under the influence of the ayahuasca, the early night sky appeared milky. The brightest of moons and shining stars punched tiny glowing holes through the billowing clouds. Although it was not cold, she felt a chill and placed her hands on her arms to rub the goosebumps away. She tried to remain calm and focus on the task at hand. Her power spirits propelled her forward. Jade moved steadily through the maize and into the entrance of the quinoa field. From here, she knew it would not be long. Before she could take a full step into the quinoa field, she was startled by the angry growl of the wolf. Jade froze on the edge of the second field as the wolf abruptly stopped to confront a pit viper. Jade's sense of alarm caused her knees to buckle. This venomous, heat-sensing snake was a nighttime hunter, seeking prey it could strike and then quickly abandon. The green snake lifted its head and focused its beady yellow eyes directly on Jade. She stepped back and gasped out loud as the condor swooped down, picked the snake up by its midsection, and flung it back toward the maize stalks where it would do them no harm. The condor rejoined Jade and the wolf for the final leg of the journey. Jade was lucid enough to realize that the pit viper had not been illusory but a very real danger commonly found in these parts.

She slowed her pace, only for a moment, to allow her heartbeat to return to its normal rhythm. Then, she opened her eyes and a translucent image of Cunac appeared before her, laughing and mocking her feeble plan to take his life. She reached out, waving her arms wildly in the air, trying to clear the image from her brain. Seeing Cunac in this manner heightened her resolve. The anger she felt knew no bounds. She was nearing the end of the quinoa field and could hear the joyous voices coming from the campfire site. She drew her knife from the underside of her tunic and gripped the handle so tightly, her hand became one with the weapon.

Jade stopped at the edge of the field. She could see clearly now. Dozens of villagers were gathered around a large fire pit. The smoke from the burning wood rose in the nighttime sky, swirling into the mix of milky clouds. The smell of smoke filled her nose as she heard the cheerful songs of Cunac's village. As she drew yet closer, she looked back to the edge of the field where the wolf and condor remained. She was on her own. This was her destiny to fulfill. She inched forward, quietly approaching, until she could see the back of Cunac's head. The thick, wavy, black and gray hair and the three feathers rising from his headdress. She felt her grip tighten even more on the knife's handle. She kept the weapon by her right thigh and tried to maintain a low profile as she crept forward from the darkest part of the field's edge. Almost upon him, she raised the knife to shoulder height so she could thrust it into the beefy neck of her seated enemy. Before the villagers around the campfire could react, Jade swooped down upon Cunac from behind and pushed the knife toward his throat. In an instant, Cunac, sensing the impending attack, turned and grabbed her right wrist with his left hand, twisting her arm until she had no choice but to release the knife. Then with his right hand, he produced his own blade from a sheath on his waist and plunged it deeply into her throat. As her life expired, Jade remained content in the ancient belief that her revenge would be exacted one day in a future lifetime.

CHAPTER 22

Dan was an average golfer. He participated in the sport mostly for fresh air, the beauty of nature, and of course, the collegiality the game promoted. This was not his first time playing at Congressional Country Club in Bethesda, but he had to admit, each time he stood on the eighteenth tee of the Blue Course, the memory of every bad drive came back into his head. A 466-yard, tree-lined par 4 with a narrow fairway was a formula for disaster, particularly for a recreational golfer with a 25 handicap. Dan considered that the difficulty of this hole might violate his constitutional rights against cruel and unusual punishment. The other three members of his foursome had already teed off. Dan stepped up, teed his ball, and did his best to relax. *A narrow fairway, trees on the left and right—really, no margin for error.* Dan exhaled and took the club back, eager to pound the ball down the fairway in a minimally respectable manner. On his downswing, his upper body lifted slightly and the club head barely made contact with the ball. The dimpled white sphere taunted him as it rolled off the small wooden peg and settled at the end of the tee box.

One of his closest colleagues in the Senate, Bobby McMillian, laughed and said, "Dan, this is a paradise hole, hit till you're happy."

Senators Raley and Reed joined in on the kidding. "Hey, Dan, if you don't hit past the ladies' tee, you gotta drop your drawers," exclaimed a laughing Will Reed.

"Oh my lord, no one wants to see that," Jed Raley replied.

After completing the "walk of shame" to retrieve his ball, Dan teed it up again, did his best to relax while keeping his head down, and calmly hit a solid drive right down the middle. Reed, a powerfully built man who at six feet eight was once an NCAA basketball champion before blowing out a knee, could boom a ball down the fairway. "Nice hit, Dan. On the ride down the fairway, I'll need to stop at the Super Walmart between our two drives," he chided.

McMillian tried to come to his aid by saying, "Hey next time, let the second guy hit first."

Dan took it all in stride. He had grown accustomed to golf humor, and it suited his personality even though his game often became the butt of the jokes. With four in the fairway, each senator managed a reasonably good second shot, They all stood at the end, looking on at the approach shot to the green.

Jed Raley decided to state the obvious. "Water on the left, water behind the green, and sand on the right. Better put it on." Dan watched as Raley proceeded to take a pitching wedge and drop a beautiful, high-arcing shot five feet from the tightly placed pin. McMillian and Reed pulled off similar shots, and they had the pin surrounded. Dan took his nine iron and, with a full backswing, hit a beauty. Along with his colleagues, Dan watched the ball traverse the bright blue sky and sail right over the pin.

"Wow," declared McMillian. "That's a pin seeker."

Dan felt the adrenaline of the rare, miraculous golf shot originating from his amateur swing. He kept his eye on the ball as it hit the green just behind the pin, which was tucked on the back left side. The momentum of the ball after checking up caused it to roll off the back of the green over the fringe and into the water. Dan's heart sank with the ball.

"Too much club, man. I would have used the wedge if I were you," said Reed.

Again trying to be the support post, McMillian said, "Beautiful shot, Dan. You'll get it next time."

Dan walked to the green with the other members of his foursome and tended the pin as his colleagues putted out. After they were all in the cup, Dan replaced the pin and as was customary after a round of golf, he shook hands with each of the other members of the foursome.

As they were walking off the green, Raley, the pear-shaped senator from Virginia with the long nose and thinning red hair, put his arm around Dan's shoulders and said, "Thanks for coming out today. It was good seeing you, and you know I always enjoy a round at Congressional."

"Thanks Jed, I appreciate the invitation. I've been under a lot of stress and this was a perfect antidote."

Raley, the chairman of the Senate Ethics Committee, replied, "We know. Bobby and Will thought this would be a good way to get you away from DC for a few hours and break the news to you gently."

"News? What? Did one of you decide to run for president?" Dan joked.

"No, Dan. This is serious. We wanted to give you a heads up. Tomorrow, the Senate Ethics Committee is opening an investigation on you."

"Ethics? I don't understand, Jed. I haven't committed any ethics violations."

At that moment, Bobby McMillian chimed in. "Dan, there is a video of you on the steps of the Lincoln Memorial. It looks like you are under the influence of something. The video has gone viral. We can't cover this up for you."

"I understand," he replied sullenly. "It's all a misunderstanding that can be cleared up in short order."

He pulled out his cell phone to call Tally. Before he could dial, the device lit up with an incoming call. Dan was puzzled—the caller ID read simply "Crisfield, MD." Apart from his father, he didn't know anyone in Crisfield. Fearing the worst, he answered tentatively, "He-llo."

The deep, accented voice from the other end said, "Good afternoon, Senator Alston. This is Chief Ferraro from the Crisfield Police Department. I hate to be the bearer of bad news, but your father was found dead this afternoon on his fishing dock."

CHAPTER 23

Maritza allowed herself to relax for the first time that day. The beginning of their elaborate plan to ruin Dan Alston was now underway. It had been a busy day. It started with an early morning meeting with Tyler Morrison, then the nearly three-hour drive to Maryland's eastern shore, overseeing the assassination of Alston's father, and five-plus hours of additional driving to Deep Creek Lake. Maryland looked so small on the map, but driving from the eastern shore to the mountains took forever.

Maritza could not take the chance that they might be seen. Not that she would ever be implicated in the assassination but, in an abundance of caution, she rented a car using one of her fake IDs and instructed Eli to do the same. She did not wish to leave a trail through the E-ZPass system or by any other means. Deep Creek was the perfect place to meet. The numerous lodges and restaurants in the town of Oakland made it easy to "hide" in short bursts. To keep from being discovered, they had agreed—no phone calls, emails, or meetings in the Baltimore-Washington corridor. Garrett County, Maryland's far western region, offered the haven they needed for their periodic update meetings, all of which were arranged using aliases and cryptic messaging through a dark web bulletin board. They both wore jeans and casual shirts to blend in. She pulled her hair into a ponytail and wore scant makeup in an attempt to look as ordinary as she could. Eli donned a burgundy Washington

Redskins ball cap. She exhaled deeply and thought about the serenity of the mountainous area and knew Eli, as an outdoorsman, liked it as well. Although they were never there long enough to partake, Deep Creek offered skiing in the winter and boating in the summer.

"When we first met at that sleazy diner in Miami on the outskirts of Little Havana, you thought I was nuts," Maritza proclaimed while pouring refills of the sauvignon blanc.

"Of course I thought you were nuts," replied Eli. "Who wouldn't? My first instinct was to get the hell out of there. But to your credit, your outreach through Quesaré and that first meeting in Little Havana showed me that my life had some higher calling, a true purpose. The clarity has brought me inner peace I never imagined possible."

Maritza raised her glass. "Here's to clearing the decks and to fresh starts." They clinked glasses and sipped quietly. They were seated in a picturesque window overlooking the lake. It was early evening and the sun just started to set.

"So the assassination went smoothly?" he asked.

"Yes, the man we hired was an expert marksman. Everything went according to plan." She smiled a sadistic smile and continued, "And the video has now been sent to the press. By tomorrow, his sterling reputation in the Senate will be mud."

"How did you get the video?"

She displayed that evil grin and replied, "It was child's play. I seduced him, lured him back to my hotel room, drugged him with a long-acting hallucinogen inconspicuously placed in the bottom of his glass, and then discreetly followed him the next morning so I could film the video. You were right, by the way, that he might wander over to the Lincoln Memorial."

"Old habits die hard, I suppose."

The server arrived with their meals. Maritza soaked in the scent of the delectable seasoning on her rockfish. Eli had a filet mignon.

"How is the planning going with the clean food boxes?" she inquired.

"Things are lining up nicely. It's incredible how easy it is to distribute illicit material when people think our goal is to simply feed the hungry."

She smirked and said, "Fools. They will learn soon enough."

Maritza was famished. She finished every bite of her meal, downed the last of the wine, and warmed at the thought that she would be the one who would crush Dan Alston and the world and values he held so dear. She had his trust. With his best friend in tow, she saw no barriers to success. After dinner, she would make the drive back to Washington. The week's schedule would not allow her to linger. There was still so much to do.

PART II

CHAPTER 24

Bob Alston was a beloved man who lived an unpretentious life and wanted an elegant but simple ceremony. Tally felt like it was planned to perfection. As the crowd made its way out of the Maryland State House in Annapolis, Tally gazed over at Dan. The death of his father had left him tormented, wracked with an overwhelming sense of grief. Bags materialized under his bloodshot eyes and his hair seemed to have gone gray overnight. Tally knew the combination of his father's sudden passing, the Senate investigation, and his strange visions were taking a toll.

Dressed in a modest charcoal mid-length dress and black shoes with a small heel, she stood back from the crowd. The governor had been lying in state for the past twenty-four hours. Bob Alston served his country in the Vietnam War and thus his casket was adorned by both the US and Maryland state flags. Troopers lined both sides of the street along State Circle in Annapolis and watched as the Maryland National Guard carried the casket down the cement steps to the waiting hearse. Tally's eyes reverted back to the building. As a Maryland native, she admired the classic American architecture and recalled from a grade-school field trip that the Maryland State House dated back to the 1700s and was the oldest such American building to be in continuous legislative use. Tally fondly remembered learning that George Washington once spoke inside this very building to resign his commission as commander-in-chief of the Continental Army. The iconic structure served briefly as the nation's capital, and the Treaty of Paris was ratified in these halls, bringing the Revolutionary War to its final act.

Although it was a cool, overcast day, the typical Maryland humidity prompted a slight sweat. She didn't know why, but she was uptight—mostly, she supposed, out of concern for Dan. She gazed up at the much taller Joc Raymer, Dan's legislative assistant, to whom she had given a ride to the day's events. Joc reasoned that having two cars at the jam-packed event would be foolhardy. Really, she knew, he was frugal and didn't want to spend money on gas if he could bum a ride. As always, Joc was keeping it together. She took a deep breath and inhaled to relax her overworked mind. *Focus on the sweet smell of the nearby Chesapeake Bay*, she told herself.

Dan, Bri, and Dan's Aunt Rose, the younger sister of the former governor, walked slowly, heads bowed behind the casket. Following was the current governor, Denise James, and her lieutenant, Leah Ryan. Reverend Louis Polk, an Alston family friend, brought up the rear. Reverend Polk would preside over the graveside ceremony. Tally had arranged for the limo to take the immediate family members to the Old Line Memorial Cemetery in Severna Park, where Bob Alston would be laid to rest. Once the dignitaries were on their way, she would follow with Joc in her Lexus ES sedan for the fifteen-minute drive.

At the cemetery, the governor's body was placed above the ground, next to the grave that would be his final resting place. Hundreds of folding chairs were set out for family, friends, and visiting dignitaries at this invitation-only event. Tally took her seat next to Joc in the middle of the section on the side behind Dan and his daughter and aunt. She sat respectfully as Reverend Polk made his way to the lectern and took control of the wireless microphone. Reverend Polk stood silently and looked up at the sky to admire the planned flyover by four jets from nearby Andrews Air Force Base. Before the trailing smoke abated from the hazy sky, a bugler from the Maryland Defense Force Band sounded "Taps" followed by "Maryland, My Maryland." Upon the conclusion of the musical tribute, Reverend Polk led the group in a short prayer and introduced a series of speakers, including Governor James and Bob's former chief of staff, George Polski, who had faithfully served the governor through both terms. Polski injected life into the sullen activities, explaining how Governor Alston had always used humor to take the tension out of a difficult situation. Tally listened intently as Polski spoke in a low, gravelly voice highlighting his eastern shore twang.

"I once observed Governor Alston break up an argument amongst his cabinet over the administration's position on education funding. He allowed everyone to exhaust their energy expressing divergent opinions and then, when the steam had gone out of the room and he hadn't uttered a single, solitary word, finally he smiled and said, 'Well, son of a bitch, this makes you just want to spit on the sidewalk.' No one had any idea what that meant, but it was Bob's way of lightening a tense moment. Over the years, I heard him say that on a number of similar occasions."

Tally smiled. She had heard Dan recount the same story many times. They had enjoyed a few lighthearted moments over the memory. Reverend Polk then asked the attendees to bow their head for one final prayer, and Tally watched as the casket was lowered into the ground. Dan took a hand shovel full of dirt and gently lobbed it on the casket. Bri did the same and Bob's sister followed. Reverend Polk then informed everyone that they were invited to a reception at the Governor's Mansion. Tally stood and waited patiently for her turn to leave. After watching Dan, Bri, and Aunt Rose proceed slowly, heads bowed, to the waiting limo, Tally looked up at the unflappable Joc Raymer, whose shaved head was cranked to the right looking back to the last row of seats. Instantly, she knew why. Tally was beside herself with anger. *Of all days and with everything Dan had on his mind, why did that selfish bitch have to show up?* Her low-cut purple dress hardly constituted respectful funeral attire.

"How in the world did she get an invitation?" Tally inquired.

Joc, looking like a lovesick puppy dog, simply replied, "From me."

"From you . . ." Tally blurted out, trying to restrain her anger in deference to the day. "What would possess you to do such a thing?" Before he could answer, Tally looked at his face and knew the answer. "Oh shit, Joc. You slept with her, didn't you?" Like a child caught red-handed with his fingers in the cookie jar, Joc was busted. His red-faced expression gave him away.

Driving back to Annapolis gave her a few minutes to try to calm herself. She looked over at Joc and chewed into him. "I'm so pissed off, I don't know where to start. She is a lobbyist. You work for Senator Alston. The conflict of interest wasn't obvious? You had to let your zipper do your thinking for you? The woman is pure sleaze." She paused to collect herself but with anger quelling her better judgment, she unintentionally blurted out, "And I am pretty sure that the senator himself has been in bed with her, so stew on that one for a while."

Joc was stunned. Like a boxer who just incurred the final blow, he was wounded and had no good reply. As those last words rolled off her tongue, Tally felt instant regret. Letting Joc know that Dan might be involved with Coya was probably a mistake. It was a tangled mess that seemed to be getting more complicated with each passing day.

"We'll figure it out," she told him. "Just stay away from Coya. No more favors and for God's sake, keep what I told you to yourself. We don't need the press getting ahold of any of this."

ooooo

The Governor's Mansion, another iconic structure Tally admired, was located next to the State House in Annapolis. Her anger at Joc's poor judgment had begun to abate, but she was still churning. She knew she needed to get her mind back to the top of its game. Although they were gathered for a funeral reception, Tally knew that political derision never took a day off. She and Joc approached the white double front doors of the mansion nestled among a sea of classic red bricks defining the look and feel of colonial America. The two-story mansion rested under a gray slate roof with two chimneys, one flying high off each side of the home. A dormer stood upright on the roof diagonally below each chimney.

An aide to Governor James checked their names against a preapproved list and they entered the foyer, taking in the sight of the burnished hardwood partially covered by oriental rugs and the architectural beauty of the rolling grand staircase. This was not Tally's first trip to the mansion, but her keen sense of appreciation for objects of bygone eras enabled a repeated sense of enjoyment. It seemed she noticed new details every time she came and, of course, each governor added their own touch so there was always something new to see.

The mansion was already packed. Joc immediately disappeared into the crowd. *Probably in search of the buffet*, she thought. Looking around, Tally noticed Maddie Alston with her new bank VP friend in tow. The jealousy she had always felt of Maddie still riled her up. Tally was the fun-loving tomboy who yearned to be the elegant, natural beauty Maddie was. No wonder Dan fell in love with her. Across the room, she saw Eli Shepherd, Dan's best friend. Like many of the attendees, he appeared sullen. Tally couldn't be sure, but she thought she saw Eli glancing in Maddie's direction. In the recesses of her mind, she recalled a snippet of a story from Dan of how Maddie was Eli's girlfriend before she and Dan hooked up. Eli was no prize. Tally wondered what Maddie ever saw in him. Tally wasn't one of them, but she knew some women simply fell in love with a man's personality.

Moving toward the crowded dining hall, an eighteen-foot rectangular mahogany table underneath an ivory runner held a buffet feast fit for a king. No one would leave hungry. At the room's far right corner, Tally saw Dan's close friends and political allies, Stella Gresham and Bobby McMillian, enjoying mimosas. Senators Raley and Reed were nearby.

These were men Tally once respected and even admired, but now she knew they were simply part of the lynch mob forcing Dan to undergo an ethics investigation to cover their own political hides. There were few true friends in Washington. At least they had the decency to show up and pay their respects. If she were Dan, she might have told them to get the hell out and respect the privacy of the moment. Dan was a gentleman, one of the many things she loved about him. In terms of being a good person, he was everything she wanted to be. Tally carried a spiteful urge to lash out at anyone who hurt the people she loved.

She wanted to find Dan. The need to throw her arms around him and provide comfort was overwhelming. Her heart just ached for him. Nobody could absorb the climbing accident, the odd visions, a Senate ethics investigation, and the death of his father without falling to pieces. She gently pushed through the crowded room, desperately seeking Dan. She was intercepted by his daughter, teary-eyed and in need of a hug. Tally loved Bri and drew in the much taller woman for a supportive embrace.

"Your granddad was such a great man," she said. "I am so sorry for your loss."

Through the tears, Bri flicked her long hair back over her right shoulder and wiped her eyes with a saturated wad of Kleenex. "I am really going to miss him. With all Dad has going on now, losing his father was the final straw. I am so worried about him."

"Your dad is one of the strongest men I know. He'll need all the love and support he can get, but trust me, he will pull through. Do you know where he is? I want to give him a big hug."

Bri pointed her in the direction of the sitting room, which although nearby was incredibly difficult to navigate to with the flood of people in the mansion. As Tally made her way into the sitting room, she finally found Dan. He was looking vulnerable and taking comfort in the arms of the person she hated more than anyone else on earth . . . Maritza Coya.

CHAPTER 25

Dan simply couldn't sleep. Laying in the dark of his bedroom in Olney, his mind was a speeding train heading off a steep cliff where there had once been a bridge. For so many years, that bridge was Maddie. He had ruined all of that by placing his career first and in the process, completely taking her for granted. The funeral was a movie he kept replaying. The day was a blur, whizzing by so incredibly fast. Everyone tried to console him, but his main concern was consoling his daughter. Bri was in meltdown. Dan wasn't sure he had the strength to be her rock, but he had given it everything he could. He invited her to spend the night in her old room, but she had opted to return to Georgetown and dive back into her studies. He understood. Bri was like her mother in many ways, but when it came to processing stress, Dan and his daughter were both the type to wash their problems away in the busyness of normal life.

The medical examiner in Somerset County had recommended an autopsy to rule out foul play. Dan refused. Yet now, in the midst of a sleepless night, he began to wonder if he had made the right call. As he often did, he reminded himself that he was probably engaged in the dangerous and mind-numbing habit of overthinking.

Dan yawned and stretched the tired, aching muscles in his back. The faint light of the plug-in alarm clock said 11:37 p.m. The motion propelled him further awake and he realized that the notion of sleep was futile. He went down to his library and poured a scotch to reflect on the day. The serenity of his home was suddenly disturbed by the surprising sound of the front doorbell. Standing there, a bottle of Johnny Walker in hand, was Maritza. Thinking about it, he never told her where he lived, but he assumed that information was easy enough to discover in the Digital Age. Before a word was spoken, they simply fell into an embrace. They retreated to the kitchen, nibbled on the remains of the brisket he had enjoyed earlier with Bri, and talked and drank until 1:30 a.m. Hours after they had made love and fallen asleep in his bed, Dan popped awake in a chilled sweat. He remembered the momentary midnight fog that invaded his brain while carving the beef. The memory now made him shiver with fear. His hand involuntary tightened around the handle of the carving knife, and then the most errant of thoughts occurred: *Take the knife and plunge it into her throat. Where did that come from?*

He felt an overwhelming sense of guilt for having such a horrible, uncontrollable thought. Dan admitted to himself that Maritza had entered his life at the perfect time. There was no way to go through all of this crap without someone to lean on. He reached over to the other side of the bed and saw she was gone.

In his middle-of-the-night, overwrought state of anxiety, Dan questioned his relationship with Maritza. Yes, he admitted, the female companionship was great. It had been a long time and, while the so-called "last honest senator" felt guilty over his budding relationship with a lobbyist, he assured himself he could handle it. At this moment, he would have liked to roll over, pull her close to him, and just hold her.

Maritza's scent was still upon him as he got up and headed for the bathroom. He took a leak and as he stood before the antique gold-framed mirror above the navy blue ceramic basin, he noticed the bags under his eyes and the new wrinkles on his cheeks. *Is this what turning fifty does?* He ran his hand through his short-cropped hair. What were once just graying temples had given way to a white avalanche. All of the sudden it seemed he was turning into an old man. He concluded it was the stress of losing his father, the crazy visions, and getting falsely accused of being some sort of drug addict. How in the world was he going to explain the Lincoln Memorial tape? It had been captured on video and blasted around the globe in a matter of minutes.

In five hours, he would be meeting with his attorney to begin preparing for the Senate investigation and the inevitable hearing that would follow. The videotape was damning evidence. His lawyer sent the video, a copy of which Dan received, to a forensic expert to see if somehow they could argue it had been tampered with. Of course, Dan told the lawyer the truth as he knew it about the strange visions and voices. The lawyer nixed all of that talk. "Spewing that type of nonsense in the public record is the fast track to resigning your senate seat," he had been told. "And that may be the best offer you will get from your so-called friends on the Hill." Sticking to his reputation as the "last honest senator," Dan felt conflicted about distorting the truth, even for his own defense. Short of tampered video, which Dan knew they wouldn't find, the lawyer asked him to consider the claim of a medicinal side effect. Dan thought this to be ridiculous. Even if such a thing were true, why would he be at the Lincoln Memorial in the early morning? No, he decided, if push came to shove, he would tell the truth and let the chips fall where they may.

Dan felt like a hypocrite. Here he was standing on his high horse about moral integrity and he was romantically involved with a lobbyist—a clear ethics violation. His sense of moral and self-righteousness had always kept him from getting involved with Tally. Tally was a good friend who understood him at a deep level. Yes, he thought she was attractive, but he had always held back to avoid the sense of impropriety—and just as important, to not jeopardize the friendship. Maritza, however, was not a friend before they became involved. Their relationship seemed to have formed overnight in a purely raw physical attraction. He still knew very little about her. She had this knack of deflecting when he asked about her past. Well, he supposed, Raley and his lynch mob could nail him on an ethics violation for dating Maritza, but that was as far as it could go.

Dan's mind traveled back to Ausangate. The sanctity of the climb and the clean, crisp mountain air had provided a sense of direction for his future in the Senate. The reasons he first ran no longer existed. There was no unity in Washington and certainly very little loyalty. It was the Wild West—every man for himself. Still, he had decided on Ausangate to leave on his own terms, not sneaking out under a banner of shame assigned to him by his colleagues and the media. Although this was the most stressful period of his life since Maddie had left, he held tight to the belief that, somehow, it would all work out. Dan shut off the bathroom light and decided to try for a few more hours of much-needed rest. He returned to the pitch-black bedroom and climbed into bed. Almost immediately, he felt her touch; the warmth of her body against his as she nestled up behind him and rested her face against his shoulder. Dan's anxiety melted away as he lifted his head off the pillow and smiled.

"I thought you abandoned me," he said warmly. Gently, she slid back in the bed, allowing Dan to lay flat on his back. She mounted him, saying only, "Shhh."

CHAPTER 26

Eli toured many warehouses in his day. As a prominent CPA and business advisor, his clients included a wide array of manufacturers, distributors, and retailers. The facility he now walked with Earl Sanderson was different. The East Coast location of Micuna Cold Chain Logistics was large by most standards. Situated in Wilmington, Delaware, it was five hundred thousand square feet and the outsourced assembly and distribution facility for dozens of well-known food companies. For FPPL, Eli knew, Micuna had undertaken the process of "kitting," which involved the picking and packing of the clean food boxes from stocks of bulk product received from processed food suppliers and organic farms from around the region. The refrigerated facility also contained a fifty-thousand-square-foot freezer to accommodate their customers' diverse food storage needs. Eli and Sanderson wore insulated jackets and hairnets provided by their tour guide, Dani Allison. "Federal regulations," she explained, "require everyone touring the facility to wear a hairnet and safety goggles."

The floor was so clean you could eat off it. Eli observed a large banner hanging on the wall above the entrance that read, "418 consecutive days without an accident."

Allison, noting his head cranked in the direction of the banner, remarked, "A safety record we are very proud of." Sanderson doted along behind her, nodding his head in agreement as if he were some sort of logistics expert.

Allison went on with the tour, explaining, "This facility processes everything from fresh fruit and vegetables to frozen pizza and ice cream. For many of our customers, we also serve as a "crossdock" facility, meaning that suppliers drop products here for consolidation to full truckloads, eliminating numerous trucks delivering to one destination. It's easier for receivers like grocery stores if they get one shipment from multiple vendors as opposed to each vendor sending in its own truck."

"So what do you actually keep in inventory?" Eli inquired.

"As little as possible, but primarily frozen foods with longer shelf life. Needless to say, the perishables need to move through pretty quickly. We work for a lot of organic food companies that do not believe in chemical preservatives."

"Dani, take us to the section where you assemble our clean food boxes," asked Sanderson.

As they traveled the immaculate concrete floor along a walking path defined by dual rows of yellow tape, Allison cautioned them to stay within the lines to avoid being hit by a forklift operator.

Around the corner, an assembly section was cordoned off and a sign proudly displayed the green and orange FPPL logo. "These team members are dedicated full time to your account," Allison stated.

Eli watched as the three workers performed the assembly of a clean food box in perfect harmony. The first would take a prefabricated, white paperboard box and place into it a bottle of purified water. Eli admired how each box lid and the custom-designed water bottle label bore the bright green and orange logo of FPPL. A second worker received the box along the conveyor and added an apple, a package of celery, and a turkey leg sealed in shrink-wrap. The third worker placed a two-inch soft-baked oatmeal raisin cookie wrapped in cellophane and completed the box with a card stating, "This clean food box is provided with love from the Foundation for Preservation, Peace, and Light." Bright orange tissue paper covered the contents and the box was then sealed with a gold star sticker. Each completed clean food box was stacked neatly in a master carton on top of a wooden pallet for shipping.

"Where are you shipping these boxes to?" asked Eli.

"This pallet they are building now will be exported tomorrow to Ghana," replied Sanderson.

Eli shook his head. "Earl, if you want to make the most out of your hard-earned donations, why not work on feeding the hungry right here in America first? That way, you can hone your operation, build credibility, and expand internationally after you attract more donors. Sending random containers to faraway places like Ghana is like trying to boil the ocean."

Sanderson looked puzzled as if the notion of feeding the hungry closer to home had never occurred to him. "You know what, Eli? That makes a lot of sense. I guess having traveled to so many third world countries with the Peace Corps, I had it in mind that we needed to reach those folks first, but darn if you don't make good business sense."

Eli smiled. "That's why people engage me . . . to be their trusted business advisor." As they walked back toward the exit, trailing Dani Allison, who stopped to converse with an employee, Eli placed his arm around Sanderson's shoulders and said, "Here's one more thing to consider."

"What's that?" replied Sanderson.

"The Senate is contemplating the passage of a new bill to make it easier to export food products. If it passes, much of the red tape and bureaucracy will disappear, making it even easier and less expensive for FPPL to feed the hungry all over the world."

"You are right on, Eli. That's why we hired American Clean Food—to lobby for the bill's passage. I understand it's stuck in Committee."

"That is my understanding but as I told you when we met in my office, my good friend, Senator Dan Alston, is the chairman of the Senate

Committee on Agriculture, Nutrition, and Forestry. Once Dan buys in, the ANF Committee blesses the bill and it goes to the full Senate floor. Why would anyone oppose its passage? It's a completely bipartisan bill."

"Why would they oppose it? Come on, Eli. Money for one. If it isn't free, someone will object to something. And let us not forget your friend Alston seems to be on the hot seat right now with the Senate Ethics Committee."

"True enough, Earl. I am sure he will be cleared and from what you tell me, this lobbyist you hired is making good progress."

Sanderson shrugged his shoulders. "I suppose you are right. We'll just have to wait and see. In the meantime, I agree with your business assessment. I will start refocusing the clean food boxes to the needy right here at home."

Eli was satisfied. He now had Sanderson unknowingly on board with his plan. As far as the Senate bill easing export regulations for food, well, he had to admit he couldn't care less whether it passed. His only motivation had been to have a reason for Maritza to penetrate Alston's office and forge a relationship with him. Now that she was in, they could move forward with Alston's ultimate demise.

CHAPTER 27

Not sure where to start in her quest to help Dan get his life back, Tally took to the phone. "Hello, is this Madame Cece?"

"Yes, hello, and it's just 'Cece.'"

"My name is Talia Clayton. I am Dan Alston's chief of staff. The senator told me about his recent session with you. Senator Alston is in some trouble, as I am sure you know. I was hoping I could ask you a few questions."

"Ms. Clayton—" she began before being interrupted.

"Please call me Tally."

"Okay, Tally it is. While I sympathize with the senator's plight, I am afraid that the nature of my session with a client is strictly confidential."

"Oh sure, I get that. I mean, I really do. You don't need to tell me anything confidential. I was just hoping you could point me to another resource who might be able to help us figure out what is going on."

"Ms. Clayton—sorry, Tally—I am a restaurateur with the gift of psychic ability. I help people where I can but, in this case, I honestly think I have done everything I can do. I am not connected to a network of psychics. I have no one to refer you to."

Dejected, Tally gently replaced the receiver on her office handset and exhaled deeply. Not knowing where else to turn for help, she resorted to Google. The search box stared her down as she pondered what to enter. *Psychics? Mediums?* She admitted to herself that she knew absolutely nothing about the problem she was trying to solve. Tally readied herself for the monotony of endless research to find a clue on how to help Dan. After an hour, she was ready to scream. There were so many weird sites from people claiming to hold the keys to everything from communicating with the dead to predicting the future. She didn't find anything she deemed credible and was feeling frustrated when suddenly her phone rang. The caller ID read "Towson University." Tally didn't know anyone at Towson University and would ordinarily have ignored the call, but something compelled her to answer.

"Ms. Clayton, my name is Geronimo Quesaré. I am an anthropologist at Towson University and I have information that may affect Senator Alston."

Somewhat skeptically, Tally answered slowly, "Go ahead. I'm listening."

"In addition to being an anthropologist and a professor, I am what is called an Akashic reader. In short, I can help someone understand how events in one's past lives might be impacting events in their current life."

Confused but curious, Tally replied, "Past lives? I don't understand."

"You see, Ms. Clayton, everyone has a soul. That soul has inhabited many bodies and has lived many lifetimes. The soul is reborn, or more commonly, reincarnated, into a new body seeking an additional opportunity to live a more perfect existence in hopes that it will be able to one day exist eternally in what you might refer to as Heaven."

"I see," she said tentatively but hopeful that this was the break she had been waiting for. "What does any of this have to do with Senator Alston?"

"I conducted Akashic readings for Eli Shepherd, a friend of the senator, as well as for a lady you may know, a DC lobbyist named Maritza Coya. I was given the direct impression that the information was being used for illicit purposes."

"I'm trying to follow along here, Mr. Quesaré but I still don't get what Eli Shepherd has to do with Maritza Coya or why their Akashic readings, as you call them, have anything to do with Senator Alston."

"Let me explain. Maritza Coya is my cousin. After learning of her past life experience, in one specific lifetime, she was able to tie that lifetime to a present-day individual who lived with her during the previous lifetime. That person is Eli Shepherd. Maritza asked me to bring them together, which I did, but now I fear they are up to no good."

"So let me get this straight. You are telling me that Eli Shepherd and Maritza Coya not only know one another but they once lived together in some previous lifetime and now they are working together to harm the senator."

"Yes, that is correct."

Tally had heard some doozies in her time from a number of crazy people. She didn't bother to express her cynicism before slamming the phone down to end the call.

CHAPTER 28

Maritza's Georgetown apartment was a find. The hardwood floors and granite countertops were features she had not enjoyed in any previous residence. Back in her Miami days, it was more likely a three-story walk-up and being lucid enough to avoid tripping over a stoned neighbor while climbing the stairs. ACF paid handsomely for a top lobbyist, and she admitted she played the part well.

While Maritza considered herself clean for more than five years, her cocaine use now, at least in her own mind, was purely recreational or sometimes, maybe better stated, strategic. While she still liked chasing the dragon, the mix of heroin and crack, a straight line of pure coke from a high-end DC dealer helped calm her nerves and prepare her for a challenging day. The work at hand was too important. She needed to keep herself calm.

The afternoon was nothing but a routine check-in meeting at ACF with Tyler Morrison. Her morning would be dedicated to the real work, exploiting the treasure trove of information she found while exploring Alston's home in the middle of the night while he slept in the upstairs bedroom. It didn't take long to find the files marked "Tax Returns" and "Medical Records" in the cherry-stained wooden lateral file behind the desk in his home office. She still shook her head when she thought of the astounding wealth this man possessed. Old money, she supposed. But on top of that, he had founded and sold a successful business. All in all, she guessed his net worth to be in the hundreds of millions. It was almost too good to be true. Robbing him of his precious financial resources will be that much sweeter knowing the depths of his fortune. She now held a major key to making it all happen, his Social Security number. Even though Eli had this information in his own files as Dan's CPA, she happened to stumble upon the tax returns in search of the medical records. Having seen the tax returns with her own eyes meant that she didn't have to trust Eli when it came to divvying up the money. *Damn if she would just take his word on the amount.*

Maritza smiled as she imagined the possibilities. The Social Security number and the details of his Senate-sponsored medical plan were some of the final pieces. The loose hair she captured from the Watergate hotel pillow provided the DNA she needed. Maritza had researched this extensively. The plan was flawless. The ruination of Dan Alston was now a certainty.

CHAPTER 29

The law office of Robinson, Reese & Snider was one of the most respected firms in Washington, DC. The firm traced its roots back to the days of the founding fathers and laid claim to being the oldest ongoing firm in America. Over the centuries, the firm represented congressmen, senators, and even presidents. The lobby screamed unabashed wealth with its marble floor, oriental rugs, and floor-to-ceiling oil painting depicting the construction of the White House in 1792. The wall opposite the oil painting was a gold-foiled backdrop with a downpour of gently streaming water falling into a black rectangular fiberglass pool resting three feet above the marble floor. Dan didn't come here often, but when he did, he always thought the lobby offered a sense of peace, something he desperately needed at the moment as he prepared to meet with his attorney to strategize for the bogus ethics investigation.

The attorney, Remy Osterhaus, was dressed impeccably. While much of the world seemed to have gone to casual attire, Remy donned a charcoal Armani suit with a white monogrammed shirt complimented by gold cuff links. His plum-patterned necktie completed the look. Dan had more simple tastes. While he wore a suit and tie, he felt underdressed standing next to Remy. The two men shook hands, holding the embrace for a moment in a display of collegial familiarity.

"I have a conference room booked on the twenty-ninth floor. Can we get you coffee or water?"

"I'm good," Dan replied as he followed Osterhaus out of the elevator and into the conference room named "Washington's Crossing." He immediately went to the large picture window and took in the breathtaking view of the city. From this vantage point, he had a clear view of the White House.

Dan sat down in one of the high-back leather chairs at the long mahogany table and did his best to relax. The Ethics Committee had publicly announced its investigation. It would be a matter of mere weeks before the shit really hit the fan. For today, all he and Osterhaus could really do was theorize what else the committee might do with the video from the Lincoln Memorial. *Other than that, what else did they have?* To Dan, it felt like they were building a case on a house of cards.

"Remy, I know we have to take this seriously but c'mon. Doesn't my reputation count for anything?"

Osterhaus leaned in from his high-back chair at the table's head and replied, "Not even the so-called 'last honest senator' gets a pass for something like this."

"Has the committee shown its hand at all?"

"No, all we have so far is the obligatory notice stating the committee's intent to investigate and a summary of the concern. We can't expect anything else for at least a week. The media might learn more than us in that period of time. They already have their bloodhounds sniffing out the trail."

"For what, exactly?"

"For starters, they want to find the person who filmed the video and posted it to social media."

Dan had no clue who that might be. Just an innocent passerby milling around the Lincoln Memorial early on a Saturday morning who saw a guy in a tux sprawled out on the cement steps having some sort of episode? Dan looked over at Osterhaus for some expression of sympathy.

The attorney, just a few years older than he and prematurely gray with defined crow's feet around his eyes, held a stoic expression as he addressed the issues.

"Here's how I see it. If all they have is the video, we need to come up with a plausible explanation to spin this our way. We could get a doctor to substantiate side effects for medicine you were taking, disclose some sort of seizure condition—real or otherwise—or submit to voluntary tox screening and/or a polygraph."

"I am not going to lie, Remy."

"Well, I am not encouraging you to lie, just to create an alternative truth that takes the focus away from the accusation."

"Alternative truth? Is that lawyer-speak for lying?"

"Look, Dan, all I'm saying is that I have seen things like this paint innocent people into a corner. If you aren't willing to be a little flexible in your thinking, we might soon be discussing how to negotiate the resignation of your Senate seat. Is that what you want?"

"Of course not. I'd like to leave the Senate on my own terms."

"Then tell me everything. Don't omit a single detail."

Dan sighed and his posture melted into a slouch. He loosened his tie and began to tell the story. He left out no details, explaining everything including the voices and visions before, during, and after Ausangate, the session with Cece LaBello, his relationship with Maritza Coya, and even his nagging suspicion that his father's death was the result of foul play.

"Do you think someone is screwing with you?"

"I don't know. Generally, I am a trusting soul. I have difficulty believing that someone is trying to intentionally ruin me."

"Let's examine what new elements exist in your life that didn't before the trouble began."

Dan looked up at the ceiling in an effort to focus his thoughts on the question. The visions had intensified in recent months but were present on and off for years. That haunting, female voice with the crazy chant . . . he had been experiencing that for years. The only single, definable new factor in his life since all the craziness occurred was Maritza. He relayed this to Remy.

"So, what do we really know about Ms. Coya other than her brief time as a lobbyist with American Clean Food? And by the way, I know I don't need to say this, but your relationship with this woman is conflict enough to send the Ethics Committee all they need to either censure you or remove you from the Senate."

Dan paused to think. He didn't know much about Maritza. She was deceptively coy when he asked about her past. Truth be told, she had entered his life at a low point and he succumbed to lust after a chance meeting at the TOY event. Since then, he had begun to have feelings for her. Playing back everything in his mind, he questioned whether she had done or said anything that would cast her in a suspicious light. He could think of nothing. He knew the Ethics Committee wouldn't care one way or the other, but Maritza really never even talked about the food export bill that ACF was sponsoring. He had not told her this, but when the time came to render an opinion on the bill, he was going to have to recuse himself. The recusal would likely place his relationship with Maritza in the spotlight.

"I've been thinking about how I can publicly manage my relationship with Maritza to avoid conflicts of interest. And no, I can't honestly think of a single thing she has said or done that might work against me."

"To be on the safe side, would you object to my PI running down some background on your new lady friend? We will likely need to get ahead of that issue as well."

Dan flinched. He hated the idea of going behind her back. If he were to build a relationship with this woman, authorizing a background check felt like an immediate breach of her trust.

"Not yet. Let's hold off."

"Your call. What about the video? I understand about the visions, but you know that won't play well in the Senate and certainly not in the media. Give some thought to spinning this some other way."

"Great, Remy. I appreciate it." As the words rolled off his tongue, his cell phone vibrated fiercely in the breast pocket of his suit coat. Dan pulled out the phone and saw an alert from his brokerage firm. Across the screen, it simply read: "ACCOUNT BALANCE - $0.00."

CHAPTER 30

Tally was worried. When Dan walked into the office, he looked haggard, like he had seen a ghost. Uncharacteristically, he failed to greet her on the way past her door. She hightailed it out of her seat and followed him into his office.

"Dan, what's wrong? Is there something I can help with?"

Dan allowed his body to simply collapse on the leather sofa and after a huge sigh replied, "I need to talk to Eli. I have a major problem and I think he is the only person who can fix it."

"What kind of problem?"

"Someone cleaned out one of my brokerage accounts."

"Oh shit! Identity theft?"

"At this point, I can only assume it's an identity theft attempt from a run-of-the-mill crook. All I know so far is that I was sitting in Remy's office, preparing for the assault from the Ethics Committee, and I got an alert saying my account balance was zero."

Instinctively not wanting to trust Eli Shepherd even though he was Dan's best friend, she carefully waded into an alternative suggestion. "Don't the brokerage houses have services that help people who are victims of identity theft?"

"Sure, given the amount involved and the sudden reduction to zero, they called me on the way over here. They will begin an investigation, but my funds will be frozen for an undetermined amount of time."

Not wanting to pry but curious to understand the magnitude of the problem, Tally inquired, "Do you mind if I ask you how much was in the account?"

Dan's shoulders and neck muscles visibly stiffened up as he answered her.

"Just north of ten million dollars."

"Holy moly," she replied, not meaning to let that slip out. It was more money than Tally could possibly dream about. She was a working professional. While she had a modest, growing investment account, it was tough to relate to the size of the loss Dan experienced.

"And that was the smallest of the accounts I have. Thank goodness the crook doesn't have access to my entire portfolio."

Tally tried to keep her expression even. Dan was upset, sure, but she couldn't imagine not completely freaking out over ten million dollars. She went over to his door, closed it gently, and approached him on the couch. She put one knee up on the leather cushion and positioned herself behind him. Lovingly, she caressed his neck and shoulders. She was tentative at first but when it became obvious that Dan didn't mind, she gave it her all in an attempt to get him relaxed. When she was done, she turned to look him in the eye and for a brief, flickering moment, she just gazed into his light blue-gray eyes. It was a moment of vulnerability for Dan, and she wanted with all her heart to capitalize upon it. He returned her gaze.

It was only a few seconds, but Tally relished each and every one. They were fuel to propel her to a lifetime of happiness and dreams fulfilled. She waited years for the end of the marriage to Maddie. Since then, she was in another stall cycle, waiting for their work relationship to naturally conclude. Recently, Dan was making noise about not running for reelection. Her hopes had begun to rise. Then, that awful night occurred where she became sick while on the arm of the man she loved. Having to leave and then learning that that awful woman had swooped in and seduced Dan . . . *Ugh!*

But here and now, she saw an opening and decided to take it. With their eyes locked together, a spark between them began to materialize. She was sure they both felt it. Their heads moved slowly toward one another and her heart pounded in anticipation of the long-desired kiss. *Just another inch . . .*

"I am so sorry," he said. His cell phone began to vibrate repeatedly as a stream of incoming text messages invaded his screen. As he read the messages on the screen, she sat back on the couch and let her heart return to a normal rhythm. *Crap, what could be so important? Dumb thought. He was a US senator. Refocus. See what you can do to help.* Before Dan finished reading, the cell phone rang. He answered and while he was talking, two more calls tried to get through.

"I understand. This is the second one today. I know the drill. Thank you for calling. Appreciate your help."

All of the stress from a few minutes ago returned. He sighed heavily and said, "I am being systematically raided. Three other financial institutions where I hold sizable accounts have all been hit. Taken down to zero."

"Oh my God! Did they say anything helpful about how to get the money back?"

"Same story as before. They will investigate and in the meantime, all accounts are frozen. The one lady I just spoke with said that crooks in these cases often transfer the money to numbered accounts in foreign countries and the funds are never recovered."

Tally's heart was breaking for the pain he was experiencing. She wanted to reignite the spark from a few minutes ago, but she knew the time was no longer right.

"Did you ask Remy if they have any resources to help with this sort of thing?"

"No, I was so upset when I saw the first text come through in his office, I just told him I had a problem and needed to leave. But I will call him, of course. First, I will get ahold of Eli. I am betting one of his clients has been through something like this before. Plus, he files my tax returns and will already have the information he needs to investigate. Eli would run through fire for me. I trust him with my life."

She couldn't put her finger on why, but connecting all the dots, there was something about Eli she just didn't trust despite Dan's blind faith in the man. She began to remember what she heard on the strange call from Quesaré, the Towson University professor. That Eli and Maritza knew each other in a prior lifetime and were working together in present day to somehow ruin Dan. It seemed unbelievable. But now? After what she just witnessed, she couldn't help but wonder if there were some truth to it. *Eli Shepherd!* The man filed Dan's taxes. He would have detailed knowledge of all Dan's accounts and his Social Security number. Who else could launch an attack on Dan that was so deliberate and coordinated? Maybe, it occurred to her, just maybe, she owed Geronimo Quesaré an apology.

CHAPTER 31

Driving south to Washington, Eli reflected on his recent visit to Micuna Cold Chain Logistics. Sanderson was thrilled to learn that Eli had a client who owned an orchard and was willing to donate fresh apples for his clean food boxes. Eli snickered aloud as he recalled the instructions given to the orchard manager. Through the bottom of each apple, a pneumatic injection device would insert a tiny, narrow capsule. No more than a millimeter in diameter, it was large enough to hold an electromagnetic charge that could be ignited remotely with little more than a spark. The spark would come from a radio frequency identification or RFID tag applied to the bottom of each clean food box. Eli convinced the orchard manager that the "inserts" were nothing more than a dissolvable preservative that had to be kept quiet because FPPL didn't approve. Without the insert, Eli reasoned, the food simply wouldn't stay fresh through the course of its journey to feed those in need. It was amazing how easy it was to convince people of what they wanted to believe.

He chuckled to himself when he recalled telling Sanderson that tracking each clean food box was the hallmark of an efficient supply chain and would guarantee the boxes would be placed in the hands of the neediest. He made a personal donation to cover the cost of the tags. *Ruining Dan Alston and a tax deduction . . . not a bad combination.* The RFID tags were commonly available for pennies apiece, and the energy generated from their normal use would be enough to create the desired havoc at the most opportune time. Simply by tapping radio frequency waves in the air and sending them to the tags via a miniature antenna, enough energy could be created from the chip to do the job at hand. Software would enable the devices to be detonated singularly or all at once.

As he turned off the Baltimore-Washington Parkway down New York Avenue, he was struck by how devious and sinister his mind had become. If all went well, the clean food box distribution plan would commence in just two weeks with Sanderson buying into the entire plan. Free apples and advanced inventory visibility all at a grand sum of zero cost to FPPL. *How could Sanderson protest?*

The Acura navigated its way through the busy DC streets. Eli despised driving downtown. Parking options always seemed limited. The Metro wasn't much better. The thought of standing in crowded subway cars with all those people bumping into him. *No thanks!* Driving was the lesser of two evils. He made his way through the traffic in the northwest part of the city and parked in a garage adjacent to Ford's Theater. A young man in front of the theater was distributing handbills promoting the upcoming Broadway stage production about the assassination of President Lincoln. *How ironic*, he thought. *A play about Lincoln's assassination at the very site at which it occurred.* As he hiked up 10th Street toward Tutino's Italian Steakhouse, he wondered if John Wilkes Booth had dined in a classic DC eatery while plotting the fate of the sixteenth president.

Eli entered the restaurant's single oak door by pulling on the long cast-iron handle below a half-moon window and approached the hostess for the table Dan had prearranged. Back in the day, he loved grabbing the finest steak in Washington with his best friend. Since being enlightened by Maritza, the venue and the person he would be dining with caused him to feel venomous. Eli was the first to arrive. He took a seat at the senator's reserved table in the back left corner, on the other side of the room from the baby grand where a man in a tux played and sang Sinatra.

Waiting for Dan, he decided he would suck it up and play the part of the doting best friend. Dan said he had some sort of problem with identity theft. If Dan thought Eli was the answer to the problem, he could play the part. As the captain of the problem resolution team, Eli saw the advantages. While Dan was thinking that Eli had it all under control, he would effectively be doing nothing. This would serve to "run out the clock" and deny Dan the use of his frozen funds. Of course, there was no way Dan was ever seeing the money again. Eli had already moved more than $75 million from various investment accounts owned by Dan Alston. That money now resided in numbered accounts protected by false identities in Switzerland and the Cayman Islands. Only he had access to the money. He hadn't yet decided to trust Maritza with this important information. *Maybe at a later time.* For now, the money would be used to facilitate their plans. If they happened to survive the havoc, he could always grab the money down the road.

Eli opened up the eighteen-inch vertical paperboard menu from Tutino's. Eli questioned why he bothered to look at the menu. He always ordered the signature dish, a New York strip cooked in Italian seasoning and topped with diced tomatoes and lump Maryland crabmeat. Served with a one-pound loaded baked potato and a side of steamed green beans with onions, it was a meal to behold. He skipped the obligatory salad so he would have plenty of room for "the real food." Feeling more informal than the posh surroundings he occupied, Eli ordered an Amstel Light to nurse while he waited.

Fifteen minutes later, the esteemed senator arrived and Eli stood up to shake hands. Dan offered something akin to his normal excuse for being late as he ignored Eli's extended hand and drew him in for an embrace.

"Sorry, man, I couldn't get out of the office. It's been a day from hell." Dan pushed back and took in his best friend. "It's great to see you. I'm glad you could break free. I really need to unburden myself."

Eli tried to smile in a way Dan would expect. *In all likelihood,* Eli thought, *Dan would be so self-absorbed in his narcissistic world, he wouldn't notice otherwise.* "

So, what are you drinking?" Dan asked.

"Amstel."

"I'll have one of those," Dan told the server who appeared out of nowhere.

"So, you said on the phone that you think someone stole your identity?"

"It's worse than it sounds. I had multiple accounts raided this morning. By lunchtime, I was robbed of seventy-five million dollars, just about the entirety of my liquid holdings. The funny thing is, they didn't grab my checking account, just the accounts where the big bucks were. It's like someone knew where to look."

Eli did his best to feign surprise. "That's one hell of a theft. I presume you reported it to the financial institutions in question?"

"Didn't have to. They all called me before I had the chance. I also reported it to the FBI. Tally's idea."

"She always was a fast-on-her-feet thinker." Inside Eli was cursing himself. He should have assumed Dan would report it to the federal authorities. Too much money involved. Now he had to maneuver quickly. "Man, that is a mind-blowing sum. Did they freeze your accounts while an investigation is being done? Do you need cash? I can lend you anything you need."

Eli smirked inside as Dan Alston thanked him profusely for suggesting that his own money be lent to him. "No, I should be okay. Thanks, Eli. I would, however, like for you to quarterback the investigation and recover the stolen funds for me."

"Sure Dan but what can I really do if the feds are involved?"

"The FBI will concentrate on the criminal activity. I need someone who is knowledgeable about the financial world to negotiate on my behalf with the banks to get me back online. I know that there are guarantees on at least a portion of the stolen funds."

The server brought Dan's beer and took the dinner order. Once she retreated, Eli reached across the table, placed his hand on Dan's wrist in an insincere act of brotherhood, and said, "Let me take a crack at it. I have had a few clients with similar experiences." Eli then took a sip of the beer and smiled genuinely. "You can count on me, Dan."

CHAPTER 32

"Everyone wants to see the bill pass. I strongly believe Senator Alston will move it through Committee soon," Maritza explained to her boss. "I am doing everything humanly possible to get him on board."

Morrison pushed back from the small conference table in the ACF office and shrugged his shoulders. "Beyond the inevitable delay from the ethics investigation, what else do you see as a barrier?"

Maritza bristled. This meeting was a required check-in meeting. In her mind, it was a waste of time. She had a flight to catch. She was totally preoccupied. "I don't know of any other barriers, Tyler. You know how the Senate works. It's a slow-go. At some point, I have to get onto the companion bill in the House."

"Our client, FPPL, calls me once a week. He is mindful of the fortune we are charging to aid in the bill's passage."

"Tell Sanderson to keep cool. We are making progress. Alston will play along and once that happens, we will be in good shape."

She watched Morrison strike a pose of indifference. He had a job to do, but Maritza sensed he was burned out, gliding down the highway and coasting toward retirement. When she was finished with her "real work," Morrison and his once-proud lobbying firm would likely go the way of the dinosaurs.

ooooo

Maritza had been to Chicago only one other time. That was several years ago for a drug deal she would just as soon forget. Today, her business was drones—illegal drones, to be precise. Through some basic internet research, she learned of the extreme frustration experienced by Timothy Frazier. Frazier, it seemed, had invented the drone that could traverse thousands of miles. Long-range drones previously faced barriers including distance and power supply, in addition to weather. Frazier resolved all of those issues but despite his brilliance, he couldn't navigate through Washington's red tape—or for that matter, the red tape of literally every state. Years of effort and millions of dollars from his personal fortune were sunk into manufacturing a product that had no market.

Frazier, the entrepreneur, thought the long-range drone would be embraced by package delivery companies and emergency medical product suppliers, as well as banks, lawyers, and others who made daily shipments of small parcels. By all rights, the Frazier drone, initially introduced in spectacular fashion by the founder and CEO, was going to be the new gold standard for same-day and next-day deliveries. There was only one problem: the federal and state governments were scared. The bureaucrats, plainly stuck in yesterday, made the product illegal. That was two years ago. In the ensuing time, Frazier had made zero progress getting his product to market in the US or elsewhere. Maritza saw an opening.

When she pulled her rental car into the massive parking lot of the Frazier Long-Range Drone Company in the Chicago suburb of Naperville, Maritza was surprised that there were only three vehicles present. It was a Tuesday at nine thirty in the morning. She read there had been layoffs, but after seeing the dearth of employee vehicles, she wondered how this company was still in business. Probably pride or ego of the founder, she reasoned. Oh well, it would only play in her favor. She walked in through the glass door of the main entrance, picked up a lobby phone, and pressed extension 240 to reach Frazier. When he arrived, she was struck by his appearance. Only in his early forties, he was prematurely gray except for his pencil-thin moustache. Frazier was short, maybe five foot seven, she thought. In bare feet, she was taller than him. In the high heels she wore to the meeting, she towered over him. She extended her hand and shook his as she looked down at his brown eyes stationed behind nerdy gray plastic frames.

"You say you are a lobbyist that knows how to cut through red tape?"

"Yes, that's my specialty," she replied. "Is there somewhere we can sit and talk privately?"

As soon as the words left her mouth, she felt foolish. The enormous complex was effectively devoid of people. He let her off the hook. "Of course, right this way."

As they entered his office, Maritza was amazed by the large prototype of the first long-range drone. More clunky looking than the final product, it was still intriguing in its own right. The six-foot wingspan and the barrel-shaped body looked a little like a miniature WWII fighter plane. Nevertheless, it was a great conversation starter.

"Very impressive," she exclaimed.

"I thought it would change the world," Frazier lamented in a nasal tone. "But, as you can see, I have laid off almost all of my employees. The factory screeched to a halt and my company is in bankruptcy. In the next few months, I will have to sell off my inventory for scrap and close this building for good."

Maritza could feel the man's pain. "There is no reason it needs to come to a halt," she said encouragingly.

Frazier sneered. "I know you say you have a good track record as a lobbyist, but I'm afraid it's too late for that kind of effort."

Maritza lit up, hoping to spread some of her enthusiasm his way. This poor guy was a brilliant man who once had the world in the palm of his hands. Now he looked like he wanted to jump off the building. "I don't think lobbying is what you need, Mr. Frazier."

"Timothy, please."

"Timothy, what would you say if I told you I had a buyer for your entire inventory of long-range drones?"

"Yeah, sure. Like I said, I need to sell off the remaining inventory. Any sale needs to be approved by the judge overseeing the bankruptcy."

Maritza shook her head. "No, no, you don't understand. I'm talking about an off-the-books project that would pay handsomely. You could buy your way out of your current financial predicament and make a fresh start."

Frazier looked at her with curiosity as he ran his right index finger horizontally across the thin line of moustache hair above his top lip. "I'm listening."

"The people I represent want you to operate the drone fleet we will buy to conduct an environmental experiment."

Frazier was no dummy. Maritza immediately sensed his hesitance at doing anything clandestine.

"Before you reply," she chimed in, "consider that we are only doing a harmless experiment. The only thing you will be doing is operating the drone fleet at low altitudes to avoid radar. If you get caught, and you will when people see the low-flying drones, you can have your lawyers negotiate the fines. You will still walk away with more money than you ever dreamed of while proving to the world once and for all that your long-range drones are everything you promised."

Frazier's right eyebrow arched in contemplation of her assessment. A slight smile formed. "How much money are we talking about?"

It took less than an hour to complete the outline of a deal. Frazier would receive a purchase order for his entire fleet of drones and the service of operating the fleet for one mission. Drones would be deployed simultaneously from the Naperville parking lot to every major US waterway. Once above its target destination, each drone would release thousands of small rubber pellets roughly the size of marbles that would take readings of the water to assess its viability as a source for human consumption, fishing and farming. The drones, Maritza explained, were the best way to get their pellet product to all waterways for a simultaneous reading, something that heretofore had never been accomplished.

"Tomorrow, I will send you a purchase order and a brief contract to memorialize the agreement. I will then have the pellets shipped here with the hope that we can deploy the drones within the next ten days."

Maritza got back into her rental car and began the drive north to Wisconsin. There she would visit the chemical company Eli found to produce the pellets. While Frazier was desperate and believed what he wanted to, the Appleton, Wisconsin, chemical manufacturer would not be so gullible. She wasn't overly worried, although she had never before purchased bulk orders of rubber pellets filled with sulfur hexafluoride—or as the gas was more commonly known, SF_6. The Wisconsin supplier, Bantam SpecChem, was being told the pellets would be used to revitalize the Frazier drones into legal short-range models. Eli's research revealed that SF_6 was commonly found in electronics as a means to provide insulation and cooling.

All in all, she was very happy that she partnered with Eli Shepherd. She still wasn't sure if she completely trusted him, but boy, was he smart. Being the outdoorsman, Eli knew that environmentalists were concerned about too much carbon being present in American waterways. She recalled him saying that the water could become acidic and kill off all the marine life. Also, he had explained, too much carbon in the water would produce a greenhouse gas effect, causing the earth's temperature to rise quickly. In fact, the carbon effect could rapidly accelerate climate change. Scientists theorized that the earth could become like Venus, where the surface temperatures climb to 750 degrees Fahrenheit. She and Eli ruminated about the effects of speeding up climate change. In addition to heating the planet's core, people would witness drought, floods, waterborne diseases, and even spontaneous wildfires.

Their original plan was to drop supercharged carbon dioxide pellets into America's major waterways, but then Eli read about SF_6, the man-made chemical that had no color or smell and wouldn't burn. Its one redeeming quality was that it proved twenty thousand times more potent than carbon dioxide in creating a greenhouse gas effect. Better yet, once released, SF_6 would remain present in the atmosphere for more than ten generations. Since SF_6 was one of the heaviest gases in existence, the pellets would sink to the bottom where the specialty thin rubber shell would break, releasing the chemical to do its worst.

Traffic mounted on I-94W. The highway was almost at a standstill. Maritza pushed the button on the driver's side door to lower the window for some air. *It smelled like pollution now*, she thought. In less than two weeks, the air would be completely unbreathable. She put the window back up and made a voice reminder on her phone to send Timothy Frazier a purchase order when she got to her Appleton hotel.

Again, Eli was a genius. Frazier's purchase order would come from Fresh Initiatives, LLC, a Maryland single-member limited liability corporation. The single member owner was Dan Alston, and the funds required to capitalize the company were Dan's. Eli made sure to divert some of the stolen money into the new business checking account before shipping the rest overseas. This way, when anyone bothered to "follow the money," it would lead right back to the so-called "last honest senator."

CHAPTER 33

"Eli is going to take care of everything," Dan reported while sounding a bit relieved from his stress of the prior day.

Plopping down in the armchair adjacent to the restored Harry Truman desk, Tally reached her hand out to his and said, "I know this will sound awful, but are you really sure you can trust him?"

She watched the lines on his face deepen. His expression changed instantly from relief to anger. The defensive wall shot up out of nowhere. "Are you kidding me? This is my best friend we are talking about—a guy who has always had my back. Shit, he practically nursed me back to health in a Peruvian hospital after I fell off Ausangate. How can you doubt his sincerity?"

Tally bristled. She seldom heard Dan curse. She knew she had pushed the wrong button, so she attempted to recalibrate the conversation. "Dan, I know Eli has been like a brother to you and that you guys go way back, but when you consider the confluence of recent events and the weird phone call I got the other day, I don't know . . . I just can't stop thinking—"

He cut her off at the pass. "Weird phone call?"

"Yeah, the other day. Out of the blue, I get this call here at the office from an anthropologist at Towson University claiming he was Maritza Coya's cousin and that she and Eli were conspiring against you somehow."

"Anthropologist? Maritza's cousin? Tally, none of that makes a damn bit of sense."

"I know. I thought he was a crackpot and hung up on him. The theft of your personal fortune is giving me cause to second-guess myself."

Dan rotated his neck left and then right in an attempt to relieve the tension. "Tell me exactly what this man said to you."

She ran him through the two-minute conversation with Quesaré. His facial muscles appeared to visibly sink and the blood drained from his cheeks. "Oh my God," she said. "Something hit a nerve. Tell me."

"I don't know," he said hauntingly. "I'm not sure, but this could tie back to the session with Madame Cece."

"What did she say that has anything to do with Eli or Maritza?"

The lines on his forehead became creased as he plowed through a clouded memory. "I can't remember everything. It seemed so irrelevant to my visions, I disregarded it all. Something to do with a violent exchange between me and a woman with long dark hair. The problem is I have never had a violent exchange with anyone . . . in my entire life."

Tally was fascinated. Some instinct from deep within told her they were onto something. "Dan, I think this ties with everything. The visions, the voice, and the odd phone call from Quesaré."

She watched as Dan fidgeted in his office chair. For the longest time, he didn't say anything and then suddenly his spirit lifted. "Wait, I recorded the whole damn thing."

"The session with Madame Cece?"

"Yes, yes," he said as he laughed in a nervous sort of way. "It's right here on my phone."

Tally got up and retreated to Dan's office door. She gently closed it, ensuring they would not be disturbed. She then grabbed a yellow legal pad and a pen from his conference table. "Okay," she said. "Let's hear it."

It took twenty minutes to get through the recording. Tally furiously scribbled notes, at times shaking her head in disbelief. When the audio playback concluded, she looked up at Dan and said, "I want to make sure I heard everything correctly. Play it again."

He hit play and they both listened intently. From Dan's expression, she hoped he now saw the dots beginning to connect, so she waded in gently.

"The recording mentioned a wolf, a condor, and a female voice chanting, 'I am one with you.' Does that mean anything to you?"

He hesitated before speaking but she knew it struck a chord. "Yes . . . it actually does. When I was on Ausangate, trying to descend by myself, I saw a wolf. After I slipped, I was sure it was going to kill me. Later, after the fall, I was laying in the snow, semiconscious, and I saw the condor circling overhead. And the . . . the female voice . . . chanting the words Madame Cece said. Tally, I thought I was having some sort of hallucination from a concussion. I told my doctor about it in the Cusco hospital. He said there are no wolves on Ausangate . . ."

Not yet knowing how to fit all of the pieces together, Tally sat quietly for a minute with her hands steepled in front of her face. Dan continued as his memory returned.

"And there was this horrible nightmare. You were in it. You and I floated above DC and then the entire country, watching people die from fires and famine. Oceans, lakes, and rivers were polluted and at the end, you . . . oh, oh, never mind."

"Dan, you can tell me. What happened to me?"

"Throughout the dream or the vision or whatever it was, your hair, it kept . . . just flying off your head and your beautiful face . . . it turned black and then in midair, you just . . . oh my lord, it was awful . . . you just . . . disintegrated."

She moved toward him in an effort to offer physical comfort. "Dan, it was just a dream. You were hallucinating. People have bad dreams all the time, especially right after a trauma. My God, you had just fallen off a mountain. It's not surprising you had such a bad experience."

"No. No, Tally. You don't get it. It was like all the visions I have had for years and years. It's easy to tell yourself it's normal, but it's not. I try to compartmentalize it, but dammit, it's hauntingly real."

She saw him becoming upset and didn't want the conversation's momentum to be upended. She switched gears again, remaining sensitive to the fragile state of his mind.

"Quesaré said that you and Maritza lived together in a past lifetime. And that Maritza and Eli knew one another in the same time period. This sounds really hokey, but could Maritza be the woman with the long dark hair with whom you once had a violent exchange? In the past lifetime?"

He didn't reply. He looked at her quizzically. She understood that what they were discussing sounded outrageous, but nothing else made any sense. Dan looked lost. Tally knew she needed to help chart his next move.

ooooo

Tally couldn't remember the last time she was on campus at Towson University. She knew only that it was a couple of decades ago. The sleepy little campus she remembered from her youth had experienced a metamorphosis. She had recently read in the *Baltimore Sun* that Towson University was the fastest-growing school in the University of Maryland system. Enrollment now exceeded twenty-four thousand. To Tally, it looked like a formidable place of higher education. Unfortunately for the Towson Department of Anthropology, they inhabited one of the campus's older buildings.

Caskey Hall was erected way back in 1938, and while attempts to modernize the building were admirable, Tally thought it appropriate that an ancient building should house the department charged with educating students in the ways of cultures from bygone times.

She marched up the cement steps to Caskey Hall, feeling a bit winded, and realized that she had barely had time to work out. She approached the set of double yellow entry doors and thought how gracious Quesaré had been when she reached back out to him. If the roles were reversed, she concluded, she probably would have refused the meeting. When she got to Room 116, Quesaré came out to meet her in the musty hallway. Tally did not know what to expect. A tall, thin, and ragged older man with a hawk nose, heavily wrinkled face, and gray ponytail was certainly not it. He caught her in an unconscious stare.

"You were expecting someone more professorial?"

Ashamed and already feeling like she owed this man something for the way she handled his initial phone call, she tried to be as honest as she could. She felt her cheeks blush. "To be truthful, yes. But I must say, you look like someone with a lifetime of great stories to tell."

The comment appeared to have disarmed him. He smiled warmly. His eyes, set deeply into his face, were two brilliant sapphires. When he smiled, they lit up the old school hallway.

Quesaré led her down the hall to the university artifacts museum. She entered a space that was ten times the size of the average classroom. Glass display cases lined the floors across the expanse of the room. Shelves encased in glass covered every wall.

"As you can see, this building is very old. However, this room does have some modern display technology we are very proud of." A Lucite panel greeted visitors at the entrance, a map of the world engraved on its surface. Quesaré touched South America with his finger, and the continent lit up in bright green. Simultaneously, each display case housing artifacts from any South American country lit up in green with the country name illuminated above in a hologram. Quesaré guided Tally to the right, toward the cases displaying Peru. "My native land," he said proudly. "Many of these artifacts were brought to Baltimore after my yearlong sabbatical back in 2000. For twelve months, I lived amongst the Q'ero near Cusco. The Q'ero are descendants of the Incas."

Tally was impressed with the room and with Quesaré. She experienced a strange attraction to him, not in a romantic way but more in a respectful way. He was validating her sentiment from a few minutes earlier. He did have a lot of stories to tell. Who wouldn't be attracted to that energy?

"I grew up in the northern part of the country, near the Shimbe Lagoon. By the time I was eighteen, I became bored. Against my parents' wishes, I left home one night to see the world and did not return for a decade. Years later, I earned a scholarship for undergrad studies at Yale, where I stayed until I left with a PhD."

Tally was enchanted with Quesaré. She could listen to this man for hours. "What brought you to Baltimore?"

After I excelled for so many years at Yale, our department chair recommended me to the president of Towson University as someone who might be interested in starting the Department of Anthropology. Before the interview, I had never been to Baltimore. That was thirty-five years ago."

"I am fascinated by your work and career. I could listen to you all day, but I do wish to be respectful of your time."

Tally listened carefully, taking copious notes while Quesaré recounted the tale of Eli, Maritza, and Dan having lived together more than five hundred years ago. He explained the relationships as gleaned from the Akashic readings performed for Maritza and Eli. "Maritza had lived as a commoner named Jade in Cusco during the time of the Incas. She was training to be a shaman, like her adopted father, Maicu."

Tally felt a chill go down her spine but didn't know why. Maybe it was the drafty old building. She listened as Quesaré continued.

"The shamans were mostly good people, healers and seers. Well respected among the villagers. After Maicu was murdered by an evil village shaman named Cunac, Jade turned to an elderly woman from the north, near the Shimbe Lagoon where I am from. The old woman named Yanakilla was also a shaman. This is the prior life that Eli Shepherd lived. Yanakilla shifted Jade's training to sorcery. Seeking revenge and now armed with some degree of shamanic training, Jade attempted to kill Cunac, the man who murdered her adopted father. In that attempt she failed and instead was killed by Cunac. I believe, as does Maritza and Eli, that Dan Alston once lived in this time period as Cunac, the evil village shaman."

For Tally, the puzzle pieces were starting to come together. "Forgive me, but that is quite a story. What I am still wrestling with is why, even armed with the knowledge of a lifetime lived hundreds of years ago, anyone would seek to take such extreme measures in present day."

Quesaré seemed to enjoy the question. Clearly he relished his role as an educator. "It is quite simple. The Akashic Records are precise. The events of one's lifetime can cause a soul to be damaged. In its attempt to heal, it reincarnates and seeks perfection in the next lifetime. Until the soul is perfected, the process repeats over and over again. A present day life with a damaged soul can create a very troubled person."

Tally was not completely onboard. This all seemed like something from a sci-fi movie. "I never heard of Akashic Records and don't understand how you can get such vivid detail about lives presumably lived hundreds of years ago."

Quesaré did not seem put off by her comment. "It is understandable. Most people have no knowledge of the recordation of the soul's activity. Every event in your present life is recorded in the Records, and for a trained reader like myself, the information unfolds before me like a book."

"How far back can you go? How many lifetimes has the average person lived?"

"These are questions with no precise answers. The Records reveal what they have to offer and no more. I have done readings that have illustrated lifetimes from thousands of years in the past. The Records often provide information about your present life and, once in a while, the future of your present life."

Tally felt enlightened and intrigued. She wanted to know more, but her focus was helping Dan and not satisfying her own sense of wonder.

"Would you like me to do an Akashic reading for you?"

Tally considered the offer. There was a newfound sense of curiosity surrounding past lives and what eras she may have occupied. *No, today was about helping Da*n. "Perhaps another time. Would it make sense for you to do a reading for Dan? It could help us understand exactly what Maritza and Eli might be up to."

"I could do that, but let me suggest that you see a different reader. Someone with no prior knowledge of my cousin, Maritza, or her friend Eli Shepherd. When the reading validates what I have told you, your Senator Alston will become a believer."

Tally agreed with Quesaré's recommendation, thanked him profusely, and left with the contact information for Renee Palomino.

CHAPTER 34

Going to see Madame Cece on the weekend was entertaining. Visiting with an Akashic reader made Dan feel downright silly. As the BMW came through the downtown section of Bel Air, Maryland, he thought about how much he valued and trusted Tally. She insisted this was important given what she learned from the anthropologist at Towson University. Still, Dan was the type who was great at crafting solutions to big problems. It's what drew him to the Senate. Doing the investigative work was best suited to others. In this regard, he was glad he had Tally.

In so many respects, he was thankful for her. Like he once did with Maddie, he found himself taking her for granted. His mind drifted back to the almost-kiss in the office. Their lips were millimeters apart. He had felt something. Desire? Certainly. He had always found her attractive. But this was something else. It felt more like an energy force circling her body. He couldn't explain it. But he could most assuredly feel it. More and more of late, he found himself noticing an aura of energy coming from certain people. It occurred most recently with Tally, previously with Maritza, and even over dinner with Eli. Maybe the Akashic reader could explain that. *Doubt it*, he thought as he approached the two-story Victorian home on Broadway in downtown Bel Air. Once a residential area, it was obvious to Dan that the short strip off Main Street was now zoned for business. A tiny parking lot had been created where the lawn once was. Dan pulled his 750i into a space facing the gray siding of the old house. A small sign out front read:

Renee Palomino

Counselor

Dan walked up the short sidewalk to the wine-colored front door. He took note of the antique brass door knocker in the shape of a lion's head. The mane appeared to be blown back, as if the lion were walking into the wind. He considered using the knocker but reasoned that this was an establishment open for business during the workday wherein he had an appointment. He tried the doorknob instead. It turned easily and he walked in.

Dan stepped across a low-pile entry rug with a picture of a zebra running across the African plain. The rug covered a small piece of the faded and scratched wood floor. As Dan stepped across the rug onto the creaky old floorboards, still feeling like he was doing something ridiculous, he called out, "Hello, is anyone here?"

From around the corner, Dan took in the sight of Renee Palomino. She was on the shorter side, maybe five and a half feet, he surmised. A heavyset woman, Renee Palomino was around seventy years of age. Her big, puffy brown hairdo containing blonde highlights made her look younger. Dan was sure that was what she was going for. He silently wondered how much hairspray she went through in a week. As she came closer, he could see her rounded face, large brown eyes, and full lips. She wore a ton of perfume. Not wanting to judge her on sight, he admitted to himself that he wanted to make a quick excuse and escape.

Before he had the chance to react, Renee came to him, smiled, and said, "Senator Alston, it is indeed a pleasure to meet you. Welcome."

She took his hand in both of hers. Her touch was warm. He tried to take note of an energy aura around her but detected nothing. "Please," she said, "come with me and we can get started."

She led him back to a room with furnishings from a prior generation. A brown couch with thin tan stripes and hard cushioning rested along the right wall. Two end pillows contained images of giraffes. A large picture of a majestic elephant on its hind legs hung in a gaudy gold frame above the couch. On the back wall, a credenza with a sliding front cabinet door held a dusty glass vase with a single dying sunflower. In the center of the room sat a plain round table and two dark wood parlor chairs resting atop a burgundy throw rug, the kind with long fringes. She motioned for him to sit in one of the parlor chairs.

"I see you have an affinity for African wildlife."

His notice of the obvious seemed to delight her. "Yes, after I retired from my securities law practice in Baltimore, I told my husband we were going on an African safari. It was the most fascinating trip of my life. I can't explain it, but I felt like I was drawn there."

Dan was stunned by her choice of words. "Drawn there?"

"Yeah, you know, I had this nagging feeling all my life like I had lived in the African plain, but I had never been there and short of watching the National Geographic channel out of curiosity, I knew nothing about the continent."

Listening to Renee tell of her experience lightened his inhibition. He needed to explore this line of conversation a bit more. "When you went there, did anything change for you? I mean, did being there validate the nagging feelings you had before the trip?"

Renee had a comforting smile. She looked him right in the eye and said, "Of course, everything changed with that trip. I don't know anything about why you are here, but I am willing to bet from that question that you also have nagging feelings about places you have never seen or experiences you never had."

Dan didn't reply. He still wasn't sure about what he was doing there and didn't want to say too much.

"You don't have to answer. I can tell from your facial expression. Africa was so enlightening to me that when I got home, I decided to attend a lecture on African culture. The lecturer was Geronimo Quesaré, the professor from Towson University who recently met with your chief of staff. Quesaré and I became good friends. He introduced me to Akashic readings and helped unlock the mystery of my connection to Africa. It was then I learned that hundreds of years ago, I had lived as a bushman in eastern Africa in the land now known as Kenya. Once I understood this and what the Akashic Records have to teach, my present day life took on a sense of clarity and peace that had previously eluded me. A year or so went by, and I asked Quesaré to train me to do readings."

"And here you are," said Dan, somewhat relieved that he now felt a bond with this woman.

"And here I am," she replied kindly. "Shall we get started?"

Dan nodded in agreement. "Would it be okay if I record the session?"

"Certainly," she replied. He took out his cell phone, silenced the ringer, and opened the recorder app. He hit "Record" and indicated his readiness.

"So, I will open the Akashic Records by saying a prayer, once aloud and twice to myself. You will remain quiet, and when I tell you it is okay, you can begin asking questions."

"Got it," he replied.

He watched Renee as she closed her eyes. Her hands were flat on the tabletop. Slowly, he heard her recite the prayer.

"Masters of the sky and all space and energy, I seek your guidance to open the Akashic Records of Daniel Campanella Alston. Let the Divine Light shine from above as we honor the sanctity and truth we are to receive."

Dan sat silently and watched the placid expression on her face as she repeated the prayer to herself two additional times. Only a minute went by. Her eyes popped open and she stared at him, as if she were in a mild trance of some sort. "The Records are open. What would you like to know?"

Tally had relayed some coaching from Quesaré on how to ask questions. Quesaré assured her that he would share nothing with Renee on the specifics of Dan's dilemma or of Eli or Maritza. He did not want to wreck the integrity of Dan's reading with Renee. Dan felt somewhat prepared to ask questions but chose to wade in gently.

"What can the Records tell me about any past lifetimes I may have lived in Peru?"

She said nothing. He watched as her eyes closed. She was lost in concentration. He waited anxiously until finally she spoke.

"Yes, you did live in Peru. It was a mountainous area. I see now. It was in or near Cusco. You were a village leader of some sort." She stopped suddenly. To Dan it appeared as if she were collecting more information.

"You were the village shaman. Your name was Cunac."

"A shaman!" he blurted out. "You mean like a medicine man?"

With his question, Renee entered a present state of consciousness. "Yes, shamans are healers, they are seers of the future, and sometimes they are evil. The Records indicate that you were an evil shaman."

"Do you mean like a sorcerer?"

"Could have been." she replied "I see you did well for the people of your village but had some bad run-ins with the people of the neighboring village. Wait . . ."

Dan tried to sit patiently. This was starting to feel like he was on a Senate investigative committee interrogating a witness. Questions began to flood his mind.

"The Records say that you murdered the shaman from the neighboring village. His name was Maicu. You wanted to control his village. You tried to make it seem like Maicu died of natural causes, but his daughter—her name was Jade—saw through you and tried to avenge the death. You also killed her."

Dan was flabbergasted. *How could any of this be true?*

"The Records remain open. What else would you like to know?"

"When exactly was this?"

Again she paused to gather the answer from the Records. "It looks like late fifteenth century. In the final days of the Incas."

"Can the Records tell me if people in my life today may have lived with me during this time?"

"Yes, the Records should be able to tell us if this is true. What are the names you wish to research?"

"Maritza Coya."

"Hmmm . . . yes, Maritza Coya was Jade, Maicu's daughter. You killed both of them."

"Eli Shepherd?"

"Let me see . . . Eli Shepherd lived during this time. He was a shaman from the north—an older woman named Yanakilla who trained Jade before and after you murdered her father."

Dan was getting irritated. He never murdered anyone. It was becoming tough to listen to any more. Still, he had questions. "If all this is really true, why on earth would these people who have reincarnated into my present day life want to take on extreme measures to seek revenge?"

"Senator, a damaged soul remains in a state of unrest. The person in such a state can live a tormented life until they are able to perfect the soul or, at a minimum, learn to let go of the past life aggressions. My practice has been littered with troubled people possessing damaged souls."

"What do you do to help them?"

"It depends. Often, merely understanding the 'why' of what is happening is enough. With others, it is more difficult. In extreme cases, like yours, where a person you once were committed a murder, it may take many lifetimes for the soul to repair itself through the process of trying to be a better person. The soul will naturally reincarnate in search of repair in the next lifetime."

"Have you ever seen people try to repair their damaged soul by acting out aggression in the present for something that may have happened hundreds of years in the past?"

"I have not, but I have read of cases where this is possible. Is there anything else you would like to know from the Records?"

"No," he said. "I think I have heard quite enough."

Once again, she closed her eyes, recited a prayer in silence, and then stated, "The Records are now closed."

He clicked off the recording and waited. She opened her eyes and asked eagerly, "Was this helpful?"

"The question I have is how to use the information to combat the actions being taken against me."

"Senator, if you want my opinion. You need more information—information that I cannot provide. Just as I did with my African experience, you must travel to Peru. The answers you seek will be found there."

CHAPTER 35

Eli had been expecting the message posted last night by Maritza on the dark web bulletin board. Her Midwest trip was complete. She was ready to meet at Deep Creek Lake in western Maryland. Wanting to avoid being seen in the same places, Eli rented a cabin deep in the woods and far off the main road. Of course he used an alternative identity. He pulled the rental car, an unassuming pale blue Hyundai Sonata, into the gravel driveway and found the frail, unlit mountain lodging set quietly in the eerie silence of the dense forest. He was the first to arrive. He stepped out of the small sedan, a far less comfortable ride than his Acura, stretched, and then fumbled with the light on his iPhone in order to get the old-fashioned metal key into the doorknob. Once inside, he was gratified to find a modicum of electricity. He flipped the switch on the wall to his right and a single bulb illuminated to show a cobblestone fireplace, a modest stack of wood, a table, and two chairs, as well as a standing-room-only kitchen with a white basin stained orange-brown, likely from a tainted water supply. There was an upstairs with two bedrooms, but he would not be needing them. Maritza would arrive soon with some takeout food. They would sit at the tiny wooden table directly under the single light bulb, eat, and compare notes. Even though they had a lot to discuss, Eli figured he would be out of there in a couple of hours and back home by 1:00 a.m. Tomorrow was Saturday. He could sleep in.

He was tired. Keeping up the normal rigors of running his company while also helping to exact revenge on Dan Alston was exhausting. Since he had turned fifty, he found his stamina lagging behind his ambition. He sat down on the three-seat plaid sofa, threw his legs across, and shut his eyes. A short rest before Maritza arrived would do him good. A spring from the secondhand sofa pressed into his lower spine. *This piece of shit should have been thrown into a dumpster twenty years ago,* he thought. There was a wayward smell. He figured it to be a combination of fireplace smoke and musk from the poorly insulated cabin.

It was tough to relax, but he tried nonetheless. His mind wandered. He thought of Maddie and the sweet love they enjoyed in high school. Life with her then and the future they imagined together was perfect. They were best friends whose hearts were locked forever in the sort of once-in-a-lifetime love few people can only dream of. He recalled the night they first made love on a beat-up sofa in the basement of her parents' home. They were each other's first. They were both so nervous and unsure. That night, so many years ago, after they fumbled through the intimacy of young love, Eli and Maddie pledged they would be together forever. Two years later, after Dan's blonde floozy girlfriend hooked up with a foreign exchange student from Austria, Maddie ran into him outside Yoyo's Pizza in Columbia, Maryland, the local hangout where they all gathered every weekend. She became Dan's sympathetic ear for the night and shortly thereafter, something more. The pain remained with him more than thirty years after. In the time since, there were many short-term relationships, but Eli steadfastly refused to give his heart to anyone else. It remained broken forever. When Maddie finally left Dan after two decades of marriage, Eli reached out to her in an expression of friendship. He couldn't say he was surprised when she politely refused his offer of dinner. Too much had changed.

Eli was rattled back into reality by the sound of a car coming across the gravel. *So much for rest.*

Maritza came through the wooden cabin door. She held two white paper bags and her black over-the-shoulder handbag. Glancing at him on the old couch, she remarked, "Are you okay? You look like you don't feel well."

Eli rubbed his eyes and said, "I'm good, just tired. What's to eat?"

Her shoulders sagged with an apologetic shrug and she said, "Subway… best I could do out here in the middle of nowhere. I got you a six-inch turkey on whole grain with everything on it and a bottle of water."

Eli laughed to himself. He hated Subway . . . and he really despised "everything on it." His tastes were simple. He would pick at the sub only because he was hungry. "Did you get any of those big, soft oatmeal raisin cookies?"

"No," she said. "I don't do desserts."

He resigned himself to being hungry. There was an all-night Roy Rogers off I-70 in Frederick, Maryland. On his way back home, he could drive while enjoying a Double-R Bar Burger and a holster of fries. Since he infrequently binged on junk food, he might even get a large vanilla shake.

Maritza went to the bathroom while Eli unpacked the Subway bags and laid out the food. She returned, running her hands through her hair to create a ponytail. "Not much of a bathroom," she said. "I'm glad we aren't staying here overnight. The plumbing barely works."

He wasn't in the mood to be sympathetic. "It'll do," he replied mundanely. "The point is not to be seen or even noticed to the extent we can avoid it. For that purpose, this place is perfect."

They sat down at the tiny wooden table. Maritza ripped into her sub, made exactly to her liking, and ate like she had been on a month-long starvation diet. He opened his sub, took one look at the mayonnaise and tomato slopped over the bun's edge, and shoved it to the side.

"Let's review where we are. Tell me about the Midwest trip."

"It's all set. Frazier and Bantam are onboard. It's simply a matter of logistics. Once we decide on the drones' deployment date, I will contact the supplier and have them hire a motor carrier to bring the pellets to Naperville. Frazier said he and the handful of remaining employees will be able to prepare the drones according to our specifications."

"Sounds like your trip went off without a hitch."

"For the most part. I wasn't sure how Frazier would react to the offer, but desperate men do desperate things. I assured him that the ten million we promised would be wired to a numbered account in Switzerland. That is, as soon as the drones make their deliveries."

"Deployment will be in thirteen days. That would be November 22, Thanksgiving Day."

Maritza beamed. "You are something else. It's absolutely perfect. The whole country will be preoccupied."

Eli smiled in reply. "We will get things going with a bang. I will make sure the clean food boxes are delivered to every major metropolitan area in the US in time for Thanksgiving. It is logical and no one will foresee any harm in feeding the hungry on Thanksgiving."

"I love it!" she replied. "But how will the clean food boxes actually be detonated simultaneously? Last time we spoke, you hadn't figured that out."

Eli again smiled in response. "It turned out to be easier than I thought. The answer was simple: 5G."

"5G? I don't follow."

"Every major cell phone carrier is racing to be the first to implement 5G technology so they can offer lightning-fast transmissions to their customers. All of the existing cell phone carriers are essentially ready to go, but the phone manufacturers are not. All I need to do is hack into the 5G network and by using Internet of Things, or IoT, software, activate the RFID tags on each clean food box. That will create a spark to ignite the electromagnetic device in the core of each apple. When we are ready, it will be as easy as pushing a button on my cell phone."

He watched her expression. She seemed dumbfounded. "The idea is magnificent. But how do you know how to do this?"

His smile turned into a smirk. "I don't, but I know how to hire someone who does. And with Dan Alston's millions at my personal disposal, it wasn't that tough."

"Speaking of Dan Alston's millions, when will you tell me how and when I will get my share?"

Eli cringed. That was the question he was hoping she would not yet ask. He needed to punt. "Based on what your cousin told us about reincarnation and our own damaged souls, we will likely be leaving this lifetime shortly. If that happens, I have arranged for the money to be donated to the Foundation for Preservation, Peace, and Light."

"FPPL? Sanderson? Are you kidding me? What gives you the right?" she declared angrily.

He needed to get her calm. Emotion played no part in what they were trying to accomplish.

"Maritza, keep your head. First off, I had to designate a beneficiary when the accounts were opened. There was no time or even a need to consult you. Second, assuming we will survive, shortly before Thanksgiving I will post an encrypted message on our dark web bulletin board telling you exactly how to access your funds."

This seemed to pacify her, at least for the moment. He still wasn't sure if he was going to be true to his word. At the present time, his thinking was he could disappear to a corner of the world, never to be found, and live quite comfortably for the remainder of his days. If they really were successful in accelerating the warming of the earth's core, the remainder of his days wouldn't be terribly long. But who really knew if their plan would work? In Eli's mind, he needed to prepare for both survival and the end of time.

Wanting to get on the road and stop for some food, he pushed toward a summary.

"So everything is in order. Alston's father has been assassinated, his money has been stolen, effectively making him broke, we have orchestrated the Senate ethics investigation, and the Thanksgiving Day apocalypse is all set, with Alston getting blamed."

It was Maritza's turn to smile in response to Eli. "Oh, and one or two additional surprises are still in store for the good senator."

The last word belonged to Eli, who calmly replied, "Don't leave anything to chance."

CHAPTER 36

It was early on a Saturday morning. The red progress bar on the recorder app of Dan's phone moved from left to right as the horizontal line above jumped up and down with each spoken word. Dan, Tally, and Bri stared at it lying on the coffee table in Dan's DC condo as it unraveled the mystique of Dan's Akashic reading with Renee Palomino. Dan was listening but couldn't help but notice the incredulous looks on the faces of his daughter and chief of staff. This stuff was unbelievable, but there was really no other logical explanation, not even a snippet of one. They all agreed that the information must be taken seriously.

"Renee suggested I go to Peru, but how can I go back there right now? I have the Senate Ethics Committee breathing down my back and a host of legislative matters to tend to."

Tally, sitting next to him on the same sofa, moved closer, placed her hand on his shoulder in a show of sympathy, and replied, "Ninety percent of the legislative stuff can be handled without you. When the time is right, docs can be uploaded to our secure portal so we can view them from South America. The Ethics Committee hearings aren't even scheduled yet. Remy can likely get them delayed. You know as well as I do, all Senate appearances are negotiable these days in terms of when and how someone will testify. Heck, even the questions are negotiated ahead of time. Honestly, I wouldn't let that stand in the way of us going to Peru."

"Wait, 'us'? You want to go with me?"

Her face told him what he needed to know. *The almost-kiss.* Deep in his subconscious, he always knew. She didn't want to go as his chief of staff. She wanted more. He chose to stifle that for the moment, mostly because his daughter was in the room, but also the pressure of all these sudden problems was beginning to mount. "What would I even do there? Who would I see?"

Tally took control. "Let me work on that with Quesaré. I am confident he will guide us appropriately."

Bri looked dazed. He thoughtfully recalled how it was Bri who introduced him to Madame Cece. It was her interest in the spirit world that helped get him this far. To Dan, his daughter now looked scared and uncertain of how to proceed.

"Dad, do you really think Uncle Eli is behind all this?"

"I don't know, Kitten. Eli has always been like a brother to me, but..." He paused to rub the stressed neck muscles stabbing at his psyche. "I just don't know."

Then, partly to comfort Tally and partly because he knew it was the absolute right thing to do, he declared, "I am going to begin distancing myself from Maritza and reexamining everything that's happened since I met her." He looked at Tally. To say she looked relieved was an understatement. Directing his attention to Bri, he continued, "And if Eli contacts you for anything, you need to play it cool and let me know immediately."

Bri was such a strong and composed young woman. This whole mess had taken its toll. She looked like she was fighting tears. "I will Dad. I promise," she said meekly.

Dan was beginning to see the reality of his situation. Instinctively, he reverted back into leadership mode. "Bri, if you have time and feel up to it, I need some research done and I know you are really good at it."

She seemed to perk up at the prospect of lending a hand to solve her father's plight. "Name it," she said.

"Find out everything you can on shamans who lived in Peru during the days of the Incas. The more I understand about the scenario from this past life I lived, the more I can work on strategy."

"When do you need it by?"

"Yesterday," he said with resignation. He turned to Tally. "Can you get me some background research on Maritza?"

She looked spooked at the somewhat ordinary request. "I already tried. There is nothing much. It's like she created an identity with a contrived history. But I know there is something rotten about her. I can feel it in my bones."

Dan had come to rely upon Tally's people radar and was sometimes surprised that she quickly and easily pegged people for something other than what he saw. For a case like Maritza's, normal background checks wouldn't do. It was time to release the hold he placed on Remy's suggestion to investigate Maritza.

Feeling as if he had the makings of a short-term plan to turn things around, he considered that, at least temporarily, he was broke. Embarrassed, he turned to his only daughter and asked of her what he never thought imaginable. "Bri, until my accounts are unfrozen, I am essentially insolvent. Can I tap your trust fund?"

A tear streamed down his daughter's cheek. He hated asking, but he knew it was short term and easier than getting a new line set up with a bank or applying for a loan.

"Dad, you can have every penny. I don't care. I just want you to get your life back."

Dan couldn't quantify how much he cherished his daughter. At that moment, his undying paternal love caused him to well up in appreciation. He collected himself and thanked them both profusely. "Let's meet back here in two days to see where we are at."

As soon as the words left his mouth, his doorbell rang.

"Expecting company?" Tally asked.

"No, and I sure hope it's not Maritza."

Dan walked to the front door and pulled it open to see a tall, thin, silver-haired police officer donning lightweight, gold-framed eyeglasses and an immaculately groomed goatee.

"Senator Alston," he said in a deep, eastern shore drawl, "my name is Chief Ferraro from the Crisfield Police Department. "You are under arrest for the murder of Governor Robert Alston."

CHAPTER 37

Listening to the exchange at Dan's front door, Tally sprang to life like a lioness protecting her newborn cub. "This is totally outrageous. He didn't kill anyone. You are not taking him anywhere. My God, this is a US senator we are talking about."

Chief Ferraro responded politely and without emotion. "Ma'am, I appreciate the gravity of the situation. That is why I came here, at a quiet time, without fanfare, to preserve the senator's dignity."

Ferraro turned to Dan. "Senator, if you agree to come peacefully, I will refrain from cuffing you."

Tally was already feeling defeated in her vain effort to diffuse the situation. Before she could respond, Dan looked back at Ferraro and said, "I will. No problem. There has to be a logical explanation for all this."

Her mind was clouded and at that moment, she was unable to think strategically. "Where are you taking him?"

"Detention center, ma'am, in the town of Princess Anne, Maryland."

"That's nearly three hours from here," she bellowed.

"Yes, ma'am," Ferraro replied. "Once we arrive, the senator will be arraigned and bail will be set at the circuit court for Somerset County. You will be able to visit at the detention center shortly after processing is complete."

Tally glanced over at Bri, who looked frightened. She understood that feeling but knew she couldn't allow herself the luxury of falling apart.

She placed an arm around Bri, turned toward Dan, and reached out for his hand. As the three of them stood in the foyer in a brief moment of comfort, Tally locked eyes with Dan and said, "Don't worry. I will get to the bottom of this."

"Call Remy. He will need to find a criminal defense attorney." With that, Dan gave them each a hug and looked right at his daughter. "Be strong," he said. "You know this is not what it seems."

Tally knew it too. The incident lit a fuse in her gut that burned through her spine and motivated her in a way she had never before experienced. As Ferraro escorted Dan out the door and into the waiting police car, Tally promised herself she would stop at nothing to clear Dan's name and reputation.

○○○○○

The second the front door closed, Tally was on her cell phone, dialing the mobile number of Remy Osterhaus. As the phone rang three and four times, she prayed he would pick up. *Damn. Voicemail.* She left an urgent message and turned to Bri.

"Come here." She had no children of her own, but every maternal instinct was now coming through. She couldn't imagine the pain Bri felt. The whole series of events was shocking. They would need to support one another to get through the raging storm that was now Dan's life.

Bri was much taller but Tally, with her head near Bri's shoulder, could feel the tears falling softly. "Let me make you some tea and honey. My mom always did that for me when I was going through a crisis."

Bri sat down at her father's kitchen table and Tally began to explore the cabinets in search of a tea bag. Coming up empty, she found an Earl Grey K-Cup and inserted it into Dan's Keurig machine. As soon as the lever came down, puncturing the K-Cup's foil cover, Tally's cell phone lit up with an incoming call.

"Tally, its Remy Osterhaus. What can I do for you?"

The words poured out of her mouth, but in her mind, she struggled with how crazy it all sounded.

"Did they say what evidence they had?"

"No, and I was too shaken up to even think about asking that." She felt so stupid. *How could she have not asked about evidence?*

"No worries. Did they tell you where they are taking him?"

"Detention center in Princess Anne."

"That means he will be on the road for three hours. By the time they book him and schedule an arraignment, it'll be dinnertime. That gives us several hours to find a criminal defense attorney and get down to the eastern shore."

"Do you know a good criminal defense attorney?"

"I do. Old college buddy of mine. He is well known in DC. You may have heard of him. His name is Burke. Tough as nails."

Tally was relieved. Everyone knew Burke. He was the guy that handled every high-profile DC criminal defense matter. Burke had a reputation as a media crusader, but Tally admitted that she couldn't think of anyone better. His record of success spoke for itself. "Call him and tell him to call me. I will be heading down there shortly with Dan's daughter. Oh, and Remy, I am going to need you to find a private investigator."

"Burke will take care of that. Standard procedure in a criminal defense matter. He will want to get to the bottom of what happened as a matter of strategy. If Dan's father really was murdered, Burke's PI will try to figure out who actually did it while Burke works on creating reasonable doubt for the jury."

Even though she was on the phone, Tally's head instinctively bobbed up and down to acknowledge her basic understanding of criminal defense proceedings. "Yeah, I get that, but I need a PI to investigate a lobbyist who has no obvious past."

"A lobbyist? Does this have anything to do with Dan's arrest?"

"I can't prove it, but I am absolutely certain it does." She didn't have the time or inclination to go into why, but Remy put the pieces together.

"When Dan was in my office the other day preparing for the ethics hearing, he told me about visions and voices and a new woman he was seeing. Is Maritza Coya the lobbyist in question?"

"You nailed it. Remy, this woman is the devil."

"Tell Burke. The lobbyist will need to be checked out by his PI as part of the criminal defense. If she is somehow mixed up in the death of Bob Alston, Burke and his team will figure it out."

Tally clicked off with Remy and served Bri the Earl Grey in a burgundy-colored ceramic mug.

"Drink up. We are heading to the shore."

CHAPTER 38

Dan didn't need his one phone call. He would have called Tally or Remy, but Tally was with him and she was calling Remy. Now he just had to wait in a holding cell. He sat on the hard metal bench bolted to the concrete wall. Thankfully, he was alone. Alone to wallow independently in his misery. He breathed deeply and was nauseated at the faint smell of urine that someone had feebly tried to wash away with a chlorine-based cleaning product. Just sitting in the cell made him feel grimy. He longed for a hot shower and his favorite chamois robe.

As much as he kept trying to deny it, he was depressed. He had always tried to be a good person. For reasons that were tough to understand, his life was falling apart. It seemed like he had just begun to put the pieces together after Maddie left. He immersed himself in work and was feeling good about how things were going. Then, after recovering from his fall off Ausangate, he met Maritza and thought he was in love. *My God! In love with the devil?* The mere thought of her now made his skin crawl. *And Eli! It was unbelievable.* He felt sapped of strength. Never in his wildest dreams did he imagine himself in a prison cell for murdering someone—let alone his own father, a man he worshipped. Dan was vulnerable. Although he was completely alone, he resisted the urge to uncontrollably weep.

Commotion from the next room and voices brought him back into the moment. The young officer on duty called out. "Senator, you have visitors." Dan watched as Tally, Bri, and Remy walked in right behind a fireplug of a man he didn't know. He was African American, maybe five foot eight, with a potbelly and manner that took hold of the entire scene.

"Remy and I will meet with the senator alone," the portly man declared. "We will be with you ladies shortly," addressing Tally and Bri. Dan now assumed that the new man was his criminal defense attorney. The young officer opened the cell and escorted Dan into a small room designated for attorneys to meet with clients. Dan shook hands with Remy.

"Dan, meet your criminal defense attorney, Theodus Burke."

"Pleased to meet you, Mr. Burke," Dan said as warmly as he could. "Thank you for coming."

Burke was lacking in social etiquette. "There's no mister and don't use my first name. People just call me Burke."

Dan raised an eyebrow at Burke's unorthodox style. "Okay, Burke, you got it."

Remy interjected to help ease the introduction between two men who would need to work closely together to achieve success. "Burke and I met in law school. He doesn't like to talk about it, but he literally fought his way out of the toughest crime-ridden neighborhoods of DC to get where he is today. His record as a defense attorney is impeccable."

Dan could see that Burke was not one to have sunshine pumped up his ass. He was all business.

They sat down at a metal table accompanied by four aluminum folding chairs.

Remy started the session. "How are they treating you? Do you need anything, coffee, water?"

Before Dan could answer, Burke took over. "Plenty of time for all that later. Let's get down to it."

Not one to be bullied, Dan asked Remy for a bottle of water. Sure, it would taste good, and yes, he needed Burke, but he wanted to show this man that he was not one to be ordered about. Nevertheless, Burke kept plowing right through.

"Senator, I have read the complaint against you. On an anonymous tip, the police did a secondary sweep of your father's fishing dock and found this." Burke produced a photo of a small dart-like object and showed it to Dan and Remy. "They believe you have something to do with its presence on the dock and that this dart was the murder weapon."

Dan didn't even know what to say. The suggestion that he killed his father was the wildest thing anyone ever said to him. "How in the world could the police have jumped to that conclusion?"

Burke stared him down in an obvious attempt to gauge his truthfulness. "Your DNA was found on the dart."

"What?" Dan was ready to explode. "That's crazy. I've never seen anything like that dart. I didn't kill my father. I loved my father. I couldn't kill anyone."

Burke was undismayed as his eyes bored a hole through Dan's emotional outburst. "Yet, Senator, here we are."

Dan gathered his thoughts and tried to piece the puzzle together to help Burke understand his innocence. "The day my father died, I was with Senators Raley, Reed, and McMillian at Congressional Country Club in Bethesda."

"And while that's good, in and of itself, it does not clear you of murder. The presence of your DNA on the dart suggests that you could have orchestrated the murder with someone else discharging the dart gun."

Listening to this, Dan felt his blood beginning to boil. He was pissed. "And what possible motive would I have for doing such a thing?"

"Drug habit, for one," Burke replied plainly. "Remember the Ethics Committee and the video at the Lincoln Memorial?"

"I don't have a drug habit, and even if I did, I wouldn't need my father's money. I am independently wealthy."

Burke seemed to let his guard down a bit. “Senator, I am here to help you. We can’t win if I don’t know absolutely everything, and I mean *everything*. You can’t hold anything back. Are we clear?”

Dan nodded in agreement and Burke continued.

“Our first step is to get you out of this cell. Then we will need to spend a good amount of time locking down the details.”

Dan exhaled in an effort to blow off some of the stress. “Sure, sure. Just tell me what you need so I can get the hell out of here.”

“It’s Saturday evening. Your arraignment is scheduled for Monday at nine o’clock in the morning with a Judge Fred Meekins. That’s when bail will be set.”

“Monday morning! Burke, I can’t stay in this shithole all weekend.”

“Sit tight. Let me see what I can do. In the meantime, I am going to send in your daughter and Ms. Clayton to visit.”

Dan slumped dejectedly in the folding chair and resigned himself to surviving the weekend in prison.

ooooo

Comforted by Tally and Bri, ninety minutes passed quickly. Tally was working on a strategy to manage the press coverage of his arrest. Even though he trusted her, he had come to the stark realization that his career in politics was over . . . and not on his terms. That’s what bothered him the most. The small meeting room he was in wasn’t much, but it beat the cell. At least this room didn’t stink. He had a real chair to sit in and access to an actual bathroom. Still, he needed to get out and fast. Dan knew with every fiber of his being that the outcome of this multilayered crisis was his to control. Everything was beginning to crystallize: the visions of destruction and famine, Tally warning him in the dream about how he had the power to change everything, and the feelings he had toward her when she disintegrated. Dan coupled the events with what he learned from Madame Cece and Renee Palomino and what Tally had learned from Quesaré. It was all coming together in his mind. A calm befell him as a plan formed in his mind. His thoughts were suddenly disturbed by Burke's bellowing baritone.

"Well, some good news for you, Senator. You are being released."

Dan was so grateful, he stuttered at getting the words out. "That's great, but how? I mean, what about the arraignment and bail hearing?"

Burke smiled for the first time since Dan met him. "Apparently, Judge Fred Meekins was taken by your spotless record, the circumstantial nature of the evidence, and my overwhelming charm."

Dan sat silently as Remy, by the side of his longtime friend, could not resist the urge to razz him a bit. "You charmed a judge named Fred?"

Burke flipped him the bird and simply replied, "Yes, Remy, I did. Judge Frederica Meekins is quite lovely. She might be the most attractive judge I've ever met."

Dan couldn't help but smile. He loved collegial exchanges. It was one small aspect of Senate life that seemed to have gone by the wayside with the proliferation of partisan politics and zero compromise.

Burke looked back toward Dan. "You can leave now. Judge Meekins has dismissed the charges and told the prosecutor to bring a stronger case. Until then, you are a free man."

Dan never felt so relieved. Tally had told him about the need to hire a PI to investigate Maritza. Even though he was being released, it was still possible that charges might be brought against him at a later date. This begged the need for Burke's PI to discover the meaning behind the dart. If someone had tried to kill his father and blame him for it, they needed to know all the facts.

Dan authorized Burke to do a thorough investigation and turned to Remy. "Obviously, I can't rely on Eli to fix my raided bank accounts. Remy, can you take hold of that for me?

Remy nodded in agreement.

"Tally, speak with Quesaré. Get more information on contacts in Cusco. Bri, I will need that background research on shamanism ASAP."

Dan then stood up, feeling like he was back in control of his life, and declared, "Each of you has an important job to do. Let's keep in touch. And for the time being, it's critical that Eli and Maritza don't suspect we're on to them. If they think we're in the dark, we gain the upper hand."

Tally, ever the loyal number two, was the first to reply. "What are you going to do next?"

"As soon as you get the lowdown from Quesaré, I am going to Peru…" He paused for a split second and then continued, "With you."

CHAPTER 39

Maritza checked her face in the Peruvian makeup mirror that once belonged to her mother. She loved the outlined gold sunrays that gave the mirror its personality. After finishing the application of her makeup, she gently adjusted her hair on the right side and appeared satisfied. It was the best she could do to hide how tired she really was. Driving all the way back to Crisfield from the mountains to drop the anonymous tip in the mailbox at the Crisfield Post Office was exhausting. Eli told her not to leave anything to chance. As always, she had been meticulous in her planning. She had tied her hair into a tight bun and sported a navy baseball cap, a phony gray moustache, and a pair of Ray-Bans, along with a baggy olive-colored jacket and pants. Any eyewitness or video surveillance would have thought her a middle-aged man.

Her afternoon would consist of a visit with Senator Fran Delamonte from Nebraska who was, in light of Alston's recusal from deliberation on the food export bill, overseeing the committee considering its recommendation to the leadership. With the Thanksgiving Day apocalypse just ten days away, Maritza still felt obliged to keep up the pretense of her work for ACF. After the meeting with Senator Delamonte, she would insert the final nail in Dan Alston's coffin.

Upon consideration of everything she and Eli had accomplished so far, she was amazed that Dan didn't suspect either one of them, especially after his arrest. She smiled to herself at how pathetic he looked on the TV coverage of his arrest. She supposed she should call to see how he was doing, just to keep up the ruse. But she had what she needed and really didn't give a shit about Dan Alston's feelings.

In thinking about everything that had happened, Maritza was astonished at how much damage one can do to someone with a few basic pieces of information. Get ahold of someone's Social Security number and a DNA sample, and it was all over. And now, for the remaining step: it was time to call Manuel Sanchez in Miami, the forger and hacker who recreated her personal history enabling her to become a lobbyist in DC and undertake the plan to destroy Dan Alston. Not wanting her call to be traced, she purchased a burner phone from the local Walmart. She pulled the phone from her black handbag and dialed Sanchez in Miami, who answered on one ring.

"Yeah," he growled.

"Manuel, it is Maritza Coya. Tell me how to get the DNA sample to you for entry into the medical records database."

Before he responded, she could hear the long drag on his cigarette and then the raspy reply of his grizzled voice. "That won't be necessary."

She was taken aback. "What? You can't back out now. If it's a matter of money, we can make a different arrangement."

Sanchez coughed, cleared his throat, and said, "The money is not an issue. I was able to find Alston's DNA sample in one of those ancestry research databases. Apparently his daughter, Brianna, had him spit in a cup to perform research on the family lineage."

Maritza understood. The original plan was to have a physical DNA sample "typed" by a laboratory, but since it was already in a database, an expert hacker like Sanchez could access it without a problem. The physical DNA that had been essential in implicating the dart killing Alston's father would not be needed in the current phase of the plan.

"Very well," she replied. "When will the job be complete?"

Again she could hear Sanchez exhaling smoke into the phone's mic. "By the end of the day. I will have linked Alston's DNA to his medical record in a US Senate database with a report from his personal physician indicating repeated abuse with LSD. It will even be signed by the physician," he said proudly.

Maritza was not satisfied. While she knew Sanchez did excellent work, she remained concerned that the plan was flawed. "Once the record you create is seen, won't the physician simply disavow the authenticity of the report?"

Sanchez snarled like a dog foaming at the mouth before replying. "That's the beauty. The physician recently croaked. The guy was eighty-seven years old and just keeled over in his office."

Maritza smiled. No loose ends. Once this process was complete, any explanation Alston had to justify the damaging Lincoln Memorial video would be viewed merely as DC spin.

CHAPTER 40

"It's here," Joc proclaimed sullenly. He handed the FedEx envelope to his boss, and Tally reluctantly ripped it open. On top of the paper stack was a letter from Senator Jed Raley, the chairman of the Senate Ethics Committee, and underneath that, a subpoena to appear before the committee on January 10. As the letter explained, due to the holidays and the need to work on an emergency funding bill to keep the government operational, the hearing on Senator Alston would be postponed until after New Year's Day. Tally glanced up at Joc and breathed a sigh of relief. She had been concerned that Senator Raley was going to abandon Dan and make a show of the hearing or threaten to do so while extracting a promise from him to resign. In the end, friendship won out. Raley was a good man. As he told Dan, he couldn't make this all go away, but he was able to delay it for a reasonable period of time without anyone raising a fuss.

Tally asked Joc to leave and close the door behind him. She needed to call Quesaré and didn't want Joc to overhear the conversation. Ever since his lapse in judgment with the devil-woman, Tally knew she had to watch what she said and did around him. He definitely suffered a precipitous drop on her trust meter. She hated that. She liked Joc but still knew, emotion aside, she should fire his ass. She exhaled to regain her composure and dialed the phone number for Quesaré.

He answered promptly and seemed pleased to hear her voice. She gleaned from his tone that he had enjoyed her company during their meeting at the university. There really was no denying it. She and Quesaré experienced some sort of kindred spirit moment wherein she felt connected to him by more than just circumstance. It was a feeling she couldn't explain.

"Tally, I have been anxious to hear how the senator's Akashic reading went. I have been dying to call Renee and ask but I thought that might be inappropriate."

"It was interesting to say the least. I listened to a recording of it. Renee told Dan that he had lived as an evil village shaman in Peru during the final years of the Incas."

"I knew it!" Quesaré exclaimed. "Did she confirm for him what I told you?"

"Yes, with regard to your cousin and Eli. The senator is now a reluctant believer."

"Reluctant? Why would he be reluctant? It explains everything."

Tally paused before she replied. The last thing she wanted to do was offend this man. She desperately needed his help and chose her words carefully. "You must understand, Professor. The senator is a logic-based person. What we are talking about goes beyond what he deems rational."

Quesaré also paused before responding. Tally was worried she erred in her answer about Dan's reluctance. Finally, he spoke. "And you? Are you a logic-based person as well?"

Again, she slowed her breathing and took her time. In politics, in the job she had as chief of staff, telling small fibs came naturally to manage certain situations. For some reason, she was compelled to be 100 percent honest with Quesaré. "I . . . I always would have considered myself a logic-based person, but you have opened my eyes to something that feels more faith-based. There is something real about all of this I just can't deny."

"And so there is," he replied. "Is there any more credence to the theory that Maritza and Eli are up to no good?"

"I've never been more certain of anything in my entire life."

"Are Maritza and Eli tied to the senator's arrest on the eastern shore?"

"Can't prove it, but yes, I think so. I need your help to uncover what else they might be up to."

"Of course. Anything. This is why I called you in the first place. Maritza is a distant relation of mine, but when I got to know her and Eli, almost from the start I experienced a negative energy from both of them."

"Thank you. Renee told the senator that he should return to Peru to learn more about who he was in the fifteenth century. We all now believe the key to disarming Maritza and Eli lies in the heart of Cusco. We were hoping that you could guide us in the right direction."

"I would like nothing more than to take you and the senator there myself and personally assist in any way I can, but my university obligations will not permit me to do so. However, please allow me to make an introduction for you."

"Yes, thank you so much. Who are you going to introduce us to?"

"My friend, Tomás Paucara. Tomás is a powerful shaman near Cusco. I have spent much of my free time over the past ten years in his company. Tomás is a healer and seer and the wisest man I have ever known. He will be able to unlock the details you need."

CHAPTER 41

Eli sat alone in the bar at the Queen's Pub, the newest restaurant by his office building in Columbia. His back was to the picture window holding the view of Lake Kittamaqundi. Even though he couldn't see the water, he loved being near the lake. Eli was on his third "tall" beer and was beginning to feel the edge going away. He reflected on how lonely his life had been. Sure, he was able to build a successful business, but his life contained a void that had never been filled. Eli was not one to dwell on things others claimed were "meant to be." Now he wasn't so sure.

Maybe, just maybe, it was his destiny to ruin Dan and end the world. The beer slogged around his empty stomach creating a stabbing, gas-like pain in his overgrown gut. Eli found himself trying to suppress a belch to avoid public embarrassment. He was just days away from ending life as people knew it, and he was having second and third thoughts. Getting even with Dan was one thing. Stealing his fortune was child's play, but killing his father? That made him overwrought with guilt. His drone fleet and exploding clean food boxes would murder so many innocent people. And he was doing all of this to heal a damaged soul from five hundred years ago because a beautiful woman told him to? My God, what had he done? What was he about to do? Eli questioned how he would live with himself but then realized that it was a fruitless endeavor. If he actually had the guts to go through with it all, he would likely die in the aftermath of his own apocalyptic plan.

Eli's heart began to race. He was heading into panic. He couldn't bring back Bob Alston, but he could call off the drone attack. He could recall the clean food boxes. He could make up a story about a bacterial outbreak. *That would work!* No one would be the wiser and he would never get caught. But what about Dan's money? If that got tied back to him . . . *Oh shit!* The hard truth hit him in the face like a cold, damp dish rag. *Too late to turn back now.* He chugged the remaining beer and ordered another.

Sweat broke out on his forehead and a pain shot down his neck and back. The stress was too much to bear. Even if he could turn back time, what did he really have to live for? He had no family. He ruined his only meaningful relationships with Dan and Bri. *I can't turn back and I don't want to move forward.*

Sitting on the high-back wooden bar chair, Eli felt paralyzed. His body was literally gripped with fear. He decided to pay his bill and make his way home while he still could. Eli swiveled in the chair but before he could get to his feet, he discovered Maritza standing in his way. He was sure she could see the fear in his eyes. She took a single step back and he stood up. He managed to catch his breath and attempted to sound like he had control of the situation.

"I thought we agreed to never be seen together in public," he whispered forcefully.

Her smile was disarming and her perfume intoxicating. "That was before. The world as we know it will cease to exist on Thanksgiving Day. I just thought it might be time for me to give thanks to you for making my world right again."

Before he could respond, she wrapped her arms around his neck and kissed him passionately on the mouth. The sensuous kiss lasted an eternity and when he finally opened his eyes, he saw her in a different light. His doubts were eviscerated and he wondered if he had been in love with Maritza all along.

CHAPTER 42

As Dan looked out the window of the chartered jet to Cusco, he couldn't help but appreciate the irony. The plane from Dulles International was breaking through the low-lying gray clouds smothering DC and making its way into the clear blue sky. On his way back to Peru with Tally by his side, Dan was hopeful that the storm hanging over his personal life had finally begun to let up. He judged the worst to be over. If Tomás could help him harness his visions and understand the motivations behind what Eli and Maritza were up to, this trip would be a success.

He glanced over at Tally and smiled at the pair of readers hiding her alluring hazel eyes. The glasses rested on the bridge of her freckled button nose. Tally's face still held the innocent beauty of her youth. Yet she was a smart and accomplished woman who fought dearly for what she believed in. Tally stood by his side and, other than Bri, was the person who had been the most loyal, loving, and supportive . . . without fail. He felt guilty that he hadn't paid more attention to her. That would all change when this mess was over. His heart now knew the truth.

As if she had read his mind, she looked up at him and simply said, "What?"

Dan smiled warmly, leaned over to kiss her, and then, without planning to say it out loud, replied, "I was just thinking how lucky I am to have you in my life."

Tally returned the kiss and laid her head on his left shoulder. A few moments passed and she lifted her head. Taking on a serious tone, she asked, “Before you kissed me, I was thinking about your father’s death. Do you think that dart was actually a murder weapon? I mean, we all thought he died of natural causes.”

Dan hated losing the fortune he had amassed over the years, but losing his father created a raging wildfire deep inside his gut. The mere thought made him want to punch something. Not wanting to take it out on Tally, he sighed and gently replied, “According to the Crisfield Police, the dart had the remnants of a poison that would have killed my father and made it look like a heart attack. Without an autopsy, we will never know for sure.”

“Is there a possibility they could get a judge to authorize exhuming the body?”

Dan recoiled at the thought of disturbing his father’s final resting spot. “Anything is possible, but to exhume the body of the former governor of Maryland based on circumstantial evidence is unlikely.”

“But doesn’t the presence of the dart and its poison create a scenario arguing for exhumation?”

“Burke convinced Judge Meekins that the dart could have been planted on the dock after the fact by the real killer who, by the way, likely left the anonymous tip leading to my arrest.”

“The whole thing is mind-blowing.”

“Tell me about it. Now that I look back, it astounds me how comfortable we get in the cocoons we create for ourselves. Life presses on day by day, but we really have no idea what’s in store for us.”

They were silent for a few minutes, but Dan realized Tally’s brain was still on hyperdrive.

“We still have no hard evidence that Maritza and Eli were behind your father’s death or the stolen funds, for that matter.”

"No, we don't. But when you consider that everything went sour after Maritza arrived and that Eli and she were known to be acquainted through Quesaré, nothing else makes sense."

"Eli certainly had the means to steal your money. He had your account numbers, your Social Security number, and the smarts to pull it off. The question is why succumb to some story about a past life motivation? I just have trouble with that."

"No more than me," Dan replied.

Dan took a sip of his Johnny Walker Black and considered the path forward. "I read the background information Bri put together on Peruvian shamans during the days of the Incas. "These shamans are healers that enter altered states of consciousness or as they call it, 'curanderos.'"

"Altered states of consciousness? Sounds like something from a 1960s rock and roll anthology," she mused.

Dan was serious. "No, not really, although these shamans do take mind-altering substances made from plants to do their work. They view it as medicine. It's a very different approach from western philosophy, where the patient takes the medicine prescribed by the healer."

"It's a lot to understand. I had heard the word 'shaman,' but until recently had no clue as to what they do or how they do it."

"And why would you? For some inexplicable reason, we were thrown into the current set of circumstances. We are learning as we go."

"According to Quesaré, our brains may be on overload by the time we get back. He assured me that Tomás will keep it simple for us."

Dan was of the opinion he should keep an open mind but being the "last honest senator," he admitted, "I just hope this isn't a waste of time."

With the government heading to the brink of a shutdown over funding, Dan hated to leave the country. But Tally was right. In today's day and age, they could literally work from almost anywhere. Traveling to Peru held the added benefit of being in the same time zone as Washington. It was early Wednesday morning and Thanksgiving was a week away.

Things would slow down for the holiday and he could catch up over the four day weekend. This trip would be a fairly quick one, just three nights. Dan was hopeful it would lead to the evidence he needed to prove Eli and Maritza's conspiracy against him. It would help him to serve out the remaining term and step down . . . in the manner he chose. If he could somehow find the proof he needed and explain it without sounding crazy, he could make it all go away. Eli and Maritza would go to jail. He would recover his stolen funds, and most important, free his good name from the involuntary bondage into which it was thrust. It was only a matter of demonstrating that the Lincoln Memorial video was simply a physical manifestation of a past life lived. *Oh God. Listen to yourself. What am I thinking? Do I bring Tomás the shaman back from Peru to testify at the ethics hearing? Who will believe any of this?*

Dejected, Dan slumped in the seat. Tally had fallen asleep. There was no one to talk to. Dan's thoughts turned to his father. *What if Tally's notion proved correct? What if Ferraro, the police chief in Crisfield, was crazy enough to file an order for exhumation? What would happen? Would it clear my name?*

His father was always a rock. He always had time, even when he was governor, to listen and give sound advice. His father's death was so sudden, Dan had not taken time to grieve. Now, here he was, thirty thousand feet in the air, with time on his hands. A lump formed in his throat, his chest muscles constricted, and he bit his bottom lip in a vain effort to hold back the tears. Despite his best effort to remain strong, he wept uncontrollably. His body heaved and his nasal passages became stuffy. Tally awoke and held his hand.

"Dan, are you okay?"

Through the sobs, he tried his level best to nod his head. He managed to stammer out, "I just miss my dad."

Tally reached into her purse for a pack of tissues and handed it to him. He wiped his eyes and blew his nose. Embarrassed for his breakdown, he excused himself and went to the restroom. He entered, closed the door behind him, and took note of his bloodshot eyes. He blew his nose again, became dizzy, and splashed some water on his face from the small metal basin.

As the cold water collided with his pores, he fell forward, smashing his forehead into the mirror and opening a two inch cut. Blood streamed down his cheek and onto the collar of his shirt. He felt his knees buckle and then he crumpled to the floor of the small bathroom. With his shins pressed up against the toilet and his head resting uncomfortably on the aluminum door, Dan felt the world beginning to spin. He rubbed his eyes, naively thinking it would wipe away the fog. But when he opened them, everything was blurry and the light stung. His stomach was queasy and he thought he might hurl. He closed his eyes again and tried to let it pass. Like a lightning bolt, a searing pain shot through the top of his head and, for that moment, he thought that perhaps he was having a stroke. Maybe the pressure was just too much. This went beyond the limits of his other migraines.

He wanted to call for help but knew no one would be able to hear him. He opened his eyes in a squint and saw an emergency telephone mounted on the wall by the toilet. Trying to maneuver his tall frame in the narrow enclosure to reach the phone was impossible. Paralyzed, he sat with his back against the door and wondered if he could lift his arms to the door handle and unlock the door. His arms seemed to each weigh a thousand pounds. With no other option, Dan was forced to ride out the storm.

Seconds later, Dan's body transformed into a stream of black smoke. The smoke traveled underneath the bathroom door to the seam of the plane's exit hatch and left the aircraft. When the dark vapor settled, it was on the edge of a quinoa field. Dan saw himself standing on a dusty road, defending himself from a would-be attacker holding a knife. The adrenaline from the encounter made him sweat. His feet were heavy on the dusty road as he carefully approached the attacker. It was a young woman with long dark hair. She wore a simple tunic and a pair of flimsy sandals. He could smell the scent of fear emanating from her, but she did not stop coming toward him. Without thinking, he extended his long arm in a balled-up fist and smashed it into the young woman's jaw. She crumpled to the ground and as she fell, Dan's world once again began to spin out of control.

CHAPTER 43

A pocket of bad air made the plane jump, causing Tally's stomach to turn. She repositioned her laptop on the table and plowed back into the never-ending workload. After twenty minutes went by, she flagged down Rhonda, the lone flight attendant on the charter flight.

"Excuse me. Have you seen Senator Alston?"

"Yes, I did see him get up quite a while ago. He went into the restroom. He didn't come back?"

"No. I think I'll go check on him."

Tally proceeded to the restroom and knocked gently on the door.

"Dan, are you okay in there?"

Hearing no reply and no movement, she became concerned. The indicator above the handle displayed the word "Occupied." She checked the door and confirmed her suspicion that it was locked. She knocked on the door again and called his name. Still, her effort to communicate was met with silence. Alarms were sounding in her brain. Something was wrong. She could just feel it. Her adrenaline overwhelmed her and she rapped hard on the door again, calling out with greater urgency. "Dan, answer me. Are you okay?"

With no answer, Tally called for Rhonda. The charter plane was too small. He couldn't be anywhere else. "He's in there. The door is locked and he isn't answering. Can you open the door?"

The flight attendant nodded calmly. "Yes, of course." To double check, Rhonda knocked on the door. "Senator Alston? Are you in there? I am going to open the door now."

Tally waited anxiously as Rhonda unlocked the door and began to pull on the outside handle. Although the locking mechanism disengaged, the door was stuck. The two women each took turns pulling at the door until finally, on Rhonda's last ditch effort, the door flew open and with it, Dan tumbled backward. Clearly, Dan had passed out. There was a gash on his forehead and blood was running down his face. Tally felt for a pulse and was relieved to find one. On the verge of tears, she gave way to Rhonda, who possessed some level of medical emergency training.

"It's important to elevate his knees above heart level and loosen any tight clothing," she said. Tally understood. Not knowing the exact cause of what was happening, ensuring proper blood flow was critical. She reached for his belt buckle and loosened it and his trousers.

"We shouldn't get him up too quickly. I need to let the pilot know what is happening. You can find a first aid kit in the cabinet on the far wall."

Tally nodded. She retrieved the first aid kit and removed a sterile wipe from a foil packet and began cleaning the blood from Dan's face. The wound was deep but was no longer bleeding. Tally hoped it did not require stitches. In the first aid kit, she discovered a butterfly bandage and applied it to the cut. She sat on the floor by his side and just ran her hand lovingly through his hair. She glanced down the corridor and saw Rhonda on her way back.

"I just spoke with the pilot. He is going to make an emergency landing in Miami so the senator can receive proper medical attention."

Tally nodded her agreement. When they landed, she would call Bri.

"That won't be necessary," came the weakened voice. With his proclamation, Dan sat up slowly. Tally could see he was still woozy and placed her arms behind his shoulders for support.

"We are only four or five hours from Cusco. If need be, I can see Dr. Chavez at the hospital there."

In no frame of mind to debate, she said, "Dan, I think we should play it safe. Let's make a quick stop in Miami, have a doctor look at you, and we can be on our way."

Dan shook his head. "Help me back to my seat. I'll have some water and I'll be fine."

Tally thought this was foolish but had worked with Dan long enough to know when not to argue. She grudgingly looked at Rhonda and said, "Tell the pilot we will continue to Cusco."

Tally and Rhonda helped Dan back to his seat. Rhonda brought him some water and while Dan sipped the cold beverage, Tally could see his color had returned and he looked pretty normal.

"So what happened in there?"

Clear-eyed, he replied in a monotonic voice, eliciting fear like she had never known.

"Everything I ever knew about who I am is a lie. My whole presence on this earth has a meaning that I don't yet understand. I just know that my life is changing. I can feel it."

Tally didn't know how to respond. She listened to him ramble and wondered silently if a bump on the head could cause a sudden personality change. The man she loved would never say anything like that.

PART III

CHAPTER 44

"I am afraid your services are no longer needed," a stressed-out Tyler Morrison proclaimed. "We heard from Senator Delamonte's office this morning. She will not support the food export bill."

"It's going to die in committee?" Maritza questioned, although it was more like a statement of fact.

"I am afraid so. They feel there are too many country-specific issues intertwined within the bill and because of that, it will get shredded in the full Senate. The House had not even begun work on a companion bill. Our efforts have failed. Why should it be so hard to export food around the world to hungry people?"

Maritza shrugged. She had no answer. She was working the ACF lobbying job only as a means to get to Dan Alston. Now that things were in motion, getting fired from ACF wasn't the worst thing in the world. She could spend the remaining days helping Eli execute the plan without having to keep up the ruse of working for Tyler Morrison. With no regrets, Maritza bid Morrison adieu and hiked out his door for the last time.

○○○○○

For years, Maritza told herself a lie. As she formed a line across her kitchen counter, she knew she had never really been truly clean. In Maritza's own mind, her cocaine use had been purely recreational, a far cry from the habit she had twenty years ago. Back then, on the streets of Miami, she would have done just about anything for a fix. Still, she was under control. It helped her cope with the stress of the day. She snorted the line, closed her eyes and stood up straight. After a few seconds, her eyes burst open and she regained the clarity required to keep the apocalypse moving forward.

In her home office, Maritza sat down at her computer and logged into her newly created account at Bantam SpecChem, the SF_6 supplier in Appleton, Wisconsin. She entered the username of DAlston from Fresh Initiatives, LLC, into Bantam's customer portal. She clicked on the tab that read "Current Orders" and saw the update: "Ready to ship." Maritza was pleased; barring any transportation issues, the shipment of SF_6 pellets would arrive in Naperville on time.

Maritza proceeded to the website of a national third-party logistics company, where she created an account for Fresh Initiatives, LLC. She entered the pickup information for Bantam SpecChem in Appleton, Wisconsin, and the destination of the Frazier Long-Range Drone Company in Naperville, Illinois. From the Bantam SpecChem portal, she had the number of cartons on pallets, the shipment weight, and the proper way to describe the product for the bill of lading. The logistics company system returned several options displaying prices from lowest to highest. The most expensive option ensured the quickest delivery. Not caring about the money, Maritza chose the trucker that offered the fastest delivery. She clicked the dispatch button, which sent the pickup order to the selected carrier along with an electronically generated bill of lading. She paid for it with a credit card Eli procured in Dan Alston's name. All confirmations would come to an email box that only Eli and Maritza could access.

According to the logistics company, the SF_6 would be in Naperville the following day. Maritza went to her bedroom, packed a bag, and headed to BWI for the flight to Chicago. Eli insisted that she be onsite to supervise the operation. They couldn't take the chance that Frazier would pretend to do his part, receive the ten million dollars, and then take off. Maritza's job was to make sure he was kept in line. Nothing could prevent the Thanksgiving Day apocalypse from going off on time and without incident.

CHAPTER 45

Tally waited impatiently for Dan in the lobby of the Palacio Nazarenas. Once they landed, Dan refused to see Dr. Chavez at the Cusco hospital and Tally, thankfully, didn't need to offer resistance. The butterfly bandage applied to his forehead had kept the wound together. After the fifteen-minute cab drive, a porter helped them with their luggage, and they had gone to their respective suites to relax for a few hours. Now an associate of Tomás Paucara was coming to pick them up for an evening meal and some private time discussing Dan's issues. Their ride was due any second, but Dan had not yet presented himself in the hotel lobby. Although he really wasn't late, Tally began to worry that maybe he blacked out in his suite.

She paced across the large gray square marble tiles and looked down at a variety of printed throw rugs. An exquisite chair with light blue upholstery resided on one of the rugs. The wood was a walnut color and the legs and base appeared to have been hand-carved. The clerk at the ornate reservation desk smiled to a customer who was just arriving. Tally admired the high-neck forest green dress worn by the clerk. Her dark hair was neatly wrapped on top of her head with a matching ribbon as she stood behind the ornamental front desk painted in a lustrous oval pattern of gold, green, and white. In the center of the lobby, there was a stone retaining wall, clearly built by hand and preserved from a bygone era. It was not uncommon for people of this region to build around structures that were hundreds of years old.

She was getting hungry and the smell of some freshly baked snack was tempting her. Tally glanced at her watch. *Where was Dan?* She would give it a few more minutes. Then from the other side of the lobby, she heard his voice clearly speaking to someone else.

"Moises, it is good to see you again!" he proclaimed. "Are you our transport to the village?"

Tally turned and watched as Dan came across the marble floor to greet a younger man, several inches shy of six feet tall and maybe mid to late thirties with a mop of wavy black hair. Tally immediately took note of the man's muscular build. He could have been a power lifter in the Olympics, she observed. Before she could make her presence known, the man responded to Dan.

"Senator Alston, the pleasure is mine." He extended his hand and the two men shook. "My family has been friends with Tomás's for generations. I provide transport for him when my business is slow."

"Well, hello," she said as she walked up to the two men. Dan placed his arm around her shoulders and introduced her to their driver.

"Tally, meet Moises Muñoz, the owner of Escalar Montañas. Moises was our guide for the recent Ausangate climb."

She now recalled the Escalar Montañas name from the itinerary she had seen from the climb. She approached Moises and gave him a hug. "It's so nice to meet you," she said warmly.

"It is nice to see the senator back on his feet," replied Moises. He added with a playful jab, "Perhaps next time you climb a formidable mountain, you will listen when your guide says it is time to descend."

Tally smiled at the reference to Dan's stubbornness. She already heard the story of how Dan ignored Moises's urgings to descend ahead of the shift in weather.

"Come," he said. "I have a car right out in front of the hotel. It is about a thirty-minute drive to the village where Tomás lives."

Surprised and having no familiarity with Peru, Tally inquired, "Thirty minutes? Will we be leaving Cusco?"

"Yes," Moises replied. "We will be traveling to Distrito Provincia Quispicanchis on the outskirts of Cusco."

Moises had a four-wheel drive Toyota Sequoia, an SUV big enough for transporting eight people—or with seats folded down, a decent amount of supplies. From Tally's view, the vehicle was in good shape although certainly not new. It looked to be recently washed and polished, giving the metallic silver paint a reflective glow in the early evening's setting sun. Moises held the door for her, and she climbed into the spacious second row. Dan sat up front with Moises.

This being her first trip to Peru, Tally was fascinated with the scenery. The mountain ranges were breathtaking. Seeing the Andes with her own eyes made her realize why Dan was pulled to climb. As they drove farther from the urban life of Cusco, the rolling terrain held fewer houses. The few that Tally saw were simple and honest structures hand built with materials gleaned from the earth. She marveled at the purity in which these people lived and felt a strange familiarity with the land. She reasoned that it probably was a manifestation of pictures she had seen as a grade-school student or read about in *National Geographic.*

As if he could read her thoughts, Moises broke the silence by explaining, "The homes that you see here are constructed from bricks that the natives make themselves from the land. They fashion the bricks from the red soil and allow proper time for the blocks to bake in the sun."

Tally was enchanted. As Moises spoke, she saw free-range sheep and goats along the side of the road. Off in the distance, she took note of a flowering crop but couldn't identify it by sight. "What is growing over there?"

"Quinoa," Moises replied. He cracked open the windows on the passenger side of the vehicle to let the air in. "Smell it?"

Tally did and from Dan's fidgeting, he did too.

"The quinoa plant gives off a musky smell. We are used to it but if you are not, it can be a little daunting."

Although she was sitting behind him, she knew Dan had suddenly become anxious. She scooted to her left, placing herself in the middle of the bench, and reached over to his left shoulder. "Are you okay?"

He nodded and then quickly instructed Moises to put the windows back up.

"Many people don't like the odor of the quinoa plant. Do not worry. The ventilation system in the SUV will clear the scent in no time."

Tally didn't understand exactly why, but she knew something other than just the smell of the quinoa field had thrown Dan out of balance. A few minutes later, the SUV veered off the highway onto a bumpy dirt road that carried them into the village. Tally was taken with the difference from the relative modern amenities of Cusco. This village had a narrow main road made of large, hand-laid stones that offered a surprisingly smooth ride. The village artery was narrow, wide enough for only one vehicle at a time. In an American city, this would have been labeled a one-way street. As Moises gently guided the SUV down the quaint village thoroughfare, Tally noticed that she could likely stick her arm out the window and touch the modest buildings. The houses along this road were pressed together and each humble abode had a number to distinguish its location.

"This is where Tomás lives. We will come back here in just a little while. I was told to bring you to the Sacred Ground where they will be helping a man suffering from cancer."

"What constitutes Sacred Ground?" asked Dan.

"Sacred Ground is any land where temples were known to have stood. It can also be land in which rocks were carved in shapes representing the moon or birds like the condor."

Tally watched as Dan flinched at the mention of a condor. She couldn't wait to meet Tomás. She wanted to believe with all her heart that he could eradicate the poison haunting Dan. "How much longer to the Sacred Ground?" she asked.

"We are arriving now," Moises stated. "We will park and walk a short distance to where the healing ceremony will take place.

They exited the vehicle. Tally was glad she had worn comfortable chinos with a lightweight blouse and a pair of cross-trainers. Dan wore jeans and a polo shirt with a pair of Nike Air Max walking shoes. Each of them wore a jacket. As they walked toward the edge of the Sacred Ground, a small group of people was already gathered and sitting on the ground atop woven mats. The ceremony had begun. They would observe and meet Tomás immediately thereafter.

Approaching the group, Tally got her first look at a real shaman. Tomás Paucara looked nothing like she imagined. For some odd reason, Tally envisioned Tomás as an ancient-looking Amazon medicine man from the movies. In fact, Tomás was a young man, probably not much older than Moises. Tomás had short black hair draped gently along his forehead. He was clean-shaven, accentuating his rugged and masculine face. Tally could see Tomás was a man who was one with the earth. Just watching him, it was evident that he took comfort from kneeling on the ground. His dark complexion stood out against the tan-colored flute-like instrument he held to his lips. Tomás's hands each displayed two gold rings, and his head was covered by a woven cap with multicolored strings draping down along his cheeks. Over a long-sleeved gray shirt, Tomás wore a green, gray, and white patterned smock of some sort, clearly woven with a simple repeating pattern illustrating the river and moon. In front of him was an elderly man lying flat on his back on top of a straw mat.

Realizing they would have precious little comprehension of what they were seeing, Moises graciously offered insight. "The shaman will open sacred space by playing music. When he completes the song, he will say a prayer and then seek to remove the *hucha* from the sick man."

"Hucha?" Dan inquired. "I am sorry. I don't know much Spanish."

Moises laughed quietly. "It wouldn't help if you did. Hucha is a Quechua word, the ancient language spoken by the Incas and still used prominently in parts of South America. It means 'heavy energy.'"

"I thought you said he had cancer," Tally said.

"Yes, this man traveled from the neighboring village to see Tomás. He was told he had a cancerous tumor in his belly. Dr. Chavez said it was inoperable and gave him six months to live."

Tally figured that the elderly man was here as a last resort. She listened as Tomás the shaman completed his chants and watched as he produced a long-haired black guinea pig from a small box. The animal seemed scared. The shaman squeezed the guinea pig's torso in his right hand and rubbed it against the elderly man's stomach. The shaman continued to chant. A combination of Spanish and Quechua flowed from his lips. A few of the villagers quietly repeated the chanted words aloud. Even with the explanation from Moises, Tally still wasn't sure what was happening. The process continued until the small animal convulsed in the shaman's hand and died. Then, shockingly, the elderly man's body visibly relaxed and she saw his face take on a peaceful look.

Tally looked at Moises. "I think I understand. The tumor is the hucha, the heavy energy. The shaman transferred the tumor from the patient to the guinea pig."

Moises smiled at her comprehension. "That is correct."

Tally glanced over at Dan to gauge his reaction to the healing ceremony. His face held a blank expression and he looked oddly stoic after watching something so miraculous for the very first time.

"Dan, what did you think?" she asked.

He looked at her, but to Tally it seemed as if Dan were looking through her. It was almost as if he weren't really present. She waited a minute but he didn't reply. Moises broke the silence.

"The shaman will take the carcass of the guinea pig and place it in a sack to burn while the patient rests in the village. We will wait back in the village for Tomás to return."

They left the SUV parked by the edge of the Sacred Ground and walked to the main village road where Tomás lived. Moises led them to the building with the number 9 above the door and through a wrought iron gate, where they entered a small courtyard. Tally saw a cactus in a terra-cotta pot and chuckled at the chickens running loose by their feet. In the corner of the tiny courtyard, Tally smiled at a collection of cute little guinea pigs, also running freely.

Moises pointed to four chairs nestled around a small table made of clay and motioned for them to sit. "Tomás should be along in just a few minutes. We can sit here and rest." Dan sat down slowly. Tally was still worried about him. For sure, something was off. *A concussion, maybe?*

"Senator Alston, how did you come by the wound on your forehead?" Moises inquired.

Dan stared back at Moises and said plainly, "I fell in the airplane's restroom during a bout of turbulence."

Not exactly the complete truth from a man who prides himself on honesty, thought Tally.

"It doesn't look too bad," said Moises. "I have an Ausangate expedition planned for next week, a small group with room for more, if you would like another crack at it."

Tally thought the suggestion was insane. Dan was still healing from the last climb and besides, next week was Thanksgiving. Much to her surprise, Dan seemed to leave his fog behind at the idea.

"You know, I actually would. When exactly are you going?" Dan asked.

"Next Thursday. The timing is perfect. Tomás will likely want you here for a week anyway, and it will give you time to adjust to the climate before the climb."

"I didn't bring any of my gear."

"No worries, we have everything you could possibly need."

Tally was mortified. She couldn't believe what she was hearing. *How could he even consider it?*

"Dan, you know that next Thursday is Thanksgiving right? And there are a million things going on in DC that need your attention."

"Thanksgiving, for me, is spent alone. Bri goes to Maddie's for dinner and I usually make a sandwich and watch football. It's pretty depressing. The idea of conquering a mountain that kicked my ass doesn't sound too bad. Besides, you already pointed out that I can easily work from Peru."

Tally always went to her parents' for the holiday. This year, she was hoping that she would spend Thanksgiving with Dan. Obviously, this thought had never entered his head. She was hurt, but in a selfless act, she elected to table the emotion.

Suddenly, the chickens kicked up in a flutter of activity as Tomás came through the gate.

"Holá, Senator Alston, Ms. Clayton. I am Tomás. It is a privilege to make your acquaintance. Welcome to my home. Please, come inside. We will share a meal and talk."

They entered the small structure. To the right of the doorway, there was a tiny sitting room with two wooden chairs and a frail-looking couch—more like a bench with cushioning, Tally remarked to herself. Modest weavings graced the walls and one tall clay vase with dried flowers sat on the wooden slatted floor. Just beyond, Tally saw a kitchen that consisted of a small timber table with two chairs and a black pot perched over a mini fire pit where food was cooked over an open flame. The pot was suspended over the fire by a wire handle that hung from a bolt above. Tomás invited them to sit in the front room while he prepared the meal. The house was so small, the distance from where she sat and where Tomás prepared the food was maybe ten feet. He added water, chicken strips, carrots, and potatoes into the pot along with some seasoning and then placed a flat tray above it. On top of the tray, Tomás laid out four skewers, each with a compliment of meat. Tomás started a fire under the cauldron and twenty minutes later came into the room to serve the skewers.

Tally was famished and couldn't wait to sample the local fare. She took her skewer, thanking their host, and promptly took a bite. She felt slightly embarrassed as she gobbled down her skewer before the others had begun to eat. "I'm sorry, but this is delicious. What exactly is it?"

Moises looked like he was going to burst into laughter. Dan sat quietly, waiting on Tomás to fill them in.

Tomás took a bite, chewed, and swallowed before answering. "I am pleased you enjoyed it. This is a delicacy we serve only to honored guests." He waited a second longer and then added, "You are eating guinea pig."

Oh my God! Alarms in Tally's head blasted away like a glass shattering on a hard floor. *Guinea pig?* She used to have a pair as pets when she was a little girl. *Pull it together,* she told herself. The last thing she wanted to do was insult her host.

Tomás, Dan, and Moises all seemed to be having a laugh at her expense. At least no one was offended. She guessed they were used to that reaction from unassuming foreigners.

Tomás broke the lighthearted moment as he stared at Tally with a sudden rush of sobriety. "When I arrived, I welcomed you to my home. But really, I should have welcomed you back to Cusco."

Confused by his comment and the sudden change in demeanor, Tally sought to correct him. "Senator Alston was here recently, but it's my first trip to Peru."

Tomás smiled, shook his head, and replied, "But it is not true. You lived here, once upon a time, long, long ago during the days of the Inca Empire."

Tally was stunned. At a loss for words, she finally managed to stammer out some form of meager resistance. "What do you mean? How could that possibly be?"

"You question possibility yet isn't that why you are here in the first place? Because you have been told by an Akashic reader that Senator Alston once lived here during the Inca Empire?"

"Well . . . yes, I suppose that's true, but that's about Dan, not me," she proclaimed.

Tomás was resolute in his stance. "It is also about you. I knew you would both be coming to Peru before Quesaré contacted me. It was foretold to me."

Remembering the ride to Tomás's village, Tally was reminded of the strange feeling she had as she watched the scenery whiz by. It was the unexplainable sensation that she had some sort of strange connection to this place. Still in denial, she leaned back and contemplated how it could possibly be.

CHAPTER 46

By the light of the pale moon peering through the small square window in the front of Tomás's modest home, Dan told his story, concluding with a dream he'd had the night before they left for Cusco. His brain replayed the scene as if it were a video being streamed across insufficient bandwidth. Details were fuzzy and although he knew what he wanted to say, words got lost between his mind and his mouth.

"It was the middle of the night. Somehow, I was drawn to my basement. I don't know why. There was no startling noise revealing the need to open the door and go down the stairs. In this dream, I was . . ." he hesitated for just a moment and continued, ". . . strangely pulled there. Once I hit the carpet at the bottom of the stairwell, I went to the wall to flick on the lights for the main room, but they wouldn't come on. I made my way in the dark, past the bar, and stumbled over one of the high-back leather chairs. The cast iron leg hit my right knee, causing me to momentarily stumble. When I went down, I hit my head on the chair back and fell to the floor. Flat on my back, I stared upward. I felt cold and alone and although I was in my own basement, I had a sense of being lost."

Dan was tired. *Fifty? Does stamina disappear at fifty?* His whole life, he had always been a high-energy person. *Maybe it was the travel.* He paused, inhaled deeply, and took note of the look on the face of Tomás. He gently shook his head as if he were taking pity. Dan hated people feeling sorry for him. Yet he needed to get the whole story out. He was here for help and his sense was that although shamanism was new to him, there was something powerful here. Maybe it was the land steeped with its rich tradition for growth and healing. Maybe it was Tomás himself. Dan was never one for blind faith, but he was sure that somehow he would find the answers he sought right here in Peru.

"After a few minutes, I rose from the floor with a bad headache and a throbbing knee, and then from nothing more than the moonlight seeping through the sliding glass door, I found it."

Dan sat silently and didn't speak. He was collecting his thoughts, straining to get the details out of his mouth. Every word was an effort. Finally he heard Tally's voice, releasing his brain from the mud it was traveling though.

"Dan, please continue. What did you find?"

He gazed at her. It took a moment for his brain to register who she was. *Yes, Tally, I got it.*

Apologetically, he pressed on. "I found a magical pathway."

"Describe this pathway for us," Tomás gently stated.

"It was a hole in the floor. But not the way you might imagine. This hole was large with smooth edges. More like a tunnel with a soft, inviting warmth and faint light offering a welcome respite from the dark basement."

"Was there a color associated with the light?" inquired Tomás.

"Yes . . ." Dan paused to gather his thoughts. "It had a blueish-purple sort of hue."

"Go on," urged Tomás.

"Ultimately, I went through the tunnel and found a landing area where just ahead there were three stone passages. It was like a fork in the road. The landing area seemed to be some sort of waiting space. It had a serene pool of crystal blue water, beautiful flowering plants, and a cool, crisp aroma."

"Is there more?" asked Tomás.

"That's all I can remember. When I woke up, I was drenched from a cold sweat. I felt dizzy, and it took a few minutes to realize where I was and that the whole thing had only been a dream."

"And this dream occurred just the one time?"

"That's the funny thing," Dan replied. "I've had some version of this dream over and over again. Lately it has been occurring more often."

Tomás nodded confidently. "Senator Alston, in simple terms, your dream is a representation of the events you have experienced over the course of your entire life. Think of the body as a river of energy or light. If someone dammed the river, the energy flow is halted and the mind and body become unbalanced."

Dan was a smart man, but Tomás's words may well have been spoken in a language other than English. He had heard the man speak but wasn't sure what to make of the words. He needed to understand this better. "And you glean this from the dream?"

"Let me explain in terms you will understand. Shamans see the world in three dimensions. We refer to these as the lower, middle, and upper worlds. The lower world is the unconscious, the middle world is the conscious or the present, and the upper world is the superconscious. Your tunnel is a symbol of the lower world and proves that, on a subconscious level, you are wrestling with the events of a past lifetime. The lower world is the keeper of events from past lives. These are the Akashic Records you learned about before you arrived here. The indigo or violet color in the tunnel is an indication that the river of light is blocked in your head. It is why you feel distant and your brain is foggy. Does this make sense to you?"

"Yes, I think so. Your job is to remove the blockage so the river can once again flow freely."

"Correct. When I am done, your mental acuity and physical energy will be restored."

Dan smiled. A lifetime of odd visions and the haunting female voice were hopefully about to end. He had forgotten what it was like to be normal. "When can we get started?"

"Tomorrow morning. But do not be fooled into thinking that you are healed after tomorrow's session. There is much more work to do."

"More? You mean to help me learn why Eli and Maritza are tormenting me?"

"Yes, for sure, but more important, we have a greater task before us."

"These people have conspired to ruin my life. They murdered my father. What could be a greater task than seeking justice?"

"I understand your passion, Senator, and those things will resolve in time. From everything you have told me tonight, I am convinced that you were born with a piece of your soul missing. The greater task is to help you retrieve it."

CHAPTER 47

Was Dan Alston that stupid? Sitting in his office, staring at the email message, Eli could hardly believe his eyes. The email from Dan was inviting him back to Peru for another attempt to summit Ausangate on Thanksgiving Day. In Eli's mind, the email was an indication that Dan still didn't suspect him for the murder of his father—or for that matter, the stolen funds. In Dan's mind, Eli was still running point on that investigation. There was no way Dan could know anything about the Thanksgiving Day apocalypse. *So what gives? Was this as innocent as it seemed?*

Eli stared at the monitor and read the email again.

Eli,

Greetings from Cusco!

I am here with Tally visiting with a shaman in search of answers to the visions and voices I told you about. I ran into Moises, who has a group scheduled to climb Ausangate on Thanksgiving Day. I want another crack at it and hope you will fly down here and join me.

Your friend always,

Dan

Is it a ploy to get me on the perilous cliffs of Ausangate to kill me? Why would Dan do that if he didn't suspect anything? Unless . . . Dan was playing me.

Even if that were true, there was an opportunity presenting itself. The climb would give him the opening to dispense with Dan Alston. He would just fall off the mountain again, but this time he would not survive.

It could all work. Maritza would be on her way to their rendezvous point after deployment of the SF_6. He could initiate the clean food box explosions from Peru and be by Alston's side when he learned the truth. Then Eli would simply watch as Dan Alston's body hurtled down the sharp, rocky face of death from high in the Andes.

CHAPTER 48

Dan committed to staying in Peru through Thanksgiving, partly to let Tomás complete his work and partly to climb Ausangate. Tally would fly back the next day. Although she could work remotely, important matters were stacking up in Washington. The government was about to shut down unless Congress agreed to raise the federal debt ceiling, and she had to tend to several other legislative matters. Tally promised Dan she would touch base with Remy to learn more about his investigation into the stolen funds, and someone had to keep tabs on Burke and his private investigator looking into Maritza.

Tally had taken exception to Dan's idea to invite Eli to Peru for the Thanksgiving Day climb. She didn't trust Eli as far she could throw him and worried that Dan was not yet physically healed from the last climb. *What if the weather turned bad again while they were up there? What if Eli tried something on the mountain?* Dan's stamina and still-healing body were at question.

Tomás told her to come to his home an hour before the morning session scheduled for Dan's soul retrieval. He wanted to see her but would not say why. She could only assume it was to get guidance on what was happening to Dan and how she could help. Tally also considered the possibility that Tomás wanted to see her alone because of his comment from the prior night. *He said he knew we would be coming, that it had been foretold to him. Both of us, not just Dan. Could that have something to do with his request?* Sitting in the back of the cab, she couldn't help but imagine.

Deep in thought, the thirty-minute ride to Distrito Provincia Quispicanchis felt like five. The cab pulled onto the narrow village road and stopped in front of number 9. Tally paid the driver, got out of the vehicle, and went through the gate into the tiny courtyard, where she was greeted by boisterous chickens and scrambling guinea pigs. Before she could knock, Tomás answered the door.

"Welcome back, Ms. Clayton," he proclaimed with a toothy grin.

"My friends call me Tally."

"There is much to discuss, Tally."

Tomás led her into the front sitting room where they had talked during the prior evening. He offered a hot beverage, which she declined. Breakfast at the Palacio Nazarenas had been quite filling. Besides, her curiosity was overwhelming her patience.

"This morning, I will aid Senator Alston by conducting a soul retrieval. During this process, the shaman enters an altered state of consciousness while traveling to the lower world in search of who or what pervades the patient's present day life. Once we encounter the source, we can help the patient move forward."

"It sounds miraculous," she replied. "How can I help Dan?"

"Tally, you are here this morning so that I may help you."

"I don't follow exactly," she said quizzically.

"This may sound strange, but even though this is your first trip to Peru, you have been here before. Of this, I am certain."

"You said that last night and yes, it's true, since we arrived yesterday, I have felt an inexplicable connection to the land. Are you saying that I lived here in a past lifetime as well?"

He smiled gently and replied, "Yes, that is exactly what I am saying. When you met Quesaré, did he perform an Akashic reading for you?"

"He offered, but I just wanted to focus on Dan."

"If you are agreeable, I would like to work with you to find the truth in the lower world."

Tally nodded her head in the affirmative.

Tomás closed his eyes while bringing his hands together as if he were about to pray and began to chant. The words in both Spanish and Quechua were unfamiliar to Tally, but his cadence placed her at ease. It took several minutes until she realized from watching him that he had entered an alternative state of consciousness. It was a little disarming. The feeling of contentment from just a moment ago disappeared as she watched and wondered what would happen next. The whole experience was so peculiar; part of her wanted to get up and bolt for the door. But there was something honest about Tomás. Uncharacteristically, Tally felt a deep sense of trust in this man she had known for less than twenty-four hours.

Her thoughts were disturbed when Tomás opened his eyes and proclaimed that he was now present in the lower world. "I see an Inca village. You are there; so is Dan. You are both shamans in neighboring villages. You are an older, meek man with a kindly face and a good spirit."

He was quiet for a few moments as he gathered more information about the scene he had entered. "There is a village gathering. There is a young woman stationed behind you. She lives with you, although you are not her father. Her parents are gone. You are training her to be a shaman."

Tally didn't know how to respond or whether it was even permissible to do so. She sat quietly and waited for him to continue.

"Dan is there. He is the shaman from the neighboring village. He is a younger and much larger man than you. He turns to you and blows tsentsak into your mouth."

Tally now felt compelled to interrupt. "Tsentsak? I don't understand."

Tomás looked on and simply said, "The magic darts possessed by all shamans. Suppressed by good shamans, the evil shamans dispense them through regurgitation and blow them into the mouth of their foe. Tsentsak can make the victim ill or cause death."

"What happened to me?"

"You were killed by the tsentsak," he replied stoically.

"By Dan? Dan killed me?"

"That is correct."

"What else can you tell me?"

"Your name was Maicu. Dan lived as an evil shaman named Cunac. The young woman you raised as your own was named Jade."

Shocked, Tally blurted out, "But according to Quesaré, Jade is Maritza Coya. If I were Maicu, I would have been her adopted father."

"That is correct."

"And Dan killed me?"

"That is correct."

Flustered and unable to think logically, Tally asked emotionally, "What do you suggest I do with this information?"

"That, of course, is up to you. Shamans believe that damaged souls from past lives reincarnate in search of a better life. Sometimes, as with the senator, a shaman must help retrieve a piece of a missing soul. Over many lifetimes, it is hoped that evil becomes good, but sometimes, as with Maritza, good can become evil. Your quest is to understand the proper pathway and ward off the evil intent of those whose souls have failed to move forward."

Tally sat and tried to hide the trembling inside. The news gave her a frightening realization of how fragile and uncertain her understanding of life really was. She prayed that before she left Peru, she could somehow figure it all out.

CHAPTER 49

Maritza was pleased. Frazier and his small crew had zealously attacked the long-range drone fleet and had the birds ready to fly. Each unit had been retrofitted with a storage chamber to hold differing amounts of SF_6 pellets to accommodate its assigned waterway. The larger the body of water, the greater number of pellets that would be deployed. The Atlantic and Pacific oceans were assigned multiple drones with the largest pellet allocations. Just prior to Thanksgiving Day, the drone fleet would deliver its deadly contents in waterways across America. Although it was impossible to predict with certainty, Eli estimated that the irrevocable damage would commence within seventy-two hours. Within a week, the earth's core would heat hundreds of degrees. While they waited for the end of time, the clean food boxes would serve to divert attention from the real crisis.

She stood on the parking lot with Timothy Frazier, who she sensed, for the first time in recent years, had achieved something monumental. She almost felt sorry for the man. A brilliant inventor stood over his fleet of aerial vehicles armed with the chemical that would destroy the world. Yet he honestly believed they were conducting water viability studies. She correctly assessed that his ego would win out over his intelligence. They stood side by side, watching the pallets of SF_6 being unloaded from the trucking company. Frazier's men would remove the product from its packaging and carefully load each drone.

It was Friday. There was less than a week to go before Thanksgiving. Eli had insisted that the drones be deployed on Monday. If the seventy-two hour projection was accurate, the SF_6 would begin to take effect while the country was relaxing for the holiday. Maritza would hang out in Chicago over the weekend and get a plane back to DC after the drones took off. She thought she might spend her final days with Eli, but he sent her a message on the dark web bulletin board that read:

Somewhere over the rainbow, honesty takes the fall. Nunavut?

Maritza knew the message was cryptically stating his intent to travel to Peru and climb Ausangate with Dan. *The Wizard of Oz* lyric referred to Ausangate, also known as the Rainbow Mountain, and honesty was a metaphor for Dan Alston's nickname. In Nunavut, Maritza knew that Eli was planning to make his way to one of the northernmost places on earth. In normal times, the high temperature in Nunavut in late November would be twenty-five degrees below zero. For a Miami girl, that sounded dreadful. But if one were looking for the last place on earth that people might survive the crisis they were creating, Nunavut was as good a choice as any. A Canadian territory, Nunavut was north of Manitoba and Saskatchewan. Eli had purchased an eight-thousand-square-foot house that was once shared by employees of a Canadian weather station. There would be plenty of room for the two of them. He had arranged to load the house with supplies for up to two years. *But who knew if the earth would survive that long?*

Inherently, Maritza was committed to the plan. Not that it really mattered. It was too late to turn back now. Spending her last days in one of the coldest, most desolate sections of the planet didn't sound so appealing, even if the earth's core temperature were heating at a breakneck pace. Eli was brilliant, but he lacked total conviction. That was evident when she needed to ply his will with sex just a few days ago. Eli foolishly held out some degree of hope that he could ride out the storm in a place like Nunavut and then take Dan's money and start anew somewhere else.

Maritza saw that idea as a fantasy. She had come so far from the streets of Miami. She understood her destiny and would have her revenge. *After that, what was left to live for?*

She returned her attention to the unloading operation in the Naperville parking lot. She told Frazier she would return on Monday morning to watch the launch. Once in her rental car, she began the drive to her hotel and contemplated the best way to commit suicide.

CHAPTER 50

Moises dropped Dan off at Tomás's home promptly at nine o'clock in the morning. Dan was worried about Tally. She didn't answer his text messages or phone call. He was sure that Tally would have wanted to sit in on his session with Tomás. As he was walking up to the door with Moises, it opened and out walked Tally. Dan was taken aback at the look on her face.

"I was looking for you at the hotel. You came early?"

She didn't answer. To Dan, it was clear that Tally was upset. He wasn't sure, but it seemed that she might have been crying. His concern grew and he reached for her as they met on the inlaid stones of the tiny courtyard. As his arms extended, she turned away.

"Tally, what's the matter with you?"

At that moment, Tomás entered the scene and tried to offer some degree of explanation.

"Tally has just learned some of the details behind a past life she lived right here in Peru. In fact, the two of you lived during the same period in adjacent villages."

"Really?" replied Dan. "This just keeps getting better and better. Why is she so upset?"

Tomás signaled for Moises and rattled off a few lines in Spanish.

"What did you say? What's going on?"

"I simply asked Moises if he would take Tally back to the hotel to rest while you and I begin our work. Once we are done, Tally's experience can be explained in a way that will make more sense to you."

Dan saw Tally regaining composure and assuming her natural inclination to take charge.

"No, no thank you. I want to be here with Dan. This is why we came here. I want to help however I can."

Before Dan could reply, Tomás jumped in. "Splendid. We will walk to the Sacred Ground and begin at once." Tomás went back into his house and returned with a rolled-up straw mat and a small leather pouch. He tucked the mat under his right arm, holding the pouch with his left, and said, "Let's go."

When they arrived, Dan was surprised to find a handful of villagers gathered to watch the proceedings. Clouds hung low in the early morning sky, keeping the sun from breaking through. Dan was glad he wore a jacket, as the air was chilly and moist. Tomás instructed Dan to lay on the woven mat spread across the Sacred Ground. Dan complied and did his best to relax. He closed his eyes and in preparation took several deep breaths, holding each as long as he possibly could before slowly exhaling. He could see his breath in the cold morning air. Tomás opened the pouch he called a *mesa* and laid its contents on the earth. Dan saw a dozen small stones and several miniature carvings made of limestone. The carvings were of familiar things. One was a man and woman, another of just an open hand, and the others captured the majesty of the condor, the power of the jaguar, and the crafty nature of the snake. Finally, Tomás spoke to offer some indication of what he was doing. "I will place these objects around your head where the hucha resides. Hucha is what shamans call the heavy energy that keeps the river of light from flowing freely."

Dan laid perfectly still while Tomás said a prayer to open sacred space. When he was done, he clicked two of the stones together and moved them across Dan's body, starting at his feet and moving up to his head.

Dan tried to be respectful of the ancient practice even though he didn't completely understand what was happening. Tomás once again began to chant in alternating phrases of Spanish and Quechua. Dan could hear a few of the gathered villagers repeating these phrases in a similar cadence. Tomás then became quiet and rubbed the stones counterclockwise in the center of Dan's forehead. Then he brought the stones to his lips and gently blew on them.

"The hucha has been captured by the stones and by blowing upon them, I send the heavy energy upward to the mountains and sky. Slowly, Senator, I would like you to sit up. We will wait a few minutes and then begin the soul retrieval."

Dan sat up. His mind felt clearer than it had in years. A torrent of thought rushed through his brain like a computer's hard drive recently rebooted. His body surged with adrenaline.

"How do you feel?"

Dan flashed an ear-to-ear smile and replied, "I feel like I could run a mile or, for that matter, climb a mountain."

Tomás seemed pleased. The villagers cheered. "Now Senator, the real work begins."

Dan lay back down and looked up into the sky. The clouds had begun to break up and the sun shone through. Already, the temperature was on the rise. "To retrieve the piece of your soul that is lost, I will enter an alternative consciousness so that I may visit the lower world."

Again, Dan observed the shaman bring his hands together in prayer and begin to chant. A small vial of ayahuasca sat by his side. When sacred space had been opened, Tomás sang icaros to pay tribute to plant life. Upon completing the verse, he played his wooden flute and then drank the contents of the small vial. Tomás waited for the ayahuasca to aid his ability to enter the lower world, and in an unorthodox departure from the shaman's traditional practice, he spoke to Dan to explain what was happening.

"In the lower world, I shall meet a gatekeeper named Pakay. In Quechua, Pakay means 'guard' or 'protector.' I must gain authorization from Pakay to enter the lower world. The visions and voices you have been experiencing occur because the missing soul piece has been trying to come back to you. Because you did not know what was happening, you rejected the overture. Pakay will help me find the missing soul piece in the lower world."

Dan had no idea what to say, so once again he deferred to respect for the shaman and his ancient practice. Abruptly, Tomás stopped speaking. The ayahuasca had taken hold. Dan had read up on this plant derivative that acted like a hallucinogen. For a shaman, it played an important role in entering alternative states of consciousness, enabling the most intricate of healing procedures to be performed.

The earth beneath the straw mat was beginning to wreak havoc with Dan's back. Not wanting to disturb the shaman's work, he told himself to remain still and keep looking toward the sky. Dan had never been a religious man, but at that moment he found himself contemplating a higher power. It felt like forever, but finally Tomás began to make a moaning sound and uttered the name "Cunac." The moniker that Renee Palomino, the Akashic reader, told him was the name his soul once had in a prior lifetime, right here in Peru. According to Renee, Cunac had been a murderer. In fact, Cunac was the evil shaman who killed the person named Jade, now reincarnated as Maritza. *Wait, could Tomás be talking to Cunac right now?* Dan badly wanted to interrupt and ask questions, but he knew it would be counterproductive. There was nothing he could do but lie still and wait.

After what seemed an eternity, Tomás was coming back into the present.

"I was able to speak with your prior lifetime soul occupant, Cunac. He relinquished the missing soul piece but not without warning."

"Warning? About what?"

"Cunac said Jade's spirit is in a state of unrest. He told me that her soul occupies a woman in Washington, DC, named Maritza Coya. Along with her mentor from that time—an elderly woman named Yanakilla, now living in Columbia, Maryland, as a man named Eli Shepherd—they are intent on destroying the world."

Dan sat up and stared down the shaman. "You must be joking."

"Senator, I can assure you that what I am communicating is very real. I have restored your soul. Your visions and voices should now be over. I cannot, however, change the destiny of the damaged souls roaming the earth and intent on ending life as we know it."

"So you think that Maritza and Eli are trying to end the world? To get even with me?"

"Do not flatter yourself, Senator. While you are considered an enemy of these people and while they are intent on doing you harm, a damaged soul can cause unbridled horrors upon the earth and its people."

"What exactly are they planning?"

"Cunac could not tell me, but he said you would learn the answer in short order."

CHAPTER 51

Sitting in the back of Moises's SUV, Tally was in another world. Simply stated, the events of the morning blew her away. Her life had been largely about politics. Nothing had ever caused her to think about reincarnation, soul retrievals, or any of these shamanic beliefs. Souls coming back, lifetime after lifetime, often together in groups in the quest for perfection. It was all so hard to digest. Tally was not religious and had never understood anything about spiritual philosophy. Her parents were Sunday churchgoers, but she had been indifferent. Concepts like what she now faced were never in her sphere of consciousness. Yet for some inexplicable reason, hearing that she was once Maritza's father and Dan was once the man who had killed her was causing her extreme distress. *How all of the roles had changed over the course of so many lifetimes!*

Dan's soul that once lived as the evil shaman, Cunac, had evolved. Dan was a good man, the most kindhearted, genuine person she had ever known. That's why she loved him like she did. Maritza's soul that once lived as Jade had turned evil. According to Tomás, her soul remained in a damaged state, devolving from lifetime to lifetime and always seeking revenge. A good shaman, he assured her, could repair the soul and release her from this purgatory. From what Tally knew of this witch, she didn't see her submitting to shamanic healing any time soon.

Tally's mind was in a spin cycle and while she intellectually understood all of this, for some reason she found it troubling that the man she loved had murdered her in a prior lifetime. Tomás assured her that such discoveries were not uncommon. The soul, he had explained, was frequently reborn to make amends with the same people it had wronged in a prior lifetime.

"Hey, are you okay back there?" Dan asked from the passenger seat.

Jolted back into reality, she looked at him. His light blue-gray eyes usually made her heart turn to putty, but in that instance she felt a flicker of fear. *Tsentsak*! A magical dart regurgitated by a shaman and blown into the mouth of an enemy. *How would she kiss him again and keep this thought out of her head?* The SUV ran over a bump on the secondary road. Her petite frame was bounced up and down on the backseat bench.

"Sorry," Moises declared. "We will be on a paved road in just a few minutes."

She returned her attention to Dan. "Yeah, I'm fine. How are you handling all of this revelation?"

His face took on an expression she wasn't sure she had ever seen before. Dan was someone whose face always revealed kindness and honesty. This look—this was clearly something different. He finally answered her with an atypical reply. "Mountain air clears my mind. The climb will be cathartic."

"Cathartic? I don't think I have ever heard that word come out of your mouth."

"It denotes a psychological cleansing of one's troubles."

"Yes," she replied somewhat frustratedly, "I know what it means."

Who was this man speaking in such odd terms? Had Tomás hypnotized him somehow? Dan seemed different.

He broke her chain of thought by adding, "It will be good to see Eli for the climb."

"Eli? Really? After what you just heard? This man is not your friend! I know the goodness in your heart wants to forgive him and look past the trouble he has caused you, but you really need to refocus here. This man is definitively your enemy!" She found herself on the verge of yelling and tried to get herself back into a calm state of mind.

Dan just looked at her with a peaceful and confident expression and said, "I appreciate the reality check."

Moises pulled back onto the highway. She gazed out the window and took in the view of the Peruvian land to which she felt such a pull. When she first arrived, it was merely an odd feeling. Now she understood why. Her mind was drawn back to tsentsak and the way she was once murdered. *Tsentsak . . . a magical dart. A dart . . . the same instrument of death used to kill Bob Alston. Coincidence? Hardly!* Tally reconciled the two events from different lifetimes and made what she concluded was a startling revelation. Maritza was acting out the revenge for Jade, whose father, Maicu was killed by a dart. *It made perfect sense!* She avenged the death of her father by taking out the father of her father's killer . . . and having him blamed for it!

Given Dan's odd behavior before and after his soul retrieval, Tally wasn't sure he was ready to have this conversation. At that moment, she was thinking she would discuss it with Remy and Burke back in DC, but those guys would just laugh her out of the room. *How can any of this be presented in a court of law?*

They arrived back at the hotel in Cusco. Tally told Dan she had another meeting with Tomás before they would all have dinner in town. She made an excuse about having work to do and retreated to her room. As she went through the doorway to her suite, her cell phone lit up. The caller ID simply read "Burke."

"Tally, my PI has been tailing Maritza Coya. Apparently she is in Chicago at some sort of drone manufacturing company."

"Drones? What in the world is she doing with a drone company?"

"We are still working on that. My guy did say that she was standing in the parking lot with Timothy Frazier, the inventor. They were watching a truck unload something. A fleet of drones was stationed across the empty lot. He said there were dozens of them. Obviously, they are preparing for something."

Tally was miffed. "But drones? Aren't they used for spying?"

"Among other things. They can also carry materials."

"Why would someone like Frazier associate with the likes of Maritza Coya?"

"He has fallen on hard times. His company is going through a very public bankruptcy proceeding. Money is a safe bet if you are looking for a motivator."

"Thanks, Burke. What's our next move?"

"I'm having my guy look into the shipment that was being unloaded. If we can get ahold of the bill of lading or delivery receipt from the trucker, we can find out what was shipped and who shipped it."

"That makes sense. Obviously, time is of the essence. Did your guy uncover anything else on Eli?"

"Not yet. He has been following a normal business routine. Nothing out of the ordinary, although we did see him and Maritza leaving together from a Columbia pub."

"That's interesting. Do you know if Remy has learned anything about the financial transactions?"

"Haven't spoken to him."

Tally clicked off with Burke and made a mental note to follow up with Remy.

She glanced down at the phone's display and noticed she had a voicemail from an unknown number. She listened to the message.

"Hi, Ms. Clayton. My name is Tony Beamon from the *Washington Post*. I am calling for comment on Senator Alston's medical records obtained by the *Post* through a Freedom of Information Act request. You may know that the records from the senator's recently deceased physician indicate a lengthy history of LSD abuse. Please call me before noon. That's when the story will be posted online."

Tally looked at her watch. It was already twelve thirty. They were so preoccupied with Tomás, she had not checked her phone all morning. How in the world did Eli and Maritza alter the records of Dan's physician? Did Dan know the doctor was dead? Did they kill him too? Tally pondered her next move. She would meet with Tomás this afternoon, have dinner with him and Dan, and then pack her bag to head straight back to DC. Tally promised herself that she would stop these people if it were the last thing she ever did.

ooooo

Tally sat at the desk in her suite, diligently pecking away on her laptop keyboard. She had dozens of unanswered emails. Engrossed in her work, she barely heard the gentle knocking on her door. She looked at her watch and couldn't believe how fast the afternoon had whizzed by. She opened the door and greeted Tomás. After they were seated in the living room of the suite, Tomás dove in.

"I hope, over the course of the day, you have had some time to process everything we spoke of early this morning."

Tally's mind was still on overload. Had she enjoyed a quiet day with nothing to think about except her morning session with Tomás, then yes, maybe she would be in a better position to discuss it. But her immediate thoughts following the session were so conflicted. In her heart, she knew her present-day love for Dan would win out easily over the stories of past-life fatherhood of the crazy bitch now trying to ruin their lives. Those thoughts were accompanied by Dan's soul retrieval and the disturbing phone call from Burke followed by the insane voice message from the *Washington Post* reporter. She could barely concentrate on the emails she was plowing through, most of which she forwarded to others in the office for further handling.

"I wish I had. Today has been like a roller-coaster ride through hell."

"I understand. I am afraid that since you are flying home tomorrow, I must burden your mind some more."

Tally sighed. She knew he meant well. What else could he throw at her? "Go ahead, I'm listening."

"I have traveled to the upper world and have had a very disturbing experience."

"The upper world? Does that mean you have seen the future?"

"Yes, and there are things that, for now, I must first share with Senator Alston. You will understand why as time moves on. Right now, I must train you for your role in events still to come."

"Train me? For what? I don't understand."

"Tally, you once lived as a shaman, a good shaman. Inherently, you were born with the abilities to practice shamanism in the present world. I knew this the first time I saw you. The energy emanating from you was unmistakable."

"You are not making any sense. Why do I need to practice shamanism?"

"To fulfill your destiny."

CHAPTER 52

It was sunset on Friday. Prior to meeting with Tomás and Tally, Dan called Bri before she hit the DC social scene with her friends. "I just wanted to make sure you knew I am staying in Peru through Thanksgiving to climb Ausangate with Eli."

"Eli? Are you crazy? Dad, think about what you are doing!" his daughter pleaded. "Are your injuries even healed enough to make such a treacherous climb?

"I actually feel pretty good, and regarding Eli, I will have him right where I want him."

"Dad, you aren't planning to take matters into your own hands. Let the authorities do their job. You are a US senator. It's not like you are calling 911 and reporting a crime."

"I know, Kitten, but Eli and Maritza have tarnished my credibility with the insinuation I am on drugs. Who will believe me? Especially when I start yammering about past lives and revenge?"

As the words fell out of his mouth, there was silence on the other end of the phone. "Bri, are you still there?"

"Dad, have you by chance checked the news feed on your phone today or seen a TV with American news?"

"No, why? What's going on?"

"The *Post* ran a story today that's going viral. It says they obtained your medical records under a FOIA request and the records confirm longtime treatment for abuse of LSD."

"Oh my God! Now they've released phony medical records? How is that even possible? Federal laws protect the privacy of health information. It would be illegal for my physician to disclose my health history . . . even my real medical records."

"The Freedom of Information Act makes exceptions to the federal health privacy laws in the case of a public official and when the doctor is deceased." Dan knew this but admired his young attorney-to-be and her command of the law.

"Yes, I am a public official, but my doctor is not dead . . ." he paused and then came to a sickening revelation. "Or is he?"

"He died recently of natural causes. The guy was pretty old. No foul play is suspected, but with everything that's gone on, we can't be too sure."

At that moment, Dan heard the knock on his door. "Gotta go. Love you, Kitten."

Dan opened the door to his suite and invited Tally and Tomás to the living room. Frustrated, he blurted out, "Well, I was just on the phone with Bri. It seems that once again, I am the world news."

He saw the look on Tally's face giving away that she already knew. "You saw the news?"

"Not exactly," she replied with reticence. "While we were out this morning, I got a call from the *Washington Post* reporter who broke the story. He said they were running with it if they didn't hear from me by noon. I didn't hear the message until after twelve."

Dan's head felt like it was going to explode. "It's pretty frightening to think how someone can ruin your life with little more than the ability to tell lies and alter databases."

As Tally and Tomás sat on the white fabric couch, Dan paced back and forth, a habit he had picked up years ago. Motion releases stress—at least that's the line he always used to justify the action.

"Senator, as bad as this news appears, we have more pressing things to discuss."

Feeling his head begin to throb, Dan replied, "Tomás, right now that's hard to believe."

"Senator, please . . . sit down. We need to talk and what I have to say will not be easy to hear."

Dan sat down in the armchair positioned catty-corner to the couch. Tally brought him a scotch to calm his nerves. Drink in hand, he drew in a breath to prepare for more difficult news.

"Your friends Eli and Maritza are up to no good and this time, I fear it may be fatal."

"Fatal? Fatal for who?"

"The earth."

"Tomás, help me out here. What are you talking about?"

Calmly, the shaman appeared to collect himself. Dan watched his face and wished he had that sense of inner peace to be summoned whenever it was needed.

After a moment, he began, slowly and deliberately. "You both recall that shamans move between the lower, middle and upper worlds." He looked at Dan and continued. "I went to the lower world this morning to retrieve the missing piece of your soul. Based on that experience, I became troubled here in the middle world, or the present, as you would call it. And so, I traveled to the upper world to see the future. That is what we must discuss right now."

Becoming somewhat impatient, Dan stammered in a low, gravelly tone, "Go on."

"I have seen the end of the earth precipitated by Eli and Maritza."

Dan shook his head. He couldn't believe what he was hearing. Before Ausangate and meeting Madame Cece, Renee Palomino, and now Tomás, he would have immediately dismissed all of this as nonsense. But given all he had been through, how could he not take it seriously?

"Tell me more," Dan said.

"Some foreign body will be deposited in major American waterways, including the Atlantic and Pacific oceans. The foreign body will cause the core of the earth to heat beyond what is sustainable for life on this planet. Water sources will quickly become toxic before drying up. Wildfires will envelop America with other parts of the world to follow. Horrific weather events will occur . . . hurricanes, tornadoes, and typhoons. Volcanoes across the world will spontaneously erupt. The combination of extreme heat and pestilence will wipe out all life on this planet . . . in fairly short order."

Dan tried to rationally absorb the news. He ran his right hand through his graying hair.

"This sounds like global warming on steroids."

Tomás sat stoically. "Yes, in fact, if the core of the earth was heated abnormally quickly, the greenhouse gas effect would cause our atmosphere to be unbreathable. Our planet would become similar to that of Venus, where the air is toxic and surface temperatures are approximately 371 degrees Celsius." He then quickly added, "That's 700 degrees Fahrenheit."

"Tomás, how many years in the future do you believe this will occur?"

"Senator, we not talking years or even months. The future I have seen commences in days. It may have already started."

Now Dan was at a crossroads. He wanted to believe the shaman, but really, the end of the world? In uncharted water, he had no idea how to proceed. He decided he must at least try to patronize the man. Tomás seemed so sure of what he saw.

"I am glad that you brought me this information. You must realize that from where I sit, the prophecy and timing are inconceivable. How could

I go to the president with information like this? The whole world now thinks I'm a drug addict. Think about it. How could Eli and Maritza pollute American waterways and bring on the end of time?"

Before the shaman could provide the answer, Tally blurted out, "Drones."

"What?" Dan asked incredulously.

"I spoke with Burke earlier and he told me Maritza was in Chicago overseeing the preparation of a fleet of drones. They were unloading a truck."

"Unloading what?" Dan asked.

"Burke's PI is trying to find that out. I should know something soon."

Before Dan could ask any more questions, Tomás piped in. "It is in line with the future I have seen. Drones could easily deposit foreign matter in American waterways." Tomás, for the first time, showed a modicum of facial stress. "Wait, I have not told you everything. There will also be a series of explosions. Many people will die."

Tally broke in. "Explosions? Where? How?"

"I am sorry. I do not know."

Dan sat silently and reflected on the conversation. He saw Tomás reach into his pocket and retrieve a small object. "Senator, this is for you. Keep it with you always."

Dan reached out and took the object from the outstretched hand of Tomás Paucara. It was a green polished stone, about the size of an egg but relatively flat. It glistened in his palm.

"This emerald has been in my family for generations. It once belonged to a queen in the Inca Empire, and is said to have always been an agent for shamanic power. The stone will aid you in your travels between worlds. "

He thanked Tomás and clutched the stone tightly. It radiated warmth and brought a measure of comfort in a time of extreme angst. Who knew? Maybe it would be nothing more than a good luck charm, but he appreciated the gesture nonetheless.

Dan turned his thoughts back to the matter at hand. Given today's news cycle, he could hardly call the president and report such a story. Yet how odd it was that Tomás had come to him with news of the future at the same time Maritza was seen with a fleet of drones and a truck delivering unknown materials. He needed to act. Just on the tiniest chance this might be true. *Should he call Eli and confront him before he arrived in Peru? No, he would only pretend to be my friend and deny everything. Calling Maritza was out . . . same story.* He needed help and knew there was only one person who might listen to such an outlandish concern.

Tomás interrupted his train of thought. "I can see that this information has set your mind ablaze. Before you take any action, I must prepare you for the coming days. You must become a shaman and harness the power within. It is the only way."

CHAPTER 53

While they sat in Dan's suite contemplating the next move, Tally's cell phone sprang to life. It was Burke.

"Tally, the PI caught up with the truck driver and spotted him a C-note for information. I have photos of the bill of lading and delivery receipt. I'm texting them over right now."

"Thanks, Burke. Let me know when you learn more."

"Already have. When you look at the documents I just sent, you will see the shipper of the unknown material was Bantam SpecChem in Appleton, Wisconsin. The commodity is listed only as "chemicals," so I had a guy I know go onto Bantam's portal to get the details. Apparently, the product is SF_6 in dissolvable pellets."

"What do we know about SF_6?"

"Looked that one up already. Sulfur hexafluoride. It's a man-made gas. They use it to inflate tennis balls. It's also known to make voices lower in tone, the opposite of what helium does when inhaled."

"Why would SF_6 in dissolvable pellets be of value to Eli and Maritza?"

"Don't know, but there is one more piece of information you need."

"Go on."

"There was a third-party billing for the freight charges. A company called Fresh Initiatives, LLC. This is the same company that purchased the SF_6. We looked into Fresh Initiatives. It is a single-member LLC registered to Dan Alston. The company was recently formed and capitalized with a new bank account flush with millions. And it all happened right after Dan's money disappeared."

Tally sighed. "The lengths they are going to are unreal. The whole thing is a setup. Burke, see if your guy can learn when these drones are going to be launched."

"I'm on it."

"One more thing. It's a safe bet that the checking account owned by Fresh Initiatives was funded with the money stolen from Dan. See if you can figure out how the checking account was funded. If we can find out where the money came from, it may confirm Eli and Maritza as the co-conspirators."

She hung up with Burke and updated Dan and Tomás. The shaman raised one eyebrow, as if to claim vindication on his vision of the future.

Dan looked at her with despair. "Tally, grab my laptop over there. We need to learn more about SF_6."

She sat down at the desk and began to access Google. It took only a minute to learn what she needed to know. "Holy crap," she declared. "It's a man-made gas and one of the heaviest gases in existence. If this stuff is dropped in the waterways in sufficient quantities, it will accelerate the greenhouse gas effect and remain in the atmosphere for thousands of years."

Dan looked extremely troubled. What politician ever had to save his country *and* the world?

"Do we think some of these drones could also be carrying explosives?"

"Bombs?" Tally asked.

"You heard Tomás. He saw a series of explosions. What if some of the drones were the carriers?"

Tally felt sick. "Dan, I know how crazy this all sounds, but we have to get the FBI involved. Only we both know you can't be the one to call in the threat. Nor me for that matter. Can we ask Burke or Remy?"

"No, I've already thought this through. You and the lawyers are too closely tied to me, and I'm tainted. The only person I can think of who might help is Jed Raley."

CHAPTER 54

Saturday morning

"Somebody's sniffing around our business?" Eli asked suspiciously.

"Frazier called me last night. He sounded scared. He said he got a call from the FBI about his planned drone launch. The feds didn't seem to buy the water viability experiment. Asked him for permits. He seemed to panic a bit."

Eli worried that Frazier would be too much of a weak link. "Tell him that he was paid ten million for his drone fleet and for the service of deploying them. I don't give a shit if the FBI is in his shorts. We will launch early. Tonight . . . just before midnight. Tell Frazier that there is an extra million in it for him. Make it happen," he barked.

He hung up and finished packing. He booked a two o'clock flight out of Dulles. The abbreviated schedule would give him only a few days to adjust to the climate before the climb, but in the end, it didn't really matter. From Peru, he would head to the house in Nunavut. He was still hopeful that Maritza would join him. She remained noncommittal. The truth was that no one knew exactly how long the earth would have after the SF_6 was deployed. What scientists did generally agree on is that global warming would affect the earth unevenly. The northernmost part of the planet seemed the most plausible option.

Eli packed only what he needed for Peru and the climb in particular. Everything else would be left behind. Clothing and other staples had already been arranged for the Nunavut shelter. He chuckled to himself as he thought of the Arctic air up north. *Who knows? Maybe in a week or two, the Arctic will feel like the Florida winter.*

Eli rummaged through his home office desk. He needed one more thing but couldn't find it. He had purchased a special satellite phone with internet connectivity. The phone was terribly expensive, but he couldn't take the chance that it might fail in the Andes. As soon as he strapped on his climbing gear on Thanksgiving morning, he would send the signal to the RFID devices via the 5G cell towers across America. While he was on Ausangate preparing to dispose of Dan Alston, the clean food boxes would be an explosive introduction to the destruction yet to come.

To be safe, Eli had purchased the specialty phone online with his Fresh Initiatives credit card and had it shipped to Dan's house in Olney where he knew no one would be. When the tracking email came advising of the delivery date, he simply drove by and picked up the package off the front porch. *Ah, found it.* He had shoved the device into the back of his desk drawer in an abundance of caution.

Eli closed his suitcase, grabbed his climbing gear, and headed off to the commercial flight from Dulles. He wasn't a fancy US senator who was filthy stinking rich. He didn't have the luxury of chartered planes on demand. Not without attracting unwanted attention. No, the best he could safely do for this trip was a first class ticket paid for with Dan Alston's money. That was a little something.

CHAPTER 55

Sitting in his hotel suite, Dan realized just how scared and alone he really was. Tally was on a plane for DC, Bri was beginning her Thanksgiving Day break, and Eli was on his way to Peru. Dan was never a man lacking for confidence. It was one of the things that made climbing fun. It was a thrill. Fear never entered the picture. This climb, however, was something entirely different. Dan inherently knew he would need to kill his best friend on the face of the mountain. *Was there a way to do that in Cusco without having to scale an ominous peak that had already had its way with him? Probably,* he concluded, but the climb was the strategy. Tomás had foreseen it. The mountains were where he felt most at ease. Thinking about it, his love of mountain climbing likely originated with his soul's prior lifetime here in the Andes. Given everything he had been through, how could he rule it out?

Tomás gave Tally a lift to the airport and then headed back to his village. This afforded Dan the opportunity to plan.

Jed Raley had been a true blue friend. After listening to the tale, Jed could have dismissed the whole thing as a machination of Dan's alleged drug habit, but some part of their long-term friendship gave him the benefit of any doubt. Without mentioning Dan's name, Jed contacted the director of the FBI and passed on the information from an anonymous tipster coming from his office. The director would notify the president in the event that the drones were being armed with explosive devices, and local authorities would work with the FBI to contain the problem. *Thank God!* Once they found the SF_6 loaded into the drones, Maritza would be apprehended and Eli would be left to him. Maybe, just maybe, he could really save the world.

Dan looked down at the emerald given to him by Tomás. He wondered if it really held the power the shaman claimed. He prayed he would never need to find out.

His cell phone began to tweet. An incoming call. It was Jed Raley.

"Good news and bad news."

Not in a mood to play guessing games, Dan tried to be mindful that Jed was perhaps his only friend on Capitol Hill at the present time. "What have you got?"

"The good news is that the FBI paid a visit to the drone company. They spoke directly with Frazier, the famed inventor and CEO. Said he appeared to be a bit rattled. Sure enough, there is a fleet of drones stretched across a massive parking lot and the drones are loaded with some sort of cargo. The bad news is that he has paperwork from a customer proving that the launch is to conduct some sort of water validation study. The locals brought in bomb-sniffing dogs. They didn't find anything. The only possible way to hold things up is the lack of FAA and state permits to operate the fleet in the manner he described. The work order he showed the FBI said the launch is scheduled for Monday. Frazier assured them he would not launch until after he has proper permitting, which you and I both know he will never get. That's what put him in bankruptcy in the first place."

"Jed, I hope they are going to keep eyes on the facility."

"No need. The director feels we did our due diligence. They don't see a threat."

"Did they verify that the drones are full of SF_6?"

"No, they just sniffed for explosives. I don't think they took the whole SF_6 thing seriously. You can't believe everything you read on the internet, Dan."

"I know, but . . ." He was about to try to persuade Jed Raley using information from Tomás, the seer. Then he remembered a tour of the FBI when he was first elected to the Senate. The director at the time mocked the numerous "tips" they received from people claiming to be psychic. Jed was with him that day. Dan knew Jed would never buy into the whole shaman thing. He was simply helping an old friend unburden his troubled mind. "Never mind. Jed, I can't thank you enough. Happy Thanksgiving to you and your family."

The FBI had checked out the drone fleet. Eli was on his way to Peru. Burke and his PI were chasing down Maritza. Remy was working in the background to clear his name and find his stolen funds, and Tally was on her way to DC to pilot the entire effort. At that moment, the anxiety he had felt began to subside. He hadn't slept well since he arrived in Cusco. He really wanted to take a nap, but he succumbed to the pressure from Moises to get in a few days of conditioning for the climb. Dan and Eli trained for three months for the first attempt at Ausangate. Even though that was only six weeks ago, Dan's body had endured a lot in that time. His strength, agility, and stamina would be highly compromised. Moises had five days to get him back in climbing condition.

CHAPTER 56

Maritza shivered. The chilly midnight air in Naperville permeated the coat that would have been plenty warm enough for an early winter evening in DC. Even that was too cold. She missed the warm climate of her youth. *Nunavut? Northern Canada?* Eli was out of his mind, holing up in weather station housing on the notion that it might heat up and survive the disaster they were unleashing. For her part, it was all about correcting the wrongs of so many lifetimes ago. Once that was complete, she could contently leave this earth and not worry about whether there would be anything left in which to reincarnate. Her efforts were completely in focus. Nothing else mattered. Dan Alston, the environmentalist entrepreneur and senator who always did right by the planet, supporting every piece of legislation to preserve clean water and pure air and feed the hungry, was about to pay for the sins of a past lifetime. His fight against climate change was her motivation to end the world as Alston knew it. Moreover, he was Cunac, the evil shaman who was a murderer and a snake. This man's spirit had taunted her over many lifetimes. All that was coming to a close. Tonight was the beginning of the end.

She looked over at Frazier. He was an impish man with nerdy glasses and a parka that seemed to smother him. He was all smiles. The extra million was burning a hole in his pocket. He snickered about his own escape to the Caribbean to enjoy his newfound wealth and live out his life in splendor. If he only knew that he was about to crush his own dream.

"Each long-range drone is outfitted with a camera. With the tablet app I had you download, you and your people will be able to watch each drone individually deposit its contents into the waterways," Frazier stated. "The drones are equipped with powerful headlights that automatically redirect when cargo is being deployed. This technology will enable you to see the operation in the dark. For added visibility, the drones have a night vision feature similar to what the military employs."

"Impressive," was all she said.

"Sixty seconds to launch," he yelled to his crew. Maritza thought Frazier was like a giddy Boy Scout getting ready to launch his first model rocket. She looked down at her watch. Thirty seconds to go. Eli was plugged into the app. She knew he would be watching from his hotel in Cusco. She envied him. If only she had the physical prowess and experience to climb mountains, she would have done the deed herself. Having to depend on Eli to finish Alston was not her first choice. She wanted desperately to look into Alston's steely blue eyes and tell him why she was inflicting this punishment on him and the world he treasured. She envisioned his face, contorted in horror as he realized the magnitude of her words and that it was she, Maritza Coya, who did what no one else could do.

"Ignition," yelled Frazier in his nasal voice.

Maritza looked up as dozens of drones simultaneously lifted from the ground to carry out the mission. The combination of fumes and cold air burned her sinuses, but she didn't care. It was actually happening!

Frazier would lock down the building, hand his remaining staff a cash bonus, and disappear forever. Maritza got back in her rental car, drove to Midway Airport, and caught the red-eye back to DC. Unbeknownst to Eli, she had one remaining item on her to-do list: the elimination of Bri Alston.

CHAPTER 57

Even though the trip had been tiring, lying in the king-sized hotel bed with his back propped upright on a pillow against the tall headboard, Eli felt a rush of adrenaline. His tablet was perched over his chest as he watched drones delivering their poison to America's prominent lakes, rivers, and oceans. Eli stared at the screen in amazement as the first drone released SF_6 pellets into the Chicago River. Just a few minutes later, another feed displayed the same thing over Lake Michigan. It was all underway. Throughout the evening, drones would fly over every major US body of water from the Hudson and Potomac in the east, the mighty Mississippi from the Midwest to the south, the Gulf of Mexico, north to the Great Lakes, and westward to the Colorado River, the Rio Grande, the Sacramento, and everything in between. Once devoid of cargo, Frazier's long-range drones were programmed to return to the massive Naperville parking lot.

The largest deployments would be the final deliveries over the Atlantic and Pacific oceans. Eli knew, of course, that since all oceans were connected, the current would ultimately transport the toxin to every part of the planet. Once the pellets dissolved, the effects would be irreversible. SF_6 was odorless and colorless and would do its work quickly and without detection. There was no stopping this. He had set forth a runaway train traveling downhill at breakneck speed. The inevitable collision was the only way it could end.

Eli set the tablet down on the bed and closed his eyes. He once again imagined the horrors he was bringing down on the world. Heating the earth's core at such an accelerated pace would quickly make life unsustainable. No water, no life. No breathable air, no life. The events in between—the fires, floods, extreme weather, and rampant spread of disease—were just filler for his final act.

He had never thought of himself as a deranged man, but somehow, inherently, Eli knew that he wasn't normal. Throughout his entire life, he had pretty much been a loner. Only once did he experience the depth of real love from another person. Only once did he find a true friend with whom he could relish life and all it had to offer. The one love had been Maddie, and the friend was Dan. In robbing him of his one true love, the friend became his enemy. Maritza had been only a vessel with which to awaken what he had always felt deep inside. No, perhaps he wasn't quite right mentally, but that didn't change the perspective that he was doing the right thing. A few more days of pretending to be Dan Alston's friend and the pain would finally stop.

CHAPTER 58

Dan didn't realize exactly how out of shape he was. Moises's training center at Escalar Montañas contained everything a climber could possibly want to prepare for an ominous peak such as Ausangate. Dan completed his second set of squats with a barbell to build lower body strength. After returning the weight to the rig, he used a hand towel to mop the sweat off his face, grabbed some cold water from the wall-mounted fountain, and went to a treadmill for a two mile run on a high-grade incline. He jokingly told Moises to have an oxygen tank nearby. Not one to clown around when getting clients ready for a climb, he offered only this in retort: "Senator, if you aren't ready, you should not go. The last thing in the world I want to do is have you airlifted off the mountain again."

Determined and knowing what was at stake beyond the challenge of the mountain, Dan replied, "Don't you worry. I'll be ready."

Twenty minutes later and nearing the end of his run, Dan was huffing and puffing. The sweat was pouring down his face and neck. With two minutes to go, he badly wanted to quit. *You can always do more than you think. Keep working.* Just as the machine completed its cycle and the automatic cool-down began, Dan saw him. The face of his enemy walked through the door. It was the first time he had seen Eli Shepherd since he learned who was behind his stolen funds and the assassination of his father. He prayed he could play it cool.

"I see I have some catching up to do," Eli remarked with a phony smile.

Dan hesitated. He wasn't especially good at being disingenuous. He pretended to be out of breath so he could take a moment to collect his thoughts. He couldn't let Eli know that he was on to him.

"Looking at the little potbelly you have going on, I would have to agree."

Dan opted for a pithy comment. Humor was always his way to diffuse tense situations. He supposed he got that trait from his father, the man Eli Shepherd had killed. Dan felt his blood beginning to boil. He could feel his face turning red. Thankfully, the exertion from the workout would mask his physiological response to the pathetic excuse for a human being that stood before him. Dan wanted to kill him where he stood. Instead, he made his excuses and headed off to the showers.

CHAPTER 59

"It's a replica *despacho* under glass," Bri exclaimed. I read about these when I was doing research for Dad on the shamans of the Inca Empire."

Tally smiled. While she was tired from the previous day's journey home from Peru, she promised Dan she would look in on Bri and deliver his gift to her. Sitting in Bri's kitchen enjoying tea on Sunday afternoon, Tally was momentarily at peace. The more she loved Dan, the greater her affection grew for his daughter. Her natural instinct to mother this dynamic young woman was never stronger. She felt some sort of unmistakable prodding to take care of Bri. While the moment was tranquil, Tally was still on edge. All the crap with Eli and Maritza had her worried. She hated the idea of Dan going back up Ausangate with Eli.

"The despacho is a prayer bundle created by the shaman to restore balance. The despacho can contain a variety of items representing different elements of healing. The bundles sometime contain chocolate, colorful string, candles, and even incense beans."

The ingredients of a despacho piqued Tally's interest. "So what would colorful string represent?"

"The Incas believed that colorful string represented the rainbows. The top of the despacho contained red carnation petals to represent the earth and white carnation petals to represent the mountains. Then, they would add a *kintu*, which is three coca leaves placed together to represent the lower world, the middle world and the upper world."

"You did your homework," Tally remarked.

Bri was excited to continue. "The shaman sometimes places a dried llama fetus in the despacho and believes it is synonymous with the unrealized dreams of the patient." Bri paused to sip her tea. "Once the kintu is made, the shaman drinks wine from an old wooden cup, wets the kintu before rubbing it on the patient's forehead, and then blows on it. Then, he makes the sign of the Southern Cross and places the kintu in the despacho."

"You really have this all down."

"I would love to go there and see it. They still use these practices in the Andes where Dad is right now." Bri gazed down at the replica under glass before continuing.

"They finish off the ceremony by carefully closing the despacho with silver and gold string. Then the shaman makes a second kintu and blows into it for any unrecovered dreams or prayers. Finally, the second kintu is slipped under the string of the despacho and the whole thing is wrapped in hand-woven material. The shaman then moves the despacho up and down the body of the patient to remove what they call the 'heavy energy.'" Bri took another sip of her tea before gleefully relaying the balance of her knowledge. "Once the patient is healed, the shaman burns the despacho."

Tally listened in fascination. "If you were sick, would you submit to this type of healing?"

"Before I did this research for Dad, I would have told you 'no way,' but now? I'm not so sure."

"I can relate. I watched what you just described and it really opened my eyes."

"Shamans see the body as a river of light. The despacho ceremony is looking for places where heavy energy is damming up the flow. Once the blockages are removed, the patient feels better."

"When I was in Peru with your dad, we saw a shaman remove a tumor from a terminal patient who had been told by modern medicine that nothing more could be done."

Bri grinned and said, "If that doesn't get you thinking differently, nothing will." As the thought was completed, Bri's expression turned from happy to distress. "Did you hear that?" she asked. She got up quickly and went to the back of the apartment toward the bedroom. "It sounds like something fell in my closet."

"Do you have a cat? I know my Ziggy is always knocking stuff over."

"No cat," she called from the other room.

Tally sat at the table and sipped her tea, figuring something must have just shifted in the closet. One time, she recalled, the wire rack holding her clothes in a walk-in closet just pulled away from the wall and fell to the floor. Too much weight. Made one heck of a loud noise when it crashed.

A split second later, Tally heard Bri scream in terror. It was a bloodcurdling cry for help. Tally's skin tingled as she bolted out of her chair and ran into the bedroom to see what had happened. Bri was mortified. She had both hands pressed up against her closet door, attempting with great difficulty to hold it shut, desperately trying to keep someone or something inside.

"Call 911!" Bri yelled. "Maritza Coya is in the closet. She tried to come at me with a butcher knife."

Tally heard the muffled threats coming from the other side of the closet door. The sound was that of a deranged lunatic trapped and wanting nothing more than to maim and kill.

Tally whipped out her cell phone and made the emergency call. Knowing they couldn't likely hold the door closed until the police arrived, she had to do something to diffuse the situation. *God, I wish I had a gun*, she thought. She motioned for Bri to gradually step away from the closet door. Tally picked up a metal folding chair from Bri's home office desk and prepared to whack Maritza across the face as she exited the closet. With the folded chair in her hands, Tally moved to Bri's right so she would have an unobstructed swing at Maritza as she came out of the closet. Bri shifted to her left while removing the restraints represented by her hands. The door flew open and Tally swung the chair at the doorway as fast and hard as she could. The difference in their height caused Tally's effort to land across Maritza's chest and neck. The knife in her right hand dropped to the carpeted floor while Maritza fell backward into the closet. Tally looked at her with hatred in her eyes and said with a dripping sense of disdain in her voice, "The police are on the way. Make one move and I swear I'll bash your skull in." Then she motioned to Bri and said, "Get the knife."

Tally watched as Bri picked up the knife and moved it safely from Maritza's reach. Tally was relieved. The terrifying situation was now in check. As she brought her gaze back onto the wounded predator on the closet floor, Maritza sprung to life, lurching forward toward Tally with outstretched arms seeking her throat. Startled, Tally dropped the chair and fell backwards as the much stronger woman jumped on top of her, pinning her to the floor and punching her in the face over and over again. Tally was diminished to a helpless victim being beaten to within an inch of her life. She felt blackness crowd her thoughts and had no strength left with which to battle the deranged predator. Just seconds from losing consciousness, Tally felt a weight literally lift from her. Through the fog, she saw Bri pulling Maritza from her with the knife in one hand and Maritza's hair in the other. Bri looked as if she were preparing to slit Maritza's throat. Tally couldn't have that. The events as they had already occurred would be traumatic enough to stain Bri's happy disposition for the rest of her life. Tally couldn't let her commit a murder, even if it was for all the right reasons. With the remaining strength she could summon, Tally sprang up and tackled Maritza, pushing her away from Bri. With a momentary advantage, Tally sat on top of Maritza and stared down into the crazed woman's fiery eyes. Tally felt her stomach gurgle in a way she had never experienced. It felt as if something had been launched inside of her, rising through her body like a missile in the sky. Involuntarily, she opened her mouth and felt the powerful spiked dart propel itself over her tongue and through her lips. Tally's eyes locked in on the face of her enemy as the dart made its way down Maritza's throat.

Mere seconds later, the fight went out of Maritza Coya. Her body went limp. It was over. Tally crawled across the bedroom floor to where Bri sat with her arms around her knees, weeping. Tally hugged Bri in an attempt to calm her down. The two women cried in unison as the police crashed through the apartment door.

"DC Police. Is everyone okay in there?"

"Yes, back here," Tally called out. Her badly beaten body ached, and she could only imagine what her battered face looked like.

Two police officers entered the room, guns drawn ready to take action. Tally saw the lead officer conclude the threat had been neutralized. Two women, one badly beaten, holding one another in solidarity and a third woman lying still on the floor. The police officer placed her fingers on Maritza's neck to feel for a pulse. "This woman is dead. The two of you will need to come down to the station."

Tally was trembling and so was Bri. Never in her life had Tally been through anything like this. But right there, in that moment, Tally gave thanks to Tomás Paucara. He trained her to overcome this foe. He had warned her of this impending attack. Although the timing and details were ambiguous, Tomás knew. He told her, "You once lived as a shaman. You have the ability to overcome your foe with tsentsak. You must be prepared."

CHAPTER 60

"Dad, it's me. Something terrible has happened. Call me when you get this."

Dan never recalled hearing his daughter's voice sound so distraught. The voice message was left while he showered from his workout. He quickly pushed redial on his phone to see what was wrong. Bri picked up after one ring.

"Are you okay, Kitten?"

"I am. Tally is with me. We just left the police station. Maritza Coya is dead."

"Dead? Oh my God. What in the world happened?"

"Somehow Maritza broke into my apartment and was hiding in my bedroom closet with a butcher knife." Bri's voice began to break down. "Dad . . . she was planning to kill me."

Dan tried as best he could to console her over the phone. "Were you hurt?"

"I'm fine. Tally saved my life. If she hadn't been there, I don't know what would have happened. She called the police and then smashed Maritza across the chest with a folding chair."

Dan was beside himself with concern. "Is Tally okay?"

"Yes, although she was pretty badly beaten. A lot of facial bruising. The police offered to take her to the hospital but she refused medical treatment."

At that moment, with the two women he loved most having gone through such a harrowing experience, Dan wanted nothing more than to go home and protect them, nurse their wounds, and give them love. "Kitten, I am getting on the first plane home I can find."

Next thing he knew, Tally had taken the phone from Bri. "Dan, stay put. We are fine. The danger here is over. You have to deal with Eli."

Dan's blood was boiling. How could Eli and Maritza go to such lengths to cause this kind of pain? What kind of monsters was he dealing with? His father was murdered and now they attack his daughter?

"Are you sure you are okay, Tally? I'm really worried."

"I am holding up. Sore as hell, but I'm okay."

"I am going to have a protective detail assigned to both of you. Perks of being a US senator. If all goes well, I will be on a plane home before you know it."

"Dan," she said. "I love you."

Welling up from having heard those words from Tally for the first time and realizing how blessed he was to have her, he simply replied, "I love you too. Tell Bri I love her and will check in later tonight." Before he clicked off, it occurred to him. He hadn't heard the whole story. "Tally, wait. How did Maritza die?" There was nothing but silence from the other end of the phone. Dan wasn't sure they were still connected. "Tally?"

Finally, she responded. "There will be an autopsy, but the medical examiner thinks that during the stress of the moment, her heart simply failed."

CHAPTER 61

Now he was on his own to carry out the balance of a mission he didn't start but believed in deeply. Eli was monitoring his phone for news indicating the SF_6 was beginning to do its job. The headline that grabbed him was "Senator's Daughter Narrowly Escapes Murder Attempt." When he read the article and realized that it was Maritza trying to kill Bri, he felt sick. Killing Dan's daughter was not part of the plan. They had never discussed it. The one regret Eli had was that Bri had gotten caught up in his tangled web of deception and revenge toward her father. Since she was born, Eli had cared for Bri as a dedicated uncle. Thank goodness she didn't die at Maritza's hand. It was more appropriate for her to perish with the rest of humanity. For now, he would have no trouble feeling the sympathy needed to keep Dan off balance. He genuinely felt bad for Bri—just not for her narcissistic father and what he was going through.

Eli walked through the quiet lobby of the Palacio Nazarenas. It was five o'clock in the morning and not a soul was around. Eli had his gear packed and a private transport waiting to take him three hours south to Tinqui, where the Ausangate trail began. The hiking trail would serve the purpose of acclimating to the higher elevation in preparation for the real climb. Eli much preferred to train on the trail as opposed to the gym. The alternative purpose was to get up into higher ground to ensure the sat phone would be able to send the proper signal initiating the clean food box explosions. His backup plan was to have Maritza set off the explosions, but that was no longer an option. If today's test failed, he would likely place the detonations on some sort of timed delay. He didn't care for this strategy. Timers could fail. In his own mind, he needed to actually press the button on his phone and see visual confirmation.

He greeted the driver on the brightly lit hotel driveway. The morning air was chilly, even though it was summertime in Peru. Eli threw his gear into the cargo hatch of the white Hyundai Santa Fe and climbed into the passenger seat. His driver spoke only limited English, and Eli wasn't much better in Spanish. So as the sun prepared to rise in the sky, they rode in silence. Eli scanned his phone for additional headlines on SF_6. He found nothing, which he deemed both good and bad. It was good from the sense that the element of surprise was still in his favor. It was bad from the standpoint of deflating his ego.

With time to kill, he began to Google and finally got a hit on Timothy Frazier. Of course, there was the story of his long-range drone company's bankruptcy, but he also discovered a story by a local Chicago reporter about a fleet of drones that took off from the company's Naperville headquarters and returned the next day. According to the article, these flights were undertaken without proper permitting and hundreds of reports streamed into police departments across the country. People claimed they had seen UFOs, and panic set in about alien invasions. Eli laughed out loud. It was a brief little snort laugh. *People are so stupid.*

The article went on to report that when authorities came to the Naperville company parking lot to question its owner, the building had been locked down. Frazier was missing and a search of his home in Naperville indicated he had fled. The FBI issued a warrant for his arrest and, fearing that he had left the country, Interpol had been alerted. Eli chuckled to himself. He already knew Frazier was long gone. *By the time they find him, the environmental apocalypse will have begun.* Then no one would be worried about Frazier's illegal drone flights or the whereabouts of the company's CEO.

Eli sipped coffee from a thermos he filled in the hotel lobby. It was just getting cool enough to drink. He peered across the cabin of the Santa Fe and watched as the magnificent morning sun rose in the east. It was a brilliant orange breaking through the last remaining vestige of the night. To Eli, the sun seemed larger than normal. Maybe, he surmised, it was because they were closer to the equator. His mind imagined watching the fiery gases of the sun through a telescope and seeing the violence the star would soon unleash. In just a few days' time, the earth's defenses against the sun's harmful rays would be severely diminished. Region by region, the core of the planet would heat to temperatures that would make it uninhabitable for life of any kind. He wondered if he would make it to Nunavut. He wondered whether it would matter.

Now realizing how tired he was, he closed his eyes and nodded off. The hike today would be physically demanding. May as well get some rest. Halfway to Tinqui, the vibration of his cell phone caused him to wake.

"Did I wake you? I know it's early, but your text said you were heading out to the Ausangate trail."

It was Dan. He left the text late last night inviting him to come along. It was all for show. Eli knew Dan wouldn't be prepared on short notice and would prefer the training center at Escalar Montañas. The last thing he wanted was Dan Alston tagging along. The primary reason he was heading to the trail was to test the special sat phone, a task that would be immeasurably more difficult if his enemy was on his hip.

"I saw the morning news. Are Bri and Tally okay?"

"Seem to be. I wanted to charter a plane to go right home, but they both assured me they are fine. I have a protective detail on them 24/7."

"That's a good idea. Do they have any idea what her motivation was?" Eli was now fishing. He wanted to see if Dan would tip his hand.

"No, but if you ask me, she was just nuts. Our relationship started off like a ball of fire and then cooled just as fast. I stopped taking her calls and sort of froze her out my life with no real notice. I can only assume she was striking back at me through Bri."

"Nothing else makes much sense, does it?"

"No," Dan replied.

"I'm glad they are both okay. Hitting the training center today?"

"Mmm, hmm," he replied. "Training for a climb is just like golf with you. I practice on the range and you prefer to just go out on the course and play."

Eli laughed. "No better experience than real life. I'll be back too late tonight to meet up. Maybe I'll see you at Moises's gym tomorrow."

Eli clicked off and tried to resume his nap. Nothing doing. His mind was abuzz. He returned to the phone, checking for weather forecasts in different regions of the US. Interestingly, much of the country was expecting a late-November heat wave. Temperatures over the Thanksgiving holiday were expected to top ninety degrees in the Midwest, and more than one hundred in the western half of the country. The Deep South was under a heat advisory for high temperatures and one hundred percent humidity. Even in the northern half of the US—normally cool and crisp at this time of year—was forecast in the eighties. Air quality warnings were popping up all over the country. In California, earthquake warnings were issued along the San Andreas Fault. In Washington State, there were alerts about volcanic eruptions for Mount St. Helens and Mount Ranier. Similar alerts were issued for Mount Shasta in California, as well as Mount Hood and Three Sisters in Oregon. As he kept reading, volcanic eruption warnings were in effect in Alaska and Hawaii. The SF_6 was behaving as he had expected.

It was all starting. He laughed silently as he read expert accounts from scientists stating that the world was going through a temporary environmental adjustment period due to global warming caused by man-made greenhouse gases. *Let them believe it!*

An hour later, Eli began the solo trek from Tinqui up the Ausangate trail. After hiking for three hours, he reasoned he had reached an elevation high enough to conduct his test. He took off his backpack, unzipped a small side pocket, and removed the special sat phone. He went to the detonation app, and hit 'TEST.' He waited anxiously but nothing happened. Another minute went by and then . . . *yes*, there they were, the words that let Eli Shepherd know the final piece of his plan was going to work.

SIGNAL SENT.

SIGNAL RECEIVED.

TEST SUCCESSFUL.

CHAPTER 62

Tally propped the reading glasses north from the tip of her nose and looked up at Joc Raymer. Two hours in the office and she had not yet made a dent in the backlog of work. An interruption was the last thing she needed.

"You have a visitor," Joc stated.

"I don't have any appointments today," she said in retort. "Who is it?"

"It's that defense attorney. Burke."

That was one person she would need to make an exception for.

"You look terrible. Like you just went ten rounds with Mike Tyson." Clearly, Burke was a man without tact or diplomacy. He rebounded slightly with, "How are you doing?"

Tally was embarrassed at her appearance. No amount of makeup would conceal the black and purple bruising on her left cheek and eye. She didn't have the luxury of hiding at home until she healed. "I'll live. What's good with you?"

"My investigator hung around the drone company after the FBI left. He was there when the fleet took off. He saw Frazier leave in his car and followed him. He grabbed a go-bag from his house, reemerged, and drove an hour north to a private airfield in Wheeling. We checked the flight manifest. Frazier booked a private jet to Grenada in the Caribbean, to some island called Carriacou. We did some more digging. It seems Mr.

Frazier recently came into a nice little payment of eleven million dollars. Funds came from the same LLC in Maryland I told you about the other day, Fresh Initiatives. The one registered to Senator Alston."

"Have you been able to learn where the funds came from to capitalize the LLC?"

"All we know so far is that the funds were transferred in from a numbered account in Switzerland."

"Can you tie the account in Switzerland to Eli or Maritza?"

"I got someone running it down, but the Swiss are notoriously tight-lipped on information like this. It's why criminals like their banking system."

Tally shook her head in disgust. It was nauseating to think what people could get away with. Dan reported the theft to the FBI. They hadn't yet reported back with any information. One would think that when a high-profile victim gets robbed of this kind of money, some small bit of information might be forthcoming.

Burke, in an attempt to placate her, went on. "Look, we'll chase down the money. This kind of cash doesn't go missing forever. It's a safe bet that the Swiss account is the senator's money or at least part of it."

"Part of it?"

"Yeah, it's a common tactic to spread the money around to different accounts, usually in more than one country. Makes it harder to trace if amounts don't line up nice and neat from the victim's account to the criminal's account."

"Any info on Maritza Coya?"

"Yeah, on my drive in, I got a call from the ME. Cause of death was ruled a heart attack. The police are wrapping up some details, but it looks like you are in the clear."

She shrugged. Her left shoulder and neck were sore from the encounter with Maritza. "I wasn't too worried about it." Inside, she smiled. She would be forever grateful to Tomás Paucara for helping her to discover her past-life as a shaman and the present-day power that accompanied it.

"Hey, are you sure you shouldn't get an X-ray or something? You look like you are in a lot of pain."

"You know," she said as she winced in pain from a slight shift in her chair, "I probably should. We'll see where the next few days take us. Once Thanksgiving arrives, I can hopefully rest up. Anything else?"

"Nope, that's all I have at the moment." He moved to the door to leave but then stopped, turned around, and said, "Tally, there is one more thing we can do. It's unconventional, but . . ."

"Burke, come on. Out with it."

"Well, you know Remy brought me in because I get results. My methods aren't always, how shall we say, 'kosher,' and since my client here is a US senator, I didn't think it was appropriate to recommend anything that wasn't completely above board."

Growing impatient with his preamble, she said with agitation in her voice, "If you know of another way to help Dan, I'm all ears."

"Okay, okay. Since the police are no longer investigating the encounter at Bri's apartment, the heat's off, and Eli is in Peru with Dan . . . I could have someone inspect his computer at home and in his office. Maybe snoop around . . . see what we can find."

"Inspect? You mean break into his office and home?" Tally felt a chill go down her spine. Dan, the "last honest senator," would unequivocally run from such an opportunity. But Dan wasn't here. As far as she was concerned, they were at war. With stone-cold eyes, Tally looked up at Burke and said decisively, "Do it."

CHAPTER 63

Remy sounded despondent. The FBI had no credible leads in the search for the stolen funds. Dan was assured that Burke's PI would get results.

"There is good news," Remy declared. "The search of Maritza's apartment yielded a treasure trove of evidence placing her in Crisfield and behind the drone launch and SF_6 procurement."

"So it confirms what we thought, but with the FBI refusing to take the SF_6 threat seriously, what good does it really do? Maritza is dead and the SF_6 has already been deployed."

"Well, there is more. The FBI found a dark web portal on her laptop."

"What does that mean?"

"It means she was using a clandestine means of communication to avoid detection."

"Communication with who exactly?"

"They are still trying to hack in to figure that out. My guess is Eli Shepherd."

"Anything else?" inquired Dan.

"Yeah, video from the US post office in Crisfield showed a strange man dropping something in the outside mailbox. We believe it to be the anonymous tipster. The same outfit worn by the tipster was found in Maritza's apartment along with a man's wig and moustache."

"That's what ties her to Crisfield. My DNA on the dart came from her also. She was in my house. We were in a hotel together—she had ample opportunity to get a DNA sample to transfer to the dart."

Dan contemplated everything he had learned. "The more I think about it, the more I think Maritza followed me out of the Watergate and filmed me on the steps of the Lincoln Memorial. The hangover I had that morning was extreme. It felt more like I had been drugged."

Remy replied stoically, "You probably were."

"And I thought I was just having one of those terrible migraines from a night with too much scotch."

"That, my friend, might also be true."

"Did they find anything else on the laptop?"

"Oh yeah. They found a customer login for the chemical company in Wisconsin that sold her the SF_6, and they found a purchase order issued for the drone fleet. All of which were under the name Fresh Initiatives, LLC. The company that you supposedly own."

"Is that all?"

"Nope, they also discovered several car reservations in Maryland and Illinois. Rental cars all have GPS now, and the vehicle movements are all tracked. We know Maritza drove to Crisfield, to western Maryland, and from Illinois to Wisconsin to arrange the drone attack."

"Will the FBI be getting ahold of Eli's laptop anytime soon?"

"Doubt it. Unless they find something more substantive to tie him to a crime, it may be tough to get a warrant."

"The wheels of justice come to a grinding halt," Dan said sarcastically.

"When I hear more from the FBI or Burke, I'll give you a call."

After learning what was found in Maritza's apartment, there was no doubt that she and Eli were behind the murder of his father. Dan never thought he would ever say this about himself, but he was filled with hatred. Going after his daughter was the last straw. He owed Tally a debt of gratitude he could never repay. She put her life on the line to save

Bri. All these years of working side by side—how could he have been so blind? He really did love her. At this point, Dan wanted to take care of business in Peru and get home to the two women he missed so much.

With only one day to go before the climb, Dan reassessed his situation. He was determined to deal with Eli at the summit. He would confront the deranged son of a bitch and end his miserable existence on the mountain. He couldn't report Eli to the authorities. Even with the evidence reported by Remy, there was not yet enough to convict him. Maritza, yes, for sure, but she was already dead. Eli would have to die on Ausangate; away from the other climbers, Dan would have the opportunity he craved.

He sat up in the high-back leather chair in his hotel suite and pondered the release of the SF_6 in all of America's waterways. Maybe Jed was right. You can't believe everything you read on the internet. What harm could it possibly do?

CHAPTER 64

It was eight o'clock on Wednesday evening. If there were no traffic, Tally could make it to her parents' home in Havre de Grace, Maryland, inside of two hours from DC. Thankfully, she would be the only guest for Thanksgiving. This was gratifying for two reasons: one, she was exhausted and didn't feel like dealing with anyone asking her a million questions about Dan and his alleged drug habit; and two, she still looked like the victim of a severe beating. Although her mother heard the story on the news, Tally hadn't been forthcoming with either parent about the extent of her bruises. She would settle that drama when she arrived. Even at forty-seven, Tally was perfectly willing to let her mother baby her for a day or two. Her plan was to spend a couple of nights and make her way back to DC on Friday.

The holiday traffic had begun to build. As she headed north on I-95 toward Baltimore, everyone came to a sudden halt. She was not in the mood for traffic. To get her mind resettled, Tally flipped on the radio and tuned into the classic rock station. Bon Jovi began singing "Dead or Alive." She tapped her foot on the floorboard to the beat of the music and began to relax when her cell phone went off. *Damn, no rest for the weary.*

"Tally, it's Burke. We have a problem. A big problem."

Tally exhaled in an attempt to regain her composure from the stress of the day. "What kind of problem?"

"My guy just left Eli's home and office. He ghosted both computers and we just got done reviewing the files. Not much on the office computer, but at home it's another story."

"Keep talking."

"First off, Eli has the same dark web portal on his home laptop. Obviously, this is how he and Maritza were communicating. We haven't hacked in yet, but we are working on it. More important, have you ever heard of the Foundation for Preservation, Peace, and Light or FPPL?"

"It sounds vaguely familiar. Why?"

"Well, Eli is doing some pro bono work for them. Their mission is to feed the hungry, and they have distributed what they call 'clean food boxes' across the country for Thanksgiving. We think Eli rigged the clean food boxes to explode."

Tally was glad traffic was at a standstill. If she were driving, she might have lost control of the car upon hearing this news. "You are saying he has bombs planted in food boxes in soup kitchens across the country?"

"That's exactly what I am saying. I even have a picture of the clean food box I am texting you now. We can't tell from the information we have when the bombs are set to explode, but I would bet he has them rigged to go off sometime tomorrow."

"How do you conceal a bomb in a food box?"

"According to what we found, an electromagnetic device is hidden in the core of an apple within each box. It won't take more than a spark to detonate the device. It could easily be accomplished through the radio frequency ID tag on each box and a good cellular connection."

"Oh my God! Do we know where these boxes were shipped to?"

"No, we looked but couldn't find a listing. All we could find was that they were shipped from a cold logistics company called Micuna. I took the liberty of calling there for a manifest, but they are closed for the holiday."

"Thanks, Burke. I'm on it. Let me know if you find anything else."

Tally's mind was spinning. She had to think fast. There simply wasn't much time. Eli planned the whole thing for when the country would be at ease during the holiday. She had to reach the president. Even though she was chief of staff for a prominent senator, she knew he wouldn't take her call. With Dan's reputation sullied, the president would view her as a crackpot. No, she decided, her best shot was to go through Jed Raley. Thankfully, she had his cell number.

"Senator Raley, its Talia Clayton, Dan Alston's chief of staff. I have a national emergency and I need you to contact the president."

"Slow down a minute, young lady. That's a mighty tall order you are requesting. How about you tell me exactly what's going on?"

She filled him in as best she could, omitting the unnecessary details relating to reincarnation and past lives. Raley knew that Dan's father had been killed and his money stolen. Tally simply told him that the PI they hired had uncovered a plot to terrorize innocent Americans and the threat appeared very real and imminent. "We don't know where in the country these food boxes are. But we have a picture, and if we can get a national alert going, we can save everyone."

What organization distributed these food boxes?" Raley asked anxiously.

"It's called FPPL or the Foundation for Preservation, Peace, and Light."

"Never heard of it. Everyone is closed for the holiday. It would be great if we could find the person who runs this organization. Any additional details would be extremely helpful."

Tally pounded her fist against the steering wheel. Maybe the FBI could track down someone from this organization. *Damn! It would take too much time and besides, they are probably working with a skeleton crew for the holiday.* And then it came to her. . . "Senator Raley, I just remembered, Senator Alston's daughter does their legal work in association with Georgetown Law. She will be able to help."

"Excellent. Let me get the wheels in motion with the president, the FBI, and the national alert. We will need to corral all of these boxes and get them into bomb containment units. We will need local authorities around the country to help."

"I'll call Bri and text you the contact information from the person in charge at FPPL."

"Great . . . one more thing. Do you know where Eli Shepherd is now?"

Tally hesitated. She knew that Eli was with Dan in Peru. If she told Raley that, the US government would ask Peruvian officials to apprehend him immediately. She thought that to be a great idea because they would pry the information they needed out of Eli to save innocent lives and keep Dan from the danger of climbing Ausangate tomorrow. On the other hand, it would deprive Dan of his destiny: the ability to fulfill Tomás's vision for Eli's ultimate demise.

She decided it was best to buy a little time. "I have an idea where he might be. I'll get back to you."

CHAPTER 65

The call from Tally was extremely disturbing. Even though a series of explosions had been seen by Tomás, something kept Dan from believing it. *Was there no end to the destruction Eli intended to cause? Could Eli Shepherd really bring about the earth's demise?* Tomás was right about the explosions. How could he now doubt the remaining part of his horrifying prophecy?

Eli was sick. Dan kicked himself for never having seen it before. Tally had done all she could. Getting Jed Raley involved was a good move. Tally hadn't given up Eli's location—another good move. Dan would have aborted his Ausangate plan, but it sounded as if everything that could be done was being attempted. Eli would still be his to deal with. For tonight, however, it was a matter of finding the device Eli intended to use to detonate the clean food boxes and safely remove it from his room.

Dan felt like a covert ops guy from the movies. Dressed in all black, he carefully camped out in the hallway of Eli's hotel room, waiting for him to leave for dinner. Once he left the corridor, Dan made his move. He approached Eli's door and entered with a master key card he had borrowed from the cleaning cart. Entering the room, he flipped on a light and was immediately aghast. It had been a long time since he had shared quarters with Eli. He had forgotten what a slob the man was. Clothes were strewn across the bed, over the desk chair, and on the floor, but the climbing gear was perched neatly against the wall. The two places to search for a small remote control were the jacket he used to climb and the backpack. Dan spotted the jacket draped over a piece of luggage and searched the garment thoroughly. He checked every pocket inside and out and even thought to search for a hidden compartment. Maybe the device was in his luggage for safekeeping—or worse, he might have it on his person.

Dan worked quickly. He picked up the backpack and unzipped the main compartment. All of these bags had a variety of small storage spaces. To accelerate the pace, he squeezed all sides of the backpack until he felt something hard and rectangular. He unzipped a small side pocket and pulled out a device slightly larger than the standard smartphone. While it looked like a smartphone, it was a bit thicker and significantly heavier. It had a sturdy black rubber case to avoid damage if dropped. Unless the clean food boxes were on some sort of timer, the electromagnetic devices could not be detonated without this device. Dan stuck it in his pocket and flipped off the light, leaving the room exactly as he had found it.

CHAPTER 66

Tally was pleased that Jed Raley moved quickly. She heard over the radio that a nationwide emergency recall was in effect for all clean food boxes issued by FPPL. She listened as the broadcaster described the boxes from the photo she had forwarded to Raley.

> *"Each box contains an FPPL logo that is a bright green and orange. If you encounter any of these boxes, please dial 911 immediately. Do not hesitate. These boxes are extremely dangerous and could explode, causing severe injury or even death."*

Raley told her that the president activated the National Guard to help round up the boxes across America and take them to bomb containment facilities where the electromagnetic vials would be removed from each apple and carefully destroyed.

Her lower back was sore from the encounter with Maritza. Sitting in the car for this long was taking its toll. Tally was slowly making her way north through Baltimore's Harbor Tunnel when her phone rang again. It was Dan.

"Tally, I have the detonation device."

"Oh thank heaven. I think the crisis has been averted. Even if the authorities don't recover all the clean food boxes by tomorrow, there is no possible way that anyone in possession of them would miss the national alert. It's on every radio station, coming across my phone screen, and I am sure on every TV channel."

"So long as the detonation device has been recovered, the boxes can't cause any real harm. Hey, forgot to ask. When Burke called you, did he find anything on Eli's computers on SF_6?"

"If he did, he didn't mention it. Why? Are you still worried about the pellets in the waterways?"

"Intellectually, I keep thinking the whole notion is preposterous. But then again, what's the temperature like where you are?"

Tally felt queasy as she considered the implications of the question. "Unseasonably warm for late November. It's ninety-five degrees out right now and it's past ten o'clock."

"I checked the news here, and there are warnings about earthquakes and volcanic eruptions to go along with sweltering temperatures. Similar warnings have been issued in the US."

"Coincidence?"

"I don't believe in them. The question is, what to do about it?"

"If Eli and Maritza did something to precipitate global warming, how in the world would anyone reverse that?"

"All I know is that Tomás was right about the explosions and he saw the world quickly ending. The signs are everywhere. It has to be related. The government dismissed the SF_6 threat before the drones launched. I can't imagine they'd take it seriously now."

"I'll take another run at it through Raley. No one can ignore the devastating effects of the climate change. Forecasts here are calling for temps in the low one hundreds by tomorrow morning with no relief in sight."

"I agree. Call Jed. The Ausangate climb is tomorrow morning. I'll beat the truth out of Eli if I have to."

With that, static overtook the call and disconnected them. A moment later, Tally heard a howling sound as she came through the tunnel and experienced a vortex of high winds literally sucking her car forward onto the highway. Golf-ball-sized hail attacked her car with ferocity. Tally looked through her windshield and in the distance saw a frightening sight: a funnel cloud had formed in the dark sky. Tally had never seen anything like it. A translucent gray image of swirling, angry wind hell bent on destroying anything in its path. She didn't know much more about extreme weather than the average person, but she knew the tornado was approaching rapidly. She wasn't safe in the car. She needed to find shelter and fast. She saw a sign for Johns Hopkins Bayview Medical Center and decided the hospital would most certainly have an emergency shelter in its basement.

Tally exited onto O'Donnell Street. The hospital was only a few minutes away. Thankfully, the hail had stopped. She wasted no time moving through the city as the distant view of the gathering tornado caused her to quake with fear. Facing the crazed Maritza Coya in Bri's apartment was less frightening. In that instance, she knew she had Bri in a two-on-one advantage, and her love for Bri caused her to protect Dan's daughter with no regard for her own safety. Tonight, it was her against nature, a fight for which she felt defenseless.

She pulled into the hospital driveway and made her way up the steep hill to the parking lot. The high winds made it difficult to drive. She parked her car and proceeded toward the main building. A bolt of brilliant lightning crashed against the black of the night as the edge of the tornado pushed forward. The air felt heavy and had the acrid smell of a dumpster on a hot, humid day. She looked down over the city and saw something unimaginable; water from Baltimore's Inner Harbor was rising in a tidal wave and flooding the city. Tally struggled to stay on her feet in the face of the powerful wind. She watched in horror as a hospital transport bus was picked up off the parking lot as if it were a child's toy. The bus flew high and away until she completely lost sight of it. Tally moved slowly toward the hospital entrance. The winds were warm, like someone took a garden blower into a sauna. Tally grabbed hold of a lamppost in fear that she, too, would blow away. The entrance was only a few steps further. She needed to make a run for it, but what chance did her petite frame have when a bus could get carried away like a leaf on the wind? She let go of the lamppost and took one step forward. As she did, the hospital lights went out and the glass doors shattered without warning, propelling her back toward the parking lot. With shards of glass acting as projectiles and stinging her body, Tally felt her spine crash against the metal lamppost before the wind picked her up and carried her toward the flooded city and its predatory harbor.

CHAPTER 67

Mount Ausangate, Peru

Eli was sweating profusely. The group included Moises and his clients, as well as Dan and Eli. They departed Tinqui at sunrise for the five-day climb and had been at it all morning. They each remarked about the unusual heat on the mountain. Moises assured the group that the temperatures would cool as they reached higher elevation, but Eli knew it was wishful thinking.

The group stopped for a rest. It was time. Eli made his excuse about needing to relieve himself and snuck off to find a private spot to initiate the detonation of the electromagnetic devices inside the clean food boxes. He walked for nearly a quarter mile for privacy. The group had fanned out, and it seemed there was a climber at every turn. Once he was satisfied, Eli set his backpack on the hard-beaten trail and unzipped the side pocket to retrieve the sat phone. *Where was it?* Eli felt a sense of dread. He was sure he packed it. There was no way it could have fallen out. *Dan! He was playing innocent, but it had to be him. How could he have known? There was no way.*

Quickly he began rifling through the backpack, emptying its contents on the ground. It was gone. Maritza was dead. There was no backup plan. Once his test signal proved successful, he had dismissed the idea of setting a timed detonation. His meticulous planning for a Thanksgiving

Day apocalypse had all been for nothing. In the sweltering heat, he felt himself begin to anger. He picked up a rock in a fit of temper and hurled it into the canyon.

Eli willed himself to calm down. *It would all be okay.* The clean food boxes were never meant to be anything other than a distraction, a mere decoy to divert attention away from the precipitous challenge of sudden and extreme climate change.

He stood up, unzipped, and took a leak against the face of the mountain. *That's right*, he told himself. *Piss on them all.* In the distance, Eli heard a whistle. It was a signal from Moises to reconvene at the rest area. He gathered his belongings and hiked back, looking out over the morning sky and wondering if he would make it off this rock to his haven in Nunavut.

He was the last one to return. The group stood in a small circle around Moises.

"I have been monitoring weather alerts on my satellite phone. The area is under an earthquake warning and the potential eruption of Quimsachata," Moises said.

One of Moises's clients spoke up. "Señor, I am a professor of geology here in Peru. You must be mistaken. Quimsachata has not erupted for more than ten thousand years."

Eli listened as Moises replied, "It is no mistake. The warning is real. If it erupts, its effects will be felt all the way to Ausangate. Coupled with an earthquake warning, our climb must be postponed."

Eli protested. "What are you saying?"

"I am saying there is no safe alternative other than to turn back immediately."

Eli looked at Dan, who said nothing but revealed a steely eyed determination to keep going. For his part, nothing would keep Eli from fulfilling his mission. If he fell prey to the eruption of a volcano that had been dormant for ten thousand years, so be it. He watched as Moises and his clients collected their gear in preparation for the return to safety. Dan stood stoically and continued to stare Eli down.

"I am going to continue," Eli proclaimed.

"Me too," said Dan.

Moises was stunned. It was obvious to Eli that Moises couldn't believe what he was hearing. "You two guys, of all people, should know better than to ignore the warnings of your guide. I cannot stop you, but know this: in the face of an earthquake or a volcanic eruption, there will be no emergency services available to save you."

"Understood," Eli replied.

"Got it," said Dan.

With that, Moises shook his head in disbelief as he and his group departed. Eli stood alone with the man he hated as the earth began to rumble beneath their feet.

CHAPTER 68

Mount Ausangate, Peru

Dan was troubled by the thunder coming not from the sky but from underground. He had never experienced an earthquake and didn't want to now. He and Eli had been alone for nearly an hour since Moises and his group descended. Neither had spoken a single word. The earth continued to bellow beneath them. Still they continued up the mountain on a march that held only the promise of imminent doom for them both.

In Peru, seasons are spoken of in only two categories: wet and dry. Given it was late November, the rainy season, it was no surprise to Dan that it had begun to pour. Despite the heat, Dan kept his waterproof jacket, helmet, goggles, and gloves on. He took refuge inside an outcropping of rocks. It wasn't a cave but more of an overhang with sides. Dan pressed his back against the rock and tried as best he could to shield himself from the rain.

Dan was suddenly struck by the idea that he might never see Bri or Tally again. He had tried to call Tally back after they were cut off, but he couldn't get through. Internet service at the hotel was down, as was the satellite television. In the hours preceding the climb, Dan felt isolated from the rest of the world. He couldn't help but worry about the two ladies he loved so much.

Eli dropped his gear so he could remove his long-sleeved climbing jacket. Dan watched as he stripped down to an Under Armour T-shirt and removed his protective helmet. The heat was unbearable. Normally, one could expect the rain to cool things down. This rain was unusual. The drops were hot. He saw the rain pelting the rock and noticed that each drop produced a hint of smoke. *Was it a heat reaction against the normally cold rock? No, this was something different.* Dan had read about the phenomenon of acid rain, and now he and Eli were trapped in its clutches.

As each drop hit the exposed skin of Eli Shepherd, his flesh burned away, bit by bit. The rain ripped through the T-shirt, and slowly but surely, Eli's upper torso and face resembled the worst imaginable burn victim pulled from a house engulfed in flames. He screamed, over and over. Clearly, he was in agony as he fell to the ground and writhed in pain. Even if Dan still felt brotherly love for this man and wanted to save him, there was nothing he could have done. *Let the bastard suffer.* For what he has done to me, the people I love, and the planet, no one ever deserved to suffer more.

Just as suddenly as it had begun, the rain stopped. Unlike what one would normally expect, there was no parting of the clouds and no emergent sunshine. Instead, the sky turned a dark, hazy shade of gray. Winds whipped about and created a macabre, demonic sky. Dan looked down at his now unrecognizable foe. He was still alive, moaning in pain.

"Dan, kill me," he pleaded. "No one should have to go through this."

"Except you!" He replied in a tone of disgust.

Through a raspy voice, Eli managed to say, "It was you who brought us to this point. You, the past-life murderer and present-life narcissist. You stole Maddie from me and made me feel like your two-bit sidekick. Like I was worthless."

Dan stared down at what appeared to be a talking corpse. He thought how pathetic it was that this sick son of a bitch had endangered the entire planet in some delusional plan to reconcile lives lived hundreds of years ago and his own lack of self-esteem. Dan reached into his pocket and held up Eli's sat phone. "Has the acid rain blinded you? Can you see this? I prevented your clean food box scheme from taking place. The authorities recalled the whole lot. You may have gotten away with killing my father, stealing my money, and ruining my reputation, but in the end, you are nothing more than what you always saw yourself as—a total loser. You failed!"

Dan looked down at Eli Shepherd. His face was essentially melted away. What returned his gaze was two bulging eyes and a set of teeth melted into severely charred flesh. A wheezing sound came from a hole in his throat. Dan guessed he was trying to laugh. Finally, with great difficulty, he managed to get his last words out. "Look around. Maritza and I set out to destroy the world. Your world and everything you valued. The earth will perish in short order and with it, the great Dan Alston."

Dan now wanted to oblige Eli in his request to be killed. There was no doubt now. The SF_6 threat had been real. As he contemplated his next move, the earth began to rumble. The tremor caused a rock slide from high above. Dan took cover and watched as a boulder smashed down squarely on the grotesque remains of Eli Shepherd's head.

When he deemed it safe, he walked over to the corpse, bent down, and shoved the small boulder off the body. With that, he stood over a man he once loved as a brother and kicked his remains over the edge of the mountain. Dan watched as the body slammed against the rock below like a pinball in an arcade machine.

"Good riddance," he said aloud.

Dan took the sat phone he had removed from Eli's hotel room and prayed he could get a signal. He remembered Moises's warning but he had to try and get help. He hit the power button, but the display read 'NO SIGNAL.'"

Damn!

The only thing left to do was to descend Ausangate. Maybe Tomás was mistaken. He could find his way home and see if there were any way to reverse the planet's perilous course. After an hour's journey, he was beyond hot. He reached for his thermos and sipped some water. He had to stay hydrated. Even though the sky looked frightening and he knew his chances of survival were slim, he needed to keep moving. He paused for a moment to look around. The air had taken on an unusual odor. Dan couldn't quite place it. It smelled like burning plants. He guessed it was the aftermath of the acid rain hitting the vegetation in the valley. From his vantage point, the rolling colors of the Rainbow Mountain had all been scorched by the toxic precipitation. In the distance, he could see smoke and lots of it. It was far away, but he instantly realized that the chaotic sky was a volcanic eruption. Quimsachata had awakened after a ten-thousand-year hiatus. Through the smoke, Dan thought he saw lava pouring into the valley.

Dan removed his helmet and goggles. The heat was unbearable. He lifted his right forearm across his face to keep the sweat from stinging his eyes. The earth rumbled again. Before he could react, the ground beneath his feet cracked open. Dan quickly got both feet onto the same ledge and tried to brace himself against the face of the mountain. Without warning, the earthquake commanded the mountainous terrain to once again separate beneath him, and Dan plunged to the bottom of the canyon. His body landed hard on a bed of rock. He was in excruciating pain, but he was alive. He looked up at the ominous gray sky and tried to think of a plan to survive. Before a cogent thought could be formed, he felt another tremor. The last thing Dan Alston saw was the rocks barreling down the mountain and burying him alive.

CHAPTER 69

Lying beneath the rubble, Dan opened his eyes. He knew where he was and remembered the earthquake and the resulting avalanche. He also realized that he had been unconscious for an undetermined period of time. Barely able to move due to the flood of rocks trapping him in place, Dan thanked God that miraculously, he somehow survived. *How much time had he lost?* Tomás had seen this moment. As a logic-based person, a prophecy foretelling the world's end—and specifically oneself falling prey to an avalanche—was pretty easy to disregard. Still, he had taken it all seriously and prepared for this exact moment.

Dan looked around but saw mostly darkness. Slivers of the angry gray sky broke through faint separations in his makeshift mountain grave. His eyes stung from the combination of sweat and soot from the mountain's remnants. It wasn't easy, but he was able to move his hands from his sides to his eyes to gently rub them, seeking a bit of relief. Breathing was difficult. The air was heavy and stale. Even with the faint cracks of daylight peeking through the top of the rocks, Dan worried about running out of oxygen. Inhaling was a chore. His state of consciousness was returning, and his body told him there was a problem. Dan couldn't move his legs. The force of the mountain slide dumped him hard on his back. Unlike his first accident on Ausangate, there was no bank of snow to cushion his fall. He was sure his spine had taken the brunt this time and feared the worst. He was paralyzed from the waist down.

If Tomás had seen this part, he kept it to himself. At least his mind was intact. *Think! Assess your situation and solve the problem.* Trapped in a canyon underneath a pile of rock, he was paralyzed from the waist down and was running out of oxygen while the world outside was coming to an end. He thought of everything at stake; the survival of the planet, all mankind, and for him personally, his two reasons to live. His little kitten, Bri, and Tally, his newfound love. Their faces and thoughts of the future propelled him to act. Even without the apocalypse, no search crew would ever be able to find him buried in rocks at the bottom of a canyon in a perilous region of the Andes. His situation was dire and he knew it. He could feel sorry for himself. He could give in and succumb to circumstances that would have prevailed over any man, or he could fulfill his destiny.

Dan slowly moved his right hand to his pants pocket and with great difficulty tried to work his fingers down to the bottom of the cloth enclosure. The joints of his fingers were stiff and sore. He could feel the pain in his hand, but his leg was unresponsive. He felt nothing against his right leg as his hand wormed its way through the pocket. He calmed himself. Yes, he was paralyzed, but his legs would not be needed for this rescue. He willed his hand to keep working until he felt it: the polished edge of the flat, egged-shaped emerald. It was the vessel that would help transport him back home. He vividly recalled how Tomás had explained that the power of the emerald dated back five generations and was once possessed by a queen in the Inca Empire. Inside his pocket, his hand took hold of the gem and clutched it tightly inside his palm. Slowly he brought the polished stone out of his pocket, laid it on top of his chest, and began his next maneuver.

With his left hand, he reached into the opposite pocket in search of the other tool needed to save his life and preserve the planet. His fingers danced around inside the pocket until he found what he was looking for. The ayahuasca!

Dan picked up the stone from his chest and placed it in between his hands as he began, in the manner he had been taught, to open sacred space. The memorized words in Spanish and Quechua flowed freely from his lips as he said them aloud. Dan then retrieved the small vial from his pocket and with great difficulty unscrewed the black cap and moved the container to his lips. As Tomás had instructed, Dan drank the contents, closed his eyes, and waited for what seemed an eternity before the elixir began to take hold. All at once, his rocky enclosure cooled. Dan felt a light, refreshing breeze blow through the tight space. Remarkably, it became easier to breathe. His upper torso relaxed and the sweat enveloping his body evaporated.

Dan opened his eyes and watched while the rocky enclosure melted away and transformed into a serene mountain pond. He found himself lying comfortably on a grass-laden marsh beneath the shade of a kapok tree. He called upon his power spirit, and before him a magnificent and muscular jaguar appeared. With the jaguar at his side, he rose and walked without difficulty to an opening in the ground where he spotted a stairwell made of sun-dried red bricks and a crooked railing constructed from tree branches. Together, Dan and the jaguar descended the stairwell where they met Pakay, the guard of the lower world. Pakay, in a golden headdress, looked at Dan stoically.

"What is your business in Ukhupacha?"

Remembering that 'Ukhupacha' was a Quechua term for the lower world, Dan replied, "Pakay, I seek permission to enter Ukhupacha to save the earth."

As if Pakay already knew the reason without having been asked, he replied in a deep monotone. "You may enter."

With the jaguar in tow, Dan walked slowly through a spiderweb of stone-faced corridors. Every direction looked the same, and there was seemingly no correct choice. It reminded him of a corn maze he and Maddie once walked through with Bri when she was four years old. The walk through the maze always began with confidence, but after a few minutes, you realized you were hopelessly lost. Not knowing what to do next, Dan paused and rotated, seeking some sort of clue from the plain stone walls. The chambers of Ukhupacha had no clues to reveal. Instinctively, Dan felt the pressure of time just ticking away. While he was making the shaman's crossing through the lower world in search of something to help, the present-day earth was being ravaged by the effects of a supercharged core.

While he was feeling helpless and lost, the jaguar gently nudged him to his right. There were two tunnels. Each looked identical. Again, the jaguar gently guided Dan to the far right entrance. They walked together and as they proceeded farther and farther, the corridor went dark, so dark that Dan could no longer see his hand in front of his face. Now he was scared. He had made the wrong choice. The answer he sought was not in this passageway. Dan concluded that the tunnel's darkness signified the end. He screamed out loud, even though he knew no one would hear him. His cry was a release from the pressure of literally carrying the world on his shoulders. Despite his shamanic training from Tomás, Dan resigned himself to failure. In his heart, he knew he had tried his best. Time simply ran out. Exhausted, Dan sat down on the ground, closed his eyes, and elected to wait for his own demise.

Minutes passed and nothing happened. The jaguar butted its head on Dan's shoulder, causing him to open his eyes. It was at this moment that he took note of a light coming from the far end of the dark tunnel. He got up and walked toward the illumination. At the end of the corridor, Dan found himself walking out of a cave onto a grassy field, where in the distance he saw a man sitting alone on the edge of a forest by a dormant fire pit.

The muscular-looking man was clearly upset. He ran his huge hands through a graying head of wiry hair that was parted in the middle. On the ground, Dan saw a headband with three long colored feathers. His beard and moustache, although bushy, failed to divert attention from the hook nose.

Dan called out to him. The man looked up and Dan took note of his eyes—shockingly black irises offset with distinct flecks of gray. The man looked hurt, not physically but emotionally.

"Who are you?" Dan asked.

"My name is Cunac. I am the village shaman."

EPILOGUE

At an elevation of nearly eight thousand feet, Dan stood with Tally on the Inca citadel known as Machu Picchu. They held hands and looked out over the Urubamba River Valley as Tomás administered the rites of marriage. Dan looked into his bride's hazel eyes and lovingly admired her cute button nose. He considered himself the happiest man on earth. Tally was glowing in her white wedding dress adorned with embroidered flowers on its lowest hem. Dan wore a classic Armani tuxedo. Bri served as maid of honor and was simply stunning with her long brown hair flowing in the breeze against her royal blue dress. Dan stole a gaze at his best man. Eli, also in a classic black tux, never looked better. Despite the secret he shared with only Tomás, Dan was once again able to claim brotherly love for the man who, for more than three decades, had been the best friend anyone could ever ask for.

Dan was overjoyed at being able to help his bride realize her lifelong dream of a destination wedding on a mountain top. When he suggested Machu Picchu and showed her pictures, she had simply fallen in love with the idea. The bride and groom were offered the opportunity to dress in Peruvian wedding clothes, but Tally insisted that on this point they go American. The ceremony, on the other hand, was Q'ero, in the spirit of the Incas. To honor the marriage, Tomás prepared a despacho and presented it to the happy couple as he spoke the words that would seal their love forever.

Dan kissed his bride. In his heart, he knew he would never tire of loving Tally. Her kind spirit, intelligence, and giving heart were his foundations of energizing light. When the ceremony concluded, the small gathering of guests including Tally's parents. Dan's beloved father, Bob Alston, Moises, Joc Raymer, and Senators Raley, Reed, and McMillian applauded and hugged them both as they made their way down the makeshift aisle.

Over his shoulder, Dan shared a quick wink of the eye with Tomás. To everyone else, they were meeting for the first time. Only the two of them knew. The sacred practice of shamanic destiny retrieval enabled Dan to help Cunac find kindness in his heart. Tomás bet on the fact that Cunac, being a shaman himself, would understand the presence of Dan Alston visiting his past-life self with news of the world's end. Cunac did understand. Dan Alston did too. His father had always taught him that every action had a reaction. One small pebble tossed into a lake could cause a thousand ripples.

Author's Note

Writing, for me, is a part-time endeavor and most certainly a labor of love. Being the CEO of a dynamic supply chain engineering and technology company (www.nexterus.com) leaves only the wee hours of the morning and some weekend time to pen my novels. My writing career would not be possible were it not for the love and support from my wife, Denise, to whom this book is dedicated. She is the first to listen to off-the-wall ideas for storylines and plot twists and is always my first reader. After reading an early draft of Shaman, Denise suggested the idea that had Tally reincarnating from Maicu. She is one of the smartest people I know and is adept at figuring out the end of a novel or a movie long before it concludes. If I can keep her guessing, I know I have something special. She is my rock and her love, friendship, and encouragement help make my stories better.

The love and support of my son, Ryan and my daughter, Leah is immeasurable. Each, in their own way, helped to make this novel what it is. Each of them read drafts of the story and offered valuable insight into the direction and its components. Leah helped greatly by editing an early draft which turned me around on many points and enabled me to keep the novel focused. I love you both more than words can express. No father could ever feel more pride for the fine young adults you have become.

The idea for Shaman was born from a discussion with my executive coach, Wayne Caskey. After a long business conversation in a crowded

Starbucks in Towson, Maryland, he began telling me about some of his side interests, namely the study and practice of shamanism and Akashic readings. Prior to this conversation, I had heard of shamanism but not the Akashic Records. Wayne gave me source material to read and introduced me to Jen Eramith, an Akashic reader, and Heidi McBratney, a practicing shaman in Canada. He also helped by connecting me to Tom Fahy, a DC lobbyist. Wayne read multiple drafts of this story and was a steady hand in guiding me through the writing process. He also took the time to perform an Akashic reading for me which was extremely helpful in crafting the scene with Dan and Renee Palomino. It should also be noted that Wayne introduced me to the concepts of shamanic soul and destiny retrieval which assisted greatly in creating an exciting and hopefully, unpredictable ending.

Heidi McBratney became my de facto technical consultant for this story. Heidi is a full-time shaman with a practice in Ontario. She has made numerous trips to the Cusco region of Peru to work with modern-day shamans. Heidi's insights were greater than any research an author could do. She read the novel as it came together and spent hours writing helpful comments and suggestions as well as talking on the phone to make sure I got things right. Heidi told me stories of her adventures, shared photos and helped me understand a world previously unknown. It should be stated that the practice of shamanism is far more complex than what is depicted in this novel. To create a story that flows, I took extensive creative liberty and any omission, error or departure from fact is solely my doing.

Every author has a group of people who act as the early readers of a novel. Chief amongst this group is my mother, Sheila Weinstock, who may just be the world's best proofreader. She definitely gets the award for finding typos that everyone else, including me, seemed to have glossed over. Mom read multiple drafts of this story and made sure to add her delicate contrarian view where needed. My other early readers were

Bruce Savadkin, Greg Tutino, Chuck Ferraro, Bill McComas, and Greg Harmis. All of your time and feedback was greatly appreciated.

My brother, Ed Polakoff, the professional photographer, was kind enough to engage in our traditional brother's barter system in taking the author photo that appears on the back cover of this book.

My father, Jay Polakoff, always asked how the book was going and read the early chapters to ensure the novel was off to a captivating start.

I would like to acknowledge the efforts of Jen Eramith, the Akashic reader who read all my chapters dealing with her area of expertise. Jen was gracious in validating that my knowledge and expression of her profession were accurate. Where there are departures from fact, again, as the author, I made a choice to exercise creative license.

When I was writing the scene involving Bob Alston's funeral, I researched the history of funerals for former governors of Maryland. I found a stirring essay written by the man who planned the 2011 funeral for William Donald Schaefer, Maryland's governor from 1987-1995. The author of that essay was Jari Villanueva. I contacted Jari and he was extremely helpful in reading a draft of the funeral chapter. Jari was gracious in his efforts to help me fine tune the details and make it as authentic as possible.

In my earliest days of drafting this novel, I met Juan Carlos Alamo, a native of Peru and, at the time, a student at Towson University in Baltimore. Juan Carlos was kind enough to read some of my early chapters and helped me to capture the details of his native land.

Before the novel really got going, Tom Fahy spent time with me by phone to give me a crash course on being a lobbyist in Washington, DC. This help was sorely needed when I was in the formative stages of the story's development.

It's been said that you can't judge a book by its cover which is true however, an excellent cover does grab the reader's attention. No one does book cover designs better than Gwyn Snider of GKS Creative. Gwyn takes the time to really understand the story and then creates a design capturing the imagination of the reader. When I first saw her concept for Shaman, I was blown away. Gwyn also handled the design and layout for this book.

When someone finishes a book, I doubt anyone stops to say, "Hey, that copyeditor did an amazing job." Perhaps they should. Copyeditors are the unsung heroes who make sure that everything is in pristine order from punctuation to overall grammar and word choice. Here's a shout out to my copyeditor, Kim Bookless, whose meticulous nature results in an excellent reading experience.

I am a proud graduate of Towson University. Until recently, I chaired the Advisory Board for the College of Business and Economics. The university is thriving and I am glad to have played a small role in its progress. I was also pleased to have incorporated Towson University into my story. It should be noted, however, that Caskey Hall is fictitious as is Professor Quesaré and all of the details surrounding the Anthropology program.

In the closing lines of the epilogue, I attributed adapted quotes to Dan Alston's father. The quote about a single pebble causing many ripples was from the Dalai Lama. The other reference was to Isaac Newton's theory that every action has a separate and distinct reaction.

Finally, I should point out that Tally's cat, Ziggy, is really our cat, Ziggy. He is as described in the novel and lives happily as a spoiled house cat with his good friend, Eli, our German Shepherd/Chow mix. And yes, that is where the name Eli Shepherd came from.

Shaman was a challenging story to write. I threw my heart and soul into it and only hope that it was the light-hearted entertainment you sought when you began reading.

Sam Polakoff
April 30, 2019

ALSO FROM SAM POLAKOFF

Hiatus

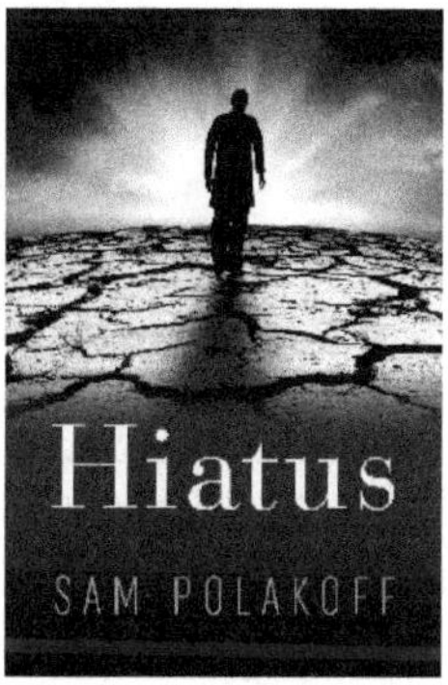

As a young boy, Dr. Benjamin Abraham is devastated by the premature death of his grandfather. The loss of his grandfather motivates Ben, a scientific prodigy, to create the Liferay making it possible for the dead to live again...but only once a year for 24 hours.

Using this technology, Dr. Abraham becomes the founder of Hiatus Centers where people can reunite with their deceased loved ones in a controlled environment. Things go terribly wrong when the technology falls into improper hands with disastrous results.

When his chief rival, Dr. Anstrov Rinaldi, learns Ben's deepest secret, information that threatens the safety of all mankind, Ben and his scientific assistant, Rachel Larkin, must work side by side in an effort to save the world.

An enthralling sci-fi thriller, Hiatus encompasses life, death and rebirth across the globe culminating in a plot threatening the very essence of human existence. To combat the unintended consequences of achieving what was once impossible, Ben Abraham must wager everything to save the world and the company he founded.

Hiatus may be purchased at www.sampolakoff.com, Amazon, Barnes & Noble or via your favorite online bookseller.

CPSIA information can be obtained
at www.ICGtesting.com
Printed in the USA
BVHW040017030919
557295BV00004B/5/P

9 781733 889803